RASSELAS

SAMUEL JOHNSON was born in 1709 in Lichfield, Staffordshire. The son of an impecunious bookseller, he experienced poverty throughout the first part of his life, and, in spite of his formidable mental endowments, was able to attend Pembroke College, Oxford, for only a year. After moving to London in 1737, he earned his living by miscellaneous journalism for many years, until his *Rambler* essays of 1750–2 and the first historical dictionary of the English language (1755) brought him fame. *Rasselas*, Johnson's one extended work of prose fiction, was published towards the end of this decade, and from 1762 a government pension of £300 a year relieved him from necessity. In the later part of his life, marked especially by his 1765 edition of Shakespeare's plays and *The Lives of the Poets* (1779–81), he came to be regarded as the greatest literary figure of his time in England. Also among his most celebrated works are the verse satires *London* and *The Vanity of Human Wishes*, his periodical essays in the *Adventurer* and *Idler*, and *A Journey to the Western Islands of Scotland*, which records his celebrated tour of the Hebrides in 1773 with his friend and later biographer, James Boswell. Johnson died in 1784 and was buried in Westminster Abbey.

THOMAS KEYMER is Chancellor Jackman Professor of English at the University of Toronto and a Supernumerary Fellow of St Anne's College, Oxford. His books include *Richardson's Clarissa and the Eighteenth-Century Reader* (1992), *Sterne, the Moderns, and the Novel* (2002), *The Cambridge Companion to English Literature from 1740 to 1830* (co-edited with Jon Mee, 2004), and the Oxford World's Classics editions of Fielding's *Joseph Andrews and Shamela* (1999), Richardson's *Pamela* (2001), and Defoe's *Robinson Crusoe* (2007).

OXFORD WORLD'S CLASSICS

*For over 100 years Oxford World's Classics have brought
readers closer to the world's great literature. Now with over 700
titles — from the 4,000-year-old myths of Mesopotamia to the
twentieth century's greatest novels — the series makes available
lesser-known as well as celebrated writing.*

*The pocket-sized hardbacks of the early years contained
introductions by Virginia Woolf, T. S. Eliot, Graham Greene,
and other literary figures which enriched the experience of reading.
Today the series is recognized for its fine scholarship and
reliability in texts that span world literature, drama and poetry,
religion, philosophy, and politics. Each edition includes perceptive
commentary and essential background information to meet the
changing needs of readers.*

OXFORD WORLD'S CLASSICS

━━

SAMUEL JOHNSON

The History of Rasselas Prince of Abissinia

━━

Edited with an Introduction and Notes by
THOMAS KEYMER

OXFORD
UNIVERSITY PRESS

OXFORD
UNIVERSITY PRESS

Great Clarendon Street, Oxford OX2 6DP

Oxford University Press is a department of the University of Oxford.
It furthers the University's objective of excellence in research, scholarship,
and education by publishing worldwide in

Oxford New York

Auckland Cape Town Dar es Salaam Hong Kong Karachi
Kuala Lumpur Madrid Melbourne Mexico City Nairobi
New Delhi Shanghai Taipei Toronto

With offices in

Argentina Austria Brazil Chile Czech Republic France Greece
Guatemala Hungary Italy Japan Poland Portugal Singapore
South Korea Switzerland Thailand Turkey Ukraine Vietnam

Oxford is a registered trade mark of Oxford University Press
in the UK and in certain other countries

Published in the United States
by Oxford University Press Inc., New York

British Library Cataloguing in Publication Data

Data available

Library of Congress Cataloging-in-Publication Data

Johnson, Samuel, 1709–1784.
[Rasselas]
The history of Rasselas, Prince of Abissinia / Samuel Johnson ; edited with an
introduction and notes by
Thomas Keymer. — New ed.
p. cm. — (Oxford World's Classics)
Includes bibliographical references.
ISBN 978–0–19–922997–0
1. Happiness—Fiction. I. Keymer, Tom. II. Title.
PR3529.A2H375 2009
823'.6—dc22
2009005383

Typeset by Cepha Imaging Private Ltd., Bangalore, India
Printed in Great Britain
on acid-free paper
Clays Ltd., St Ives plc

ISBN 978–0–19–922997–0

CONTENTS

Acknowledgements	vii
Introduction	ix
Note on the Text	xxxv
Select Bibliography	xxxviii
A Chronology of Samuel Johnson	xliv
THE HISTORY OF RASSELAS, PRINCE OF ABISSINIA	1
Explanatory Notes	111
Glossary	153

ACKNOWLEDGEMENTS

MODERN editions of Samuel Johnson rest on the learning and labour of generations of scholars, and I am indebted to two previous editors of *Rasselas*, J. P. Hardy and the late Gwin J. Kolb, and to the many contributors to the Yale Edition of the Works of Samuel Johnson. Isobel Grundy, Heather Jackson, Jack Lynch, Jim McLaverty, Adam Potkay, and Peter Sabor gave valuable advice and information at just the right moments, and Darryl Domingo and Erin Parker have been exemplary research assistants. Eva Guggemos and Laurie Klein kindly facilitated access to the Kern and other early copies of *Rasselas* at the Beinecke Library, Yale University, and the title page reproduced from Johnson's first edition was generously supplied by Carl Spadoni from the William Ready Division of Archives and Research Collections, McMaster University Library. I am grateful as ever to Judith Luna and her colleagues at Oxford University Press for their enthusiasm and expertise, and for trusting that things would in time be finished, though not concluded.

INTRODUCTION

Rasselas is a book about happiness, and for all the famous despondency of its author it caught the mood of its time. Three London editions and a Dublin reprint were in circulation within a year of first publication in 1759, and translations into Dutch, French, German, Italian, and Russian followed over the next five years. No early edition so clearly reflects the practical as well as philosophical importance that early readers found in Johnson's theme as the first American edition, brought out in 1768 by Robert Bell, a radical Irish bookseller who had moved to Philadelphia on the bankruptcy of his business in Dublin. Bell's *Rasselas* was a noisily transatlantic, democratizing affair ('AMERICA: PRINTED FOR EVERY PURCHASER', screams the imprint), and his title page features a further appeal to the common reader by inserting a maxim from the seventeenth-century moralist La Rochefoucauld: 'The Labour or Exercise of the Body, freeth Men from Pains of the Mind; and 'tis this that constitutes the Happiness of the Poor.'[1] Never mind that the narrative to follow was conspicuously less sanguine than this about the blessings of poverty, and indeed about everything else. Bell's choice of *Rasselas* as the inaugural publication of his new career in a new world, and as a text that might open the way to felicity for even the humblest of his fellow colonists, was inspired. At a time when the pursuit of happiness was shortly to be defined by Thomas Jefferson as an inalienable individual right and a collective political goal, here was a work that directly addressed, with formidable wisdom and eloquence, the most enduring yet also the most pressing of human concerns.

Johnson was quick to grasp the implications of Bell's edition on seeing a copy some years later, and he expressed pleasure 'because the Printer seems to have expected that it would be scattered

[1] See J. D. Fleeman, *A Bibliography of the Works of Samuel Johnson*, 2 vols. (Oxford: Clarendon Press, 2000), i, 793. Bell probably adapted his maxim from the English translation published by Andrew Millar in 1749: see La Rochefoucauld, *Moral Maxims*, ed. Irwin Primer (Newark: University of Delaware Press, 2003), 169.

among the People'.[2] But he would certainly have deplored any attempt to find common ground between his most celebrated imaginative work and the Declaration of Independence in 1776, based as it was on the 'self-evident' truth—self-evident, though with meanings that continue to be disputed—'that all men are created equal; that they are endowed by their creator with certain inalienable rights; that among these are life, liberty, & the pursuit of happiness'.[3] Duties, not rights, were at the centre of Johnson's ethics, and in *Rasselas* he ends his narrative with the homecoming of a rebel son: a son who recognizes, moreover, that the political sovereignty he desires will not be obtained. A staunch conservative who was also a vocal abolitionist and a tireless enemy of cant, Johnson became the foremost British polemicist against the American Continental Congress in the 1770s, so scathing in his denunciation of congressional proceedings that his rhetoric had to be softened by government officials. Pieties about equality for all enraged him especially, and even after the revisions imposed on Johnson's best-known political pamphlet, *Taxation No Tyranny* (1775), he continues to ask, with thunderous frankness, 'how is it that we hear the loudest yelps for liberty among the drivers of negroes?'[4]

Yet Johnson and Jefferson may have been closer to one another in their thinking about the pursuit of happiness, if not about equality or slavery, than either would have cared to admit. Even before *Rasselas*, in an argument based squarely on the principle that 'the end of all human actions is happiness', Johnson was writing about communal as well as personal felicity as a necessary and legitimate project for the American colonies, no less than for the mother country. 'Every man and every society is intitled to all the happiness that can be enjoyed with the security of the whole community', he declares in an essay of 1756, as war for colonial

---

[2] *The Letters of Samuel Johnson*, ed. Bruce Redford, 5 vols. (Oxford: Clarendon Press, 1992), ii, 13 (to William White, 4 March 1773).

[3] *The Essential Jefferson*, ed. Jean M. Yarbrough (Indianapolis: Hackett, 2006), 18.

[4] *The Yale Edition of the Works of Samuel Johnson*, ed. Allen T. Hazen, John H. Middendorf et al., 18 vols. to date (New Haven: Yale University Press, 1958–), x, 454; hereafter *YW*. Johnson is unlikely to have known of the anti-slavery passage (directed against British traders, not American owners) that was removed from Jefferson's original draft at the insistence of southern delegates.

supremacy was being waged between Britain and France, and 'from this general claim the Americans ought not to be excluded' (*YW*, x, 212). Even more interesting is the likelihood that Jefferson shared with Johnson the central insight of *Rasselas* that, although pursuing happiness was a necessary endeavour, obtaining it was something else. A standard formula about 'pursuing and obtaining happiness and safety' is common to several key documents in the swirl of republican rhetoric from which the Declaration emerged, but it was 'pursuit' only that entered the text prepared by Jefferson and adopted by the Congress, amplified in Jefferson's draft by a similarly open-ended reference to 'the road to happiness & to glory'.[5] No mention was made of secure possession, and, as historians of American independence have observed, to speak of 'pursuit' alone was to problematize our relationship to the happiness we seek, and to emphasize our distance from it. Darrin M. McMahon quotes the unsettling primary definitions of *pursue* and *pursuit* that Johnson himself included in his great *Dictionary* of 1755—'To chase; to follow in hostility'; 'The act of following with hostile intention'—and notes the etymological and semantic links with notions of prosecution and persecution.[6] Johnson's manuscript of *Rasselas* does not survive, but further connotations are called to mind by the frequent (indeed majority) use in early editions of alternative spellings, *persue* and *persuit*. In the solemnity with which these usages line up—'Yet what, said she, is to be expected from our persuit of happiness, when . . . happiness itself is the cause of misery?' (p. 78)—it is hard not to sense that perseverance, and persistent self-persuasion, must also form part of the quest. Pursuing happiness here is an arduous endeavour, not to be confused with comfortably obtaining it, and—as *Rasselas* implies with its 'conclusion, in which nothing is concluded' (p. 108)—more

---

[5] *Essential Jefferson*, 21.

[6] Darrin M. McMahon, *Happiness: A History* (New York: Grove Press, 2006), 320; see also Garry Wills, *Inventing America: Jefferson's Declaration of Independence* (New York: Vintage, 1979), 245. It is worth adding that Johnson illustrated the verb *pursue* (sense 4: 'To endeavour to attain') with a couplet by Matthew Prior that had lodged in his mind: 'We happiness *pursue*; we fly from pain; | Yet the pursuit, and yet the flight is vain.'

salutary as an activity in itself than in its prospects of reaching completion.

All the evidence suggests that, as a matter of both personal experience and philosophical outlook, happiness was far from Johnson's reach at the time when *Rasselas* was composed. Ten years earlier, in his great poem *The Vanity of Human Wishes* (1749), he had intensified a satire by Juvenal, his classical model, into a monumental yet also heartfelt poetic statement about the inevitable defeat of sublunary desire. Life in this poem is a condition of flight or denial, and also—in natural human reaction—of relentless, unavailing struggle; it is a vale of tears in which mankind 'Hides from himself his state, and shuns to know, | That life protracted is protracted woe' (*YW*, vi, 104 (line 258)). This famous couplet, with its unflinching, chiastic equation between living and suffering, set the tone of Johnson's writing for the decade to follow. Closer in time to *Rasselas*, his pulverizing review of Soame Jenyns's *Free Enquiry into the Nature and Origin of Evil* (1757), a fatuous Panglossian treatise on the benevolence of Providence, features his memorably downbeat assertion that 'the only end of writing is to enable the readers better to enjoy life, or better to endure it' (*YW*, xvii, 421). Here was a formula that would re-emerge in *Rasselas*, in even more grimly antithetical style, with the poet Imlac's account of life as 'every where a state in which much is to be endured, and little to be enjoyed' (p. 32).

Yet if authorship might alleviate a condition that was otherwise cheerless, in Johnson's case the payoff for the author himself was hard to locate. After eight years of strenuous labour to produce the *Dictionary*—labour as heroic yet also as doomed, Johnson implies at one point, as that of the conquering Xerxes in *The Vanity of Human Wishes*[7]—he concludes his Preface with an arresting shift from the instability of language and meaning to the painful mutability of life in general, and especially his own. In the 'gloom of solitude' that now afflicts him as the *Dictionary* goes

[7] 'To enchain syllables, and to lash the wind, are equally the undertakings of pride, unwilling to measure its desires by its strength', Johnson declares in the Preface to the *Dictionary* (*YW*, xviii, 105), echoing *The Vanity of Human Wishes* on the fury of Xerxes at the Hellespont: 'The waves he lashes, and enchains the wind' (*YW*, vi, 103 (line 232)).

through the press, fulfilment seems further than ever beyond reach, and the life of authorship is in personal terms a state of mere joyless endurance. 'I have protracted my work till most of those whom I wished to please, have sunk into the grave, and success and miscarriage are empty sounds', reads Johnson's plangent envoy to the *Dictionary*: 'I therefore dismiss it with frigid tranquillity, having little to fear or hope from censure or from praise' (*YW*, xviii, 113).

If censure and praise were of no account, however, other kinds of compensation continued to matter. It is one of the many ironies of *Rasselas* that we owe Johnson's tale from a world without money—'the ladies could not...comprehend what the merchants did with small pieces of gold and silver' (p. 41)—to the author's pressing need for ready cash. At the height of his fame Johnson liked to shock admirers by posing as a mercenary hack: a man in whose gruff opinion, as James Boswell reports with obvious dismay, 'No man but a blockhead ever wrote, except for money'.[8] In this case necessity really was a leading motive, however. Early biographers of Johnson, including several memoirists writing before Boswell's massive *Life* of 1791, competed with one another to tell exaggerated stories about *Rasselas* as a masterpiece dashed off in grief to meet the costs of his mother's last illness and death, and in the process the origins of the work became permanently blurred. But a broadly compatible story is told by Johnson himself in a letter to his printer William Strahan, dated Saturday 20 January 1759, and now sandwiched in editions of his correspondence between a valedictory letter to his mother and a grief-stricken note to his stepdaughter three days later. 'I shall send a bill of twenty pounds in a few days, which I thought to have brought to my mother; but God suffered it not', he tells Lucy Porter on 23 January: 'I have not power or composure to say much more.'[9] Instead the power and composure were channelled into *Rasselas*, which Johnson had been hoping to complete and deliver on 22 January—the eve of his mother's funeral, as things

[8] *Boswell's Life of Johnson*, ed. G. B. Hill, rev. L. F. Powell, 6 vols. (Oxford: Clarendon Press, 1934–64), iii, 19.

[9] *The Letters of Samuel Johnson*, ed. Bruce Redford, 5 vols. (Oxford: Clarendon Press, 1992), i, 180 (23 January 1759).

turned out—and as he may, even in the circumstances, have managed to do. The exact chronology of composition will always be a matter of conjecture, but from the available evidence it is not unreasonable to imagine Johnson writing the closing chapters of *Rasselas*, including the visit to the catacombs and his magisterial dialogue on death and the soul, as he waited for confirmation of his bereavement to reach him in London from Lichfield (his place of birth, some 120 miles to the north).

The letter to Strahan is worth quoting in full:

Sir:
When I was with you last night I told you of a thing which I was preparing for the press. The title will be The choice of Life or The History of —— Prince of Abissinia.

It will make about two volumes like little Pompadour that is about one middling volume. The bargain which I made with Mr. Johnston was seventy five pounds (or guineas) a volume, and twenty five pounds for the second Edition. I will sell this either at that price or for sixty, the first edition of which he shall himself fix the number, and the property then to revert to me, or for forty pounds, and share the profit that is retain half the copy. I shall have occasion for thirty pounds on Monday night when I shall deliver the book which I must entreat you upon such delivery to procure me. I would have it offered to Mr. Johnston, but have no doubt of selling it, on some of the terms mentioned.

I will not print my name, but expect it to be known. I am, Dear sir, your most humble servant,

SAM. JOHNSON

Get me the money if you can.[10]

Several points are worth pulling out of this no-nonsense letter, the most obvious being the urgency, almost importunate in tone, of Johnson's postscript. In the event, *Rasselas* did not appear in print for three more months, and later stages of Johnson's negotiations with Strahan and the booksellers who joined him in the project (William Johnston, mentioned in the letter, and the fashionable Pall Mall publisher Robert Dodsley) remain obscure. The likelihood is that Johnson eventually sold the copyright of both volumes together for £75, with a further £25 to be paid on

[10] *Letters*, i, 178–9 (20 January 1759).

publication of a second edition. Boswell's talk of a larger sum is still sometimes cited as the conclusive source, but these are the figures recorded in recently discovered legal proceedings arising from an alleged piracy (in the *Grand Magazine of Magazines* for April 1759), and Johnson's document assigning copyright appears to have been shown in court.[11] The amount of £100 in total was solid remuneration for a work of fiction at a time when what we now call 'the rise of the novel' was by no means a one-way bet, and when the hard-nosed Dodsley was reportedly 'one of those Booksellers, who think the Day of Novels is over'.[12] But it evidently represented a climbdown on Johnson's part, and it looks a disappointing figure alongside the £250 that Dodsley's brother James was shortly to pay Laurence Sterne for the opening two volumes of *Tristram Shandy*.[13] Perhaps Johnson's need to make money from books was more acute than his skill in negotiating for it with booksellers. Another well-placed observer was of the opinion that 'any other person with the degree of reputation he then possessed would have got 400*l*. for that work, but he never understood the art of making the most of his productions'.[14]

That said, Johnson's letter to Strahan is in other respects the work of a pragmatic book-trade professional. Like the serene surface of *Rasselas* itself, the unruffled, businesslike tone of the letter gives little hint of emotional duress or the turmoil within, and Johnson's robust manner effectively screens what he elsewhere calls the 'invisible riot of the mind' (*YW*, iv, 106). Instead he focuses directly on publishing practicalities such as the form and content of his title page and the length and arrangement of his copy. Much debate has surrounded the generic identity of *Rasselas* ('moral fable', 'philosophical romance', and 'satirical apologue' are terms

[11] Nancy A. Mace, 'What Was Johnson Paid for *Rasselas*?', *Modern Philology*, 91 (1994), 455–8.

[12] Samuel Richardson to Lady Barbara Montagu, 17 February 1759, Harvard University, Houghton Library, MS Hyde 77 (6.75).

[13] Sterne's first edition of volumes i–ii was privately published in York in late 1759; £250 is the figure negotiated in March 1760 for the second edition of volumes i–ii, with a further £380 to follow for volumes iii–iv (Arthur H. Cash, *Laurence Sterne: The Later Years* (London: Methuen, 1986), 9–10).

[14] Sir James Prior, *Life of Edmond Malone* (1860), 161, paraphrasing the judgement of Johnson's friend Giuseppe Baretti.

sometimes used to distinguish *Rasselas* from the mainstream novel), and in proposing his title Johnson firmly privileges the rational and discursive aspects of his work over its imaginative content. The title will be *The Choice of Life*, a bold statement of philosophical theme, and only with his proposed subtitle does Johnson identify the manuscript—here, a generically indeterminate 'thing'—as a work of narrative fiction. Even the name of his hero is undecided or unimportant, and although the broadly novelistic identity of *Rasselas* was reasserted by the time of publication, perhaps at the insistence of the booksellers ('*The Prince of Abissinia. A Tale*' is the published title, with 'The History of Rasselas, Prince of Abissinia' on the half-title page), Johnson's working title perfectly reflects the thematic structure of his text. The 'choice of life' formula occurs no fewer than eleven times as the narrative unfolds, beginning with the hero's regret that the imprisoning paradise of the Happy Valley denies him 'the choice of life' (p. 32), and progressing through the alternative critiques of his pursuit of happiness voiced by his companions in the search. Before the visit to the pyramids, Rasselas's mentor Imlac offers the worldly advice that 'while you are making the choice of life, you neglect to live' (p. 66); after the visit to the catacombs comes the other-worldly renunciation of his sister Nekayah, for whom at last 'the choice of life is become less important; I hope hereafter to think only on the choice of eternity' (p. 108).

The title page of *Rasselas* is otherwise envisaged by Johnson as spare and austere, uncluttered even by the claim to authorship that he clearly wanted to make. The same goes for the text itself, in length amounting to a 'middling volume' but enough to be spread economically across two (the model Johnson mentions, *The History of the Marchioness of Pompadour*, was a slender two-volume duodecimo of 1758[15]), so inflating the price. Perhaps Johnson was simply hoping to increase the value of his copyright by having his printer manufacture the illusion of a longer work; if so, the plan failed, since, though *Rasselas* was indeed published in two volumes, he was paid on the basis of just one. But Johnson

---

[15] See Fleeman, *Bibliography*, i, 780–1; Johnson may have revised the second edition of 1759.

was interested in general in *mise en page*, and he understood that
the material presentation of literature was integral to its communication of meaning.[16] His real priority may well have been to
create exactly the visual effect that Strahan then duly achieved,
with the almost lapidary impression conveyed by the composi-
tor's use of disproportionately large type in a small octavo format
('Two Pocket Volumes', said the newspaper advertisements),
with just twenty lines of text on a typical page. The fount used
was Caslon Pica, a harmonious and distinctly modern typeface,
rarely used at the time for fiction and often thought more suitable
for poetry than for prose (though its best-known eighteenth-
century outing was for the Declaration of Independence). Caslon
was the first native fount to break significantly with prevailing
Dutch models, and in its conspicuous Englishness it sorted well
with the medium used to carry the print, a superfine writing
paper watermarked with a traditional Britannia motif and the
motto 'Pro Patria'.[17]

None of these niceties of production was missed by Sterne,
a writer whose alertness to the expressive potential of the material
book is obvious throughout *Tristram Shandy*. Six months after
Rasselas appeared, Sterne told Robert Dodsley that he was proposing 'to print a lean edition, in two small volumes, of the size of
Rasselas, and on the same paper and type', and this indeed was
the form in which the self-published York volumes of *Tristram
Shandy* appeared a few weeks later.[18] No doubt Sterne wanted to
make his work visually reminiscent of a current success, but he
may also have hoped to signal, by echoing Johnson's format, a
meaningful intertextual connection. Related to *Rasselas* in the
first place by visual and physical resemblance, *Tristram Shandy* is
a work that comically enacts, in extended form, some of the most

[16] On the relationship between Johnson's intentions and the published format of the
Dictionary, see Paul Luna, 'The Typographic Design of Johnson's *Dictionary*', in Jack
Lynch and Anne McDermott (eds.), *Anniversary Essays on Johnson's Dictionary*
(Cambridge: Cambridge University Press, 2005), 175–97.

[17] See Fleeman, *Bibliography*, i, 785–8.

[18] *The Letters of Laurence Sterne*, ed. Lewis Perry Curtis (Oxford: Clarendon Press,
1935), 80 (Sterne to Robert Dodsley, 5 October 1759); see also Peter J. de Voogd,
'*Tristram Shandy* as Aesthetic Object', in Thomas Keymer (ed.), *Laurence Sterne's
Tristram Shandy: A Casebook* (New York: Oxford University Press, 2006), 113–14.

unsettling themes of Johnson's text: our shared vulnerability to that kind of madness in which 'false opinions fasten upon the mind, and life passes in dreams of rapture or of anguish' (p. 94); the unattainability of anything more complete in life than a conclusion in which nothing is concluded.

The last and most revealing detail in Johnson's letter about *Rasselas* is his desire to be recognized as author. Vanity was surely a spur to this human wish, and as reprints of his celebrated *Rambler* essays of 1750–2 began to accumulate, Johnson must have been aware of the growing marketability of his name. But he was also indicating here that *Rasselas* depended for its impact and meaning on its status as a work by Johnson (or, in a formulation that was fast becoming standard, 'the author of the *Rambler*'), and as the culmination to date of an evolving canon. Reviews make clear that he got his wish, in part through the mechanisms of hint and whisper that worked at the time to counterbalance conventions of anonymity in print, but also as a consequence of unmistakable internal evidence. With its emphatic periodic sentence structures and its sonorous literary cadences, Johnson's prose style was more or less inimitable, and the range and rigour of his lexical choices — honed in the masterpiece of nuanced definition that he had compiled in the *Dictionary* — were unlike anything else in prose fiction at the time. Early reviewers immediately heard 'the learned and sensible author of the *Rambler*', with 'his usual nervous and sententious Stile', and in the *Monthly Review* Owen Ruffhead ridiculed the incongruity of Johnson's philosophic words in what might otherwise have seemed a modish exercise in lightweight oriental fiction. 'He wants that graceful ease, which is the ornament of romance; and he stalk[s] in the solemn buskin, when he ought to tread in the light sock', wrote Ruffhead, a professional rival and political enemy: 'His stile is so tumid and pompous, that he sometimes deals in *sesquipedalia*, such as *excogitation*, *exaggeratory*, &c. with other hard compounds, which it is difficult to pronounce with composed features — as *multifarious*, *transcendental*, *indiscerpible*, &c.'[19]

[19] *Critical Review*, vii (April 1759), 373; *London Magazine* xxviii (May 1759), 258; *Monthly Review* xx (May 1759), 428; all quoted by Gwin J. Kolb, 'The Early Reception

Other readers were struck by the distinctively Johnsonian mood that darkened the happiness theme, and one even thought the work a 'black diamond', a jewel disfigured by an inherited condition of 'malevolent melancholy' that its author was unable to throw off. For Sir John Hawkins, another biographer, *Rasselas* was a work in which 'he poured out his sorrow in gloomy reflection, and being destitute of comfort himself, described the world as nearly without it'.[20] Later readers and critics have taken this line of thinking a stage further, sensing a unique psychobiography on the loose in the subtext of *Rasselas*, there as a more or less unconscious side-effect of rapid composition in a mood of anguish. From this perspective it is not simply that major episodes, such as Johnson's chapters about flying (pp. 17–20) and madness (pp. 93–5), express personal obsessions, though they certainly do: the fascination with flight that made the inaugural ballooning voyages of 1783–4 a pervasive topic in Johnson's last letters (bound up with the dropsical, asthmatic state of his earthbound body), or the fear of insanity that made him look with such dismay and dread on the predicament of Christopher Smart, the friend and fellow poet he visited in the madhouse during the *Rasselas* period.[21] Rather, the acts of repression involved for Johnson in transforming private agonies of guilt and loss into generalizing exploration of large abstractions—the nature of happiness, the stability of reason, the immortality of souls—left traces of specific trauma in the text, or generated a return of the repressed at key moments. For Irvin Ehrenpreis, *Rasselas*'s self-imposed exile from the Happy Valley expressed an ageing city-dweller's rueful sense of lost provincial youth, and his arrival in Cairo at the age of twenty-eight exactly mirrored Johnson's watershed move to London in 1737. The name Imlac was an

of *Rasselas*', in Paul J. Korshin and Robert R. Allen (eds.), *Greene Centennial Studies* (Charlottesville: University Press of Virginia, 1984), 219–21.

[20] William Hayley, *Two Dialogues* (1787), 107; Sir John Hawkins, *The Life of Samuel Johnson, LL.D.* (1787), 367.

[21] For more on ballooning and madness respectively, see Keymer, ' "Letters about nothing": Johnson and Epistolary Writing', in Greg Clingham (ed.), *The Cambridge Companion to Samuel Johnson* (Cambridge: Cambridge University Press, 1997), 236–8, and 'Johnson, Madness, and Smart', in Clement Hawes (ed.), *Christopher Smart and the Enlightenment* (New York: St Martin's Press, 1999), 177–94.

unconscious anagram of Michael, the long-dead father whose memory was still haunting Johnson when, years after *Rasselas* and at the height of his fame, he returned to a marketplace where he had once refused to help at his father's bookstall and stood in expiation at the scene for hours, bare-headed in the driving rain.[22] For Hester Thrale Piozzi, who knew the tormented private Johnson more intimately than anyone else, an alternative identification was in play where Imlac describes the lacerating rejection of his courtship by a class-conscious social superior. 'Poor Imlac! but how Dr. Johnson knew the World', Piozzi wrote in the margin of her copy sixty years later: 'He meant Imlac as his own Representative to *his own* feelings; The Lady was Miss Molly Aston . . .'[23]

Yet there is also a more important and, on the author's part, a much more deliberate sense in which *Rasselas* demands to be read as specifically a book by Johnson. If *Rasselas* took just a week to set down, there is also a sense in which its author had been preparing to write it for decades, drawing for theme and technique alike on resources he had been developing over half his lifetime. Here too Hawkins gives a useful lead:

The fact, respecting the writing and publishing the story of Rasselas is, that finding the Eastern Tales written by himself in the Rambler, and by Hawkesworth in the Adventurer, had been well received, he had been for some time meditating a fictitious history, of a greater extent than any that had appeared in either of those papers, which might serve as a vehicle to convey to the world his sentiments of human life and the dispensations of Providence, and having digested his thoughts on the subject, he obeyed the spur of that necessity which now pressed him, and sat down to compose the tale above-mentioned, laying the scene of it in a country that he had before occasion to contemplate, in his translation of Padre Lobo's voyage.[24]

[22] Irvin Ehrenpreis, '*Rasselas* and some Meanings of "Structure" in Literary Criticism', *Novel*, 14 (1981), 101–2; for Johnson's penance in the marketplace at Uttoxeter, see *Boswell's Life of Johnson*, iv, 373.

[23] Marginalia by Hester Thrale Piozzi in her 1818 edition of *Rasselas*, now at the Houghton Library, Harvard University, quoted by H. J. Jackson, *Marginalia: Readers Writing in Books* (New Haven: Yale University Press, 2001), 107–8.

[24] Hawkins, *Life of Johnson*, 366.

Hawkins is not always an accurate source, but unlike Boswell he already knew Johnson quite well in this period, and we should take seriously his suggestion that *Rasselas* had been in gestation since the time of the *Rambler* and the *Adventurer* (a periodical of 1752–4, managed by John Hawkesworth, to which Johnson also contributed). Others who knew Johnson later in life trace the origins of the work at least as far back as this, and the usually reliable William Shaw, a Gaelic scholar whose career Johnson promoted, reports it as 'known to many of the Doctor's friends, that his *Rasselas or Prince of Abyssinia* was an early conception, on which his ideas were matured long before the completion of the work'.[25] Whatever the facts, it can be no coincidence that Johnson's first published book was *A Voyage to Abyssinia* (1735), the English translation of a travel narrative by Father Jerónimo Lobo, a Portuguese Jesuit involved in seventeenth-century attempts to subject the Abyssinian Patriarchate, which had cut itself off from mainstream Christianity following the Council of Chalcedon in 451, to doctrinal and political control by the Papacy in Rome. Further information about Ethiopian geography, natural history, religion, and culture—with, as one might expect at the time, the occasional exotic dose of disinformation—was known to Johnson from other sources, and he also had a lifelong interest in the various Islamic cultures and settings toured by his protagonists in *Rasselas*, whom he implicitly establishes—though this is easy for modern readers to miss—as Monophysite African Christians. Years later, Johnson identified Lady Mary Wortley Montagu's posthumously published account of life at the Ottoman court as the only non-obligatory book that he had ever read cover to cover, and in the year of *Rasselas* he was the obvious choice to write a preface to *The World Displayed* (1759–61), a multi-volume collection of voyage narratives, many of them concerning the East. Rather than define the new worlds documented in these narratives as promising sites for colonial adventure, Johnson introduces the work with a characteristic effect of eloquent, measured outrage: 'The *Europeans* have scarcely visited any coast, but to gratify avarice,

---

[25] William Shaw, *Memoirs of the Life and Writings of the Late Dr. Samuel Johnson*, 133.

and extend corruption; to arrogate dominion without right, and practise cruelty without incentive.'[26]

Mingling with Johnson's memories of Lobo and his ongoing reading about Africa and Asia were his occasional exercises in the popular eighteenth-century form of the oriental or eastern tale (which, in Johnson's hands, sometimes becomes an African tale). As early as 1748 he had contributed an allegorical fiction entitled 'The Vision of Theodore, The Hermit of Teneriffe' to an educational textbook published by Robert Dodsley, and although the *Rambler* remains the most important repository of Johnson's oriental tales, he continued to produce fiction in this vein for the *Idler* (1758–60), the periodical he was writing with one hand while *Rasselas* was written with the other. By including this material in periodicals otherwise mainly devoted to moral, critical, and philosophical essays, and to socially satirical pieces about manners and taste, Johnson tapped into an enduring vogue, already discernible in seventeenth-century English literature but traceable in particular to the widely imitated 'Grubstreet' translation (1704–17) of Antoine Galland's *Arabian Nights' Entertainments*. Exotic and sensuous, exuberantly unbound by the conventions of realism and moral decorum that regulated the emergent novel, the oriental tale provided an alternative space in narrative fiction for the fabulous and supernatural, and for the play of imagination and dream. The intoxicating blend of extravagant fantasy and luxuriant hyperbole that characterized the most successful oriental tales of the period—works such as Hawkesworth's *Almoran and Hamet* (1761), Frances Sheridan's *The History of Nourjahad* (1767), and William Beckford's scandalous *Vathek* (1786)—also suggests the opportunities for symbolic patterning that were inherent in the mode, free as it was from the contingencies and clutter inherent in novelistic realism. One need only think of the presence in *Rasselas* of the Nile, which dominates the narrative as much as any human character, to see how Johnson was drawn to possibilities of this kind. Throughout the work, the Nile accompanies Rasselas and his party from its imagined source in the

---

[26] *The World Displayed*, 20 vols. (1759–61), I, xvi. For Johnson on Montagu see G. B. Hill (ed.), *Johnsonian Miscellanies*, 2 vols. (Oxford: Clarendon Press, 1897), i, 319.

uplands of Abyssinia to its climactic inundation near Cairo, and it also supplies the text as a whole—so urgent in its warnings about the need to remember 'the stream of time' and commit to 'the current of the world' (p. 77)—with its pervasive aquacities of thought and language. The river is there at the opening of the narrative, supplying the Happy Valley with 'delights and superfluities' (p. 8) and upbraiding Rasselas for failing to engage with 'the flux of life' (p. 15); it remains there at the end, flooding the Egyptian plain and teaching Imlac and the recovering astronomer to let themselves go with the flow: 'to be driven along the stream of life without directing their course' (p. 109).

Yet even the all-providing river is a reminder of the limitations placed on human fulfilment, for as Nekayah puts it, with beautiful economy, 'no man can, at the same time, fill his cup from the source and from the mouth of the Nile' (p. 66). Against the fluid, liberating energies of the father of waters, moreover, Johnson also sets the oppressive stasis of brick and stone. No less rich in symbolic and structural importance is the built environment of *Rasselas*, in which the hero's journey of the mind and soul also leads him from his palace prison in the first phase of the narrative, with its 'unsuspected cavities' and 'subterranean passages' (p. 9), through the 'dark labyrinths, and costly rooms' (p. 72) of the pyramid he enters at the end of the second phase, to the 'labyrinth of subterraneous passages' in the catacombs at the end of the third (p. 105). All these places serve different functions thematically, the first expressing the constraint and frustration of Rasselas in the Happy Valley, the second allowing Imlac to declaim against the vanity of imperial power, and the third provoking the penultimate chapter's climactic debate about the material body and the immaterial soul. Yet all these buildings also share a common vulnerability in the face of time—'palaces and temples will be demolished to make stables of granate, and cottages of porphyry' (p. 83), Pekuah learns from the Arab chief—and the claustrophobic atmosphere that characterizes them all reinforces Johnson's suggestion that his hero's pursuit of happiness will often involve change but no real progress, or will simply hit a brick wall.

Yet it was not as a poet but as a philosopher that Johnson was above all drawn to oriental fiction. Certainly the genre reached deep into his psyche, and *Rasselas* was not the only time when his instinctive reaction to anticipated loss was to write an oriental tale; the *Rambler* narrative most frequently cited as a precursor of *Rasselas*—the tale of 'Seged, lord of Ethiopia', whose efforts to dictate happiness by political fiat collapse on the death of his cherished daughter—was also produced at a point of bereavement.[27] But always Johnson's conscious motive was intellectual. Oriental fiction may have been marketable, and lyrical, and therapeutic, but he wanted in particular to exploit the hospitality of the genre to metaphysical and ethical reflection—a hospitality which, like its potential as symbolism or dream, was again an effect of its non-realist tendency 'to escape', as Carey McIntosh writes, 'from familiar contingencies into an environment almost hypothetically pure'.[28] In various *Spectator* papers of 1711–12, Joseph Addison had been one of several predecessors to transform the oriental tale into a vehicle of philosophical exposition, and in this respect the fictional element in Johnson's essay periodicals is less anomalous than at first appears. Accordingly, wherever Johnson looks to be on the cusp of a cliché of oriental fiction, his next move is to overturn generic expectations or frustrate readerly desires. The abduction of Pekuah by marauding Arabs is a case in point, at first sight a staple twist in the oriental plot, central to the atmosphere of sensual extravagance and erotic obsession that characterizes the genre. Far from raping and pillaging in the approved manner, however, the Arab chief turns out to be a world-weary Johnsonian melancholic, bored by the absence of philosophical conversation from his seraglio, and never happier than when cultivating his passion for archaeology or astronomy and polishing his rhetorical abstractions. 'The lance that is lifted at guilt and power will sometimes fall on innocence and gentleness', he tells Pekuah in his reasoned account of Arab banditry as a just mode of resistance to Turkish imperialism (p. 82), and it is he who shakes his head,

[27] See James L. Clifford, *Dictionary Johnson: Samuel Johnson's Middle Years* (New York: McGraw-Hill, 1979), 207. Johnson's wife Tetty died on the night of 17/18 March 1752; for the tale of Seged, see *Rambler* 204–5 (29 February, 3 March 1752), *YW*, v, 296–305.

[28] Carey McIntosh, *The Choice of Life: Samuel Johnson and the World of Fiction* (New Haven: Yale University Press, 1973), 89.

with connoisseurly regret, over the dilapidation of temples to make stables of granite. This violation of generic norms in *Rasselas* was Ruffhead's main point of attack in the *Monthly Review*, but he failed to see that on Johnson's part the effect was a conscious strategy, even a comic one. Referring to a well-known bookshop and circulating library that specialized in disposable fiction, Ruffhead scoffed that *Rasselas* 'will impose upon many of Mr. Noble's fair customers, who, while they expect to frolic along the flowery paths of romance, will *f*ind themselves hoisted on metaphysical stilts, and born aloft into the regions of syllogistic subtlety, and philosophical refinement'.[29]

Still less did the philosophical priorities of *Rasselas* leave room to imitate other aspects of fiction that developed in the period, including those that Johnson most admired. One of his first and most celebrated *Rambler* papers was his defence of the realist novel in *Rambler* 4 (31 March 1750), and here—his future authorship of *Rasselas* notwithstanding—Johnson singles out for praise the close commitment to everyday life of the new fiction, which 'can neither bewilder its personages in desarts, nor lodge them in imaginary castles'. As the essay proceeds, however, the capacity of realist fiction to absorb and command the imagination of readers becomes a two-edged sword, admirable in aesthetic terms, but morally hazardous. Because of their imaginative hold, novels enjoy formidable didactic potential, and 'may perhaps be made of greater use than the solemnities of professed morality, and convey the knowledge of vice and virtue with more efficacy than axioms and definitions'. As *Rasselas* reminds us in its remarkable account of the mad astronomer, however, imagination is not always subservient to reason, and can just as well mutiny against it in any mind. 'But if the power of example is so great, as to take possession of the memory by a kind of violence, and produce effects almost without the intervention of the will,' Johnson continues in *Rambler* 4, 'care ought to be taken that, when the choice is unrestrained, the best examples only should be exhibited, and that which is likely to operate so strongly, should not be mischievous in its effects' (*YW*, iii, 19, 21–2). The novelist is thus caught in

[29] *Monthly Review*, xx (May 1759), 437.

a bind, urged on the one hand to represent life as it is, warned on the other to deal only in moral absolutes, avoiding all shades of grey.

Rambler 4 is often read as a broadside against Henry Fielding's *Tom Jones* (1749), but its central anxiety—about the corruption of readers by 'splendidly wicked' characters 'whose endowments throw a brightness on their crimes' (*YW*, iii, 23)—applies as much if not more to Samuel Richardson's *Clarissa* (1747–8). As such, this essay does much to explain why, in a work committed to rational enquiry and suspicious of the imagination as a site of disease and disorder, Johnson works so hard as a practitioner of fiction to avoid the representational priorities and techniques that he elsewhere praises as a critic. Whether or not Johnson could have written a novel in the usual sense of the term is an open question, but in *Rasselas* he studiously refuses to do so, as though nothing must be allowed to complicate or jeopardize the clarity of his philosophical discourse. From the metropolitan bustle of Cairo to the gloom of the catacombs, evocations of setting are stripped of solidity of specification, and as Srinivas Aravamudan has noted, the Happy Valley in particular is represented in a generalizing style of 'romance periphrasis' that 'bypasses the open-ended empirical representation favored by novels'.[30] Instead, Johnson identifies *Rasselas* as a moral vision or thought experiment in which Richardsonian techniques of particularization and individualization have no part to play. All the characters in *Rasselas* speak the same Johnsonian language, and Johnson's refusal to equip his diverse cast with individualizing idiolects was a matter of mockery at the time: 'I hardly ever hear a sentence uttered by the Princess, or the Lady Pekuah, but I see the enormous Johnson in petticoats', wrote a critic of 1787 (Hayley, *Two Dialogues*, 106). The effect is so self-conscious, however, as to escape this kind of sneer. Where Richardson equips the servant heroine of *Pamela* (1740) with dialect expressions and a rich arsenal of homespun proverbs, her counterpart in *Rasselas* says nothing about crying over spilt milk when she breaks a porcelain cup, and instead observes, with emphatic Johnson parallelism, 'that

[30] Srinivas Aravamudan, *Tropicopolitans: Colonialism and Agency, 1688–1804* Durham, NC: Duke University Press, 1999), 203.

what cannot be repaired is not to be regretted' (p. 16). As well as countering the usual oriental stereotype of passionate simplicity, the elevated discourse or intellectual sophistication shared by all Johnson's characters, servants and bandits included, works here as a non-realist distancing device, a constant reminder to approach *Rasselas* not as absorptive fiction but as philosophical treatise.

Elsewhere, Johnson is just as keen to emphasize his distance from the comedy of Fielding. Alongside its resemblance to Johnson's own tale of Seged, early readers would immediately have recognized the sudden death of the Stoic's daughter in chapter xviii of *Rasselas*—so revealing his vaunted philosophy to be no fortification against loss—as reworking a celebrated episode from *Joseph Andrews* (1742). But where Fielding milks the episode for laughs, and eventually returns his own failed Stoic to a protected comic realm—after heartfelt laments for his supposedly drowned son, Parson Adams glimpses the boy 'in a wet Condition indeed, but alive, and running towards him'[31]—Johnson pointedly follows another method. The Stoic's daughter disappears from the narrative with an offhand finality that neatly enacts the abruptness of bereavement, and also the indifference of the unbereaved. Rasselas and his party then move on, their lesson about Stoicism learned.

It would be wrong to conclude, however, that the outcome of Johnson's resistance to the emerging conventions of the novel was simple didactic transparency. Philosophical discourse is certainly to the fore in *Rasselas*, trumping other considerations, and the work can legitimately be read as an extended resumption of *Rambler* themes, often close in argument or wording to Johnson's essays on grief, happiness, hope, patience, retirement. The episodic structure of the narrative assists this essayistic function, and by sending his characters to converse with proponents of varying conceptions of happiness, ancient and modern, Johnson produces a condensed satirical history of western philosophy, from the Stoic, Epicurean, and Aristotelian schools to post-Lockean materialism and the deist philosophy of nature. On political issues, the

---

[31] Henry Fielding, *Joseph Andrews*, ed. Thomas Keymer (Oxford: Oxford World's Classics, 1999), 271 (iv. 8).

work unquestionably gives Johnson room to strike unambiguous
positions in tune with his journalism, and here it is worth noting
the extent to which, much against the grain of oriental fiction in
general, *Rasselas* constantly implies, and sometimes makes explicit,
unyielding hostility to the imperial project. As Clement Hawes
has shown in detail, 'the term "Orientalism" . . . does not illuminate *Rasselas*',[32] and the environment of the tale, though exotic and
despotic in the usual manner, is never presented according to
orientalist stereotype as a desirable arena or a legitimate target for
colonial appropriation. From his earliest career Johnson had been
satirizing just the literary assumptions critiqued by Edward Said
and his followers in the twentieth century, and in a *Gentleman's
Magazine* column of 1738 he borrows Swift's Gulliver persona to
target the self-serving 'imaginary sovereignty' of European states,
which 'have made Conquests, and settled Colonies in very distant
Regions, the Inhabitants of which they look upon as barbarous,
though in Simplicity of Manners, Probity, and Temperance superior to themselves'.[33] Johnson intensified this kind of rhetoric on the
outbreak of the Seven Years War, famously likening the campaign
for American supremacy between Britain and France to 'the quarrel of two robbers for the spoils of a passenger' (*YW*, x, 188). At
the same time he showed no illusions about colonial adventure as
a route to happiness, whether personal or social: 'And since
the end of all human actions is happiness,' he asks at one point,
'why should any number of our inhabitants be banished from
their trades and their homes to a trackless desert, where life is
to begin anew' (*YW*, x, 211). Far from being an 'orientalist' in the
Saidian sense, one for whom lush new worlds were alluring fair
game, Johnson was notorious in the year of *Rasselas*—the 'Year
of Victories', in which the war turned decisively in Britain's
favour—as a prophet against empire, doggedly resistant to the
opportunities for domination of the globe from Asia to America
that were suddenly opening up.

[32] Clement Hawes, *The British Eighteenth Century and Global Critique* (New York: Palgrave Macmillan, 2005), 184.

[33] *Gentleman's Magazine*, viii (June 1738), 285.

Hence perhaps the defensively patriotic paper on which *Rasselas* was printed. Hence also the firm conviction of the work that oriental bliss was a pernicious myth, deserving a rebuttal that Johnson presents in a characteristic 'lose-lose' formulation: 'The Europeans, answered Imlac, are less unhappy than we, but they are not happy' (p. 32). Having confronted and debunked the literary cliché of the orient as a vast Happy Valley, Johnson then goes on to laud the achievements of eastern cultures, ancient and modern, comparing these favourably with his own: 'The old Egyptians have left behind them monuments of industry and power before which all European magnificence is confessed to fade away', Imlac declares (p. 67), while modern Persia, India, and China display virtues and accomplishments unmatched elsewhere.

But this does not mean that *Rasselas* fails to recognize the future of European domination that awaited many of the lands it describes, imminently so in the case of India. Like Gulliver in Lilliput, the would-be aviator of chapter vi envisages with alarm the exploitation of his technology in the cause of imperial annexation, and his vision of a conquering 'flight of northern savages' (p. 20) not only evokes the Ottoman Empire to the north of Abyssinia, or the northern barbarians who sacked ancient Rome, but also glances at the potent expansionist forces of modern Europe. A few chapters later, the threat of technological advance in 'the northern and western nations of Europe; the nations which are now in possession of all power and all knowledge; whose armies are irresistible, and whose fleets command the remotest parts of the globe' (p. 29), is given salient discussion. Intriguingly, it was for this passage that Johnson searched on picking up a copy of *Rasselas* in 1781 for the first time since publication (or so he announced, though he had certainly examined the American edition in 1773).[34] He might have turned to other nearby chapters for episodes of tyranny and oppression, and from the despotism of the Abyssinian emperor (against whom Rasselas rebels by leaving the Happy Valley, and whose rule he dreams of replacing with enlightened autocracy) to the exploitation of Egypt by a corrupt Ottoman bureaucracy, the narrative plays out against a

---

[34] See *Boswell's Life of Johnson*, iv, 119.

relentless background of political injustice. As Gerald MacLean has argued, the Ottoman example provided an established model, both energizing and cautionary, for thinking about empire 'at a time when the English were seeking to find a place for themselves in the larger world beyond their insular realm'.[35] Here was another opportunity provided for Johnson by the oriental form, which he exploited with recurrent reference—especially in Ottoman contexts: the Arab's speech against Turkish usurpation, or the fall of the Bassa of Egypt—to imperial overreach and misrule.

On other questions, however, *Rasselas* offers less of a straightforward route to Johnsonian opinion. Its method is dialectic, not linear exposition of pre-established truth but a relentlessly sceptical testing of arguments and positions against one another, without the easy outcomes of authorial assertion. The method is based in a conviction, as Rasselas and Imlac discuss in chapter xi, that it is from 'diversity of opinions' that wisdom emerges, and that 'we grow more happy as our minds take a wider range' (pp. 30–1), and here too, as well as in strictly thematic matters, the *Rambler* and other periodicals were essential preparation for *Rasselas*. Johnson's is in many contexts a voice of aggressive conviction, but as his subtlest modern readers have shown, he practises periodical writing in the spirit of a Montaigne essay or a Cicero dialogue, as a mode of provisional argument or intellectual testing, displaying as he does so 'a mind perpetually in movement, a mind that never reposes on the stability of truth'. Adam Potkay writes of Johnson's 'fine art of propositional counterpoint' as 'the dialogue of a doubled self', and for Fred Parker the periodical essay is in his hands 'a form which interrogates an opening position, "sees more", and modifies or complicates it, without pretence to finality or system, since implicit in the genre is the awareness that another day will bring another essay with a different starting-point'.[36] *Rasselas* pursues this exploratory method to extremes, not least by

---

[35] Gerald MacLean, *Looking East: English Writing and the Ottoman Empire before 1800* (Basingstoke: Palgrave Macmillan, 2007), xi.

[36] Fred Parker, *Scepticism and Literature: An Essay on Pope, Hume, Sterne, and Johnson* (Oxford: Oxford University Press, 2003), 238; Adam Potkay, *The Passion for Happiness: Samuel Johnson and David Hume* (Ithaca: Cornell University Press, 2000), 213, 212; Parker, *Scepticism*, 238.

adding emphatic warnings against the very means of enquiry, both rational and rhetorical, on which it depends in itself. As Imlac notes of the almost Johnsonian eloquence of the Stoic, who 'reasons, and conviction closes his periods', those who set up as teachers of morality often deal in empty words—'they discourse like angels, but they live like men'—and at the end of the chapter Rasselas comes to understand 'the inefficacy of polished periods and studied sentences' (pp. 45, 46). This is a typical moment, in which, ardently searching for positive answers, Johnson's hero learns only a negative, and it is characteristic of the negative dialectic that unfolds through the work as a whole. 'The more we enquire, the less we can resolve', he despairs at one point, before returning to look on the bright side: 'Thus it happens when wrong opinions are entertained, that they mutually destroy each other, and leave the mind open to truth' (p. 62).

But what is this promised truth, in a work that also flaunts its lack of conclusion? Traditionally, readers have sought to extract secure meaning from *Rasselas* by identifying the poet Imlac as Johnson's mouthpiece: a fictional equivalent to the biographical Johnson, the pugnacious, invincible conversionalist who, at the centre of Boswell's *Life*, crushes folly and error at every turn with blasts of unanswerable dogma. Even in his special field of poetry, however, Imlac's opinions are a notably unreliable surrogate for Johnson's own, and at some points he even advances positions, such as the markedly Hobbesian view of human depravity placed in his mouth in chapter ix, that Johnson himself abhorred.[37] By the same token, beliefs that seem authentically Johnsonian are sometimes given to the unlikeliest of spokesmen, as when the ludicrous aviator of chapter vi reproduces an argument in favour of ambition and risk that Johnson had previously advanced himself (see below, note to p. 19). Given the minimalist and noncommittal presence of Johnson's narrator, there seems no consistently reliable or authoritative voice to which the reader can turn, and the text remains irreducibly open. Boswell himself attempted to cut through these difficulties by declaring Johnson's work to be

[37] See Howard D. Weinbrot, 'The Reader, the General, and the Particular: Imlac and Johnson in Chapter Ten of *Rasselas*', *Eighteenth-Century Studies*, 5 (1971), 80–96.

(in contrast with Voltaire's irreligious *Candide*, published shortly beforehand) a repeat performance of *The Vanity of Human Wishes*, in which 'Johnson meant, by shewing the unsatisfactory nature of things temporal, to direct the hopes of man to things eternal'.[38] But apart from a single remark by Nekayah, this lesson is at best implicit, and Boswell's attempt to recuperate *Rasselas* as a work of consoling Christian doctrine only points up the unsettling reticence of Johnson's ending, so unlike the emphatic religious peroration that closes the earlier poem.

It is hardly a surprise, in this context, that readers craved more certain answers. Rumours of a compensatory sequel circulated at the time, though as Hawkins points out (in wry parody of Johnsonian diction) Johnson's conviction 'that in this state of our existence all our enjoyments are fugacious, and permanent felicity unattainable' would have made it impossible to meet his readers' desires.[39] In the decades following his death in 1784, other writers responded by providing *Rasselas* with remedial sequels of their own, and the infusion of practical and religious optimism into both—Ellis Cornelia Knight's *Dinarbas: A Tale* (1790) and Elizabeth Pope Whately's *The Second Part of the History of Rasselas* (1835)—is powerful evidence of just how unsettling Johnson's inconclusiveness remained.

For some readers, however, *Rasselas* could continue to symbolize the hopeful pursuit of autonomy and happiness. Alan Richardson is right to note Johnson's 'supreme indifference to skin colour in *Rasselas*, which makes so little of the blackness of its Abyssinians . . . that readers scarcely ever register it at all',[40] but that may not have been the case for African readers in the age of Ignatius Sancho and Olaudah Equiano, when the name of Johnson's hero was occasionally adopted by emancipated slaves. It is reasonable to speculate that young men such as Rasselas Belfield (*c.*1790–1822) and Rasselas Morjan (*c.*1820–1839), both of whom ended their lives as

---

[38] *Boswell's Life of Johnson*, i, 342.

[39] Hawkins, *Life of Johnson*, 372.

[40] Alan Richardson, 'Darkness Visible? Race and Representation in Bristol Abolitionist Poetry, 1770–1810', in Tim Fulford and Peter J. Kitson (eds.), *Romanticism and Colonialism: Writing and Empire, 1780–1830* (Cambridge: Cambridge University Press, 1998), 135.

free men in England, took their Christian names not only because Johnson's hero was one of very few eligible Africans in English literature (one would hardly pick Oroonoko, or Othello), and not only because Johnson himself was revered among abolitionists for his lifelong insistence that 'No man is by nature the property of another' (as he put it in a landmark legal case against slavery of 1777).[41] *Rasselas* is among much else an ingenious variation of the familiar eighteenth-century genre of the captivity narrative, documenting the hero's deliverance or escape, and in this sense the name also connoted escape from imprisonment into a world of potential fulfilment, confronted in freedom.

'RESCUED FROM A STATE OF SLAVERY IN THIS LIFE AND ENABLED BY GOD'S GRACE TO BECOME A MEMBER OF HIS CHURCH HE RESTS HERE IN THE HOPE OF A GREATER DELIVERANCE HEREAFTER', reads the headstone of Rasselas Morjan's grave in Wanlip, Leicestershire. At Bowness on Windermere, in Cumbria, Rasselas Belfield is memorialized in more secular style, and in first-person verse: 'A Slave by birth I left my native Land | And found my Freedom on Britannia's Strand: | Blest Isle! Thou Glory of the Wise and Free, | Thy Touch alone unbinds the Chains of Slavery.'[42] We cannot know the relationship between these rather conventional inscriptions and the lives and aspirations of their subjects, and although both men had been manumitted they continued to work as domestic servants—albeit, the expense of their monuments makes clear, as valued upper servants in enlightened households. However uncertain we might be about the completeness of their emancipation, however, we may be confident that Rasselas Belfield and Rasselas Morjan had a better chance of pursuing happiness than the majority of their counterparts across the Atlantic. In this context, it is interesting to observe that, as slavery in America at last neared its end in the Civil War of 1861–5, one of the most influential abolitionists involved, the Radical Republican senator Charles Sumner, was

[41] *Boswell's Life of Johnson*, iii, 203.

[42] For a transcription of Rasselas Belfield's headstone, see the notice of its listing as a historic monument (23 August 2008) at http://www.culture.gov.uk/reference_library/media_releases/5404.aspx; Rasselas Morjan's baptismal record and headstone are displayed at http://www.leicestershire.gov.uk/the_palmer_family_of_wanlip_hall.pdf.

also put in mind of Johnson's tale. 'The last chapter of "Rasselas" is entitled "The Conclusion, in which Nothing is Concluded",' declared Sumner in his famous Boston emancipation speech of 6 October 1862; 'and this will be the proper title for the history of this war, if Slavery is allowed to endure.'[43] Perhaps Sumner forgot that conclusions for Johnson were rarely happy, but he seems to have known that, with life itself to be endured, and enjoyed, *Rasselas* would always remain a resource worth keeping in mind.

[43] *The Works of Charles Sumner*, 15 vols. (Boston: Lee and Shepard, 1870–83), vii, 229.

NOTE ON THE TEXT

JAMES BOSWELL reports Johnson as saying in 1781 that he had not looked at *Rasselas* 'since it was first published', and he also records Johnson's undated recollection 'that he composed it in the evenings of one week, sent it to the press in portions as it was written, and had never since read it over'.[1] It is now assumed, however, that these anecdotes somewhat compress a short period of more or less continuous activity over the first six months of 1759, when, following its rapid initial composition, apparently in January, *Rasselas* appeared in an accurate but sometimes hastily worded first edition of 19 or 20 April, and then went through a process of light but meticulous textual revision before reappearing in a 'corrected' second edition (strictly speaking a corrected reimpression, with type rearranged rather than reset) of 26 June 1759.[2] No subsequent edition of *Rasselas* between 3 April 1760 and Johnson's death in 1784 shows signs of authorial revision, but scholars have accepted the argument first made by O. F. Emerson in 1899 and developed by R. W. Chapman in his edition of 1927 that substantive variants in the second edition were introduced by Johnson himself.[3] Most of these changes are to single words, and none runs to more than a sentence. But they go far beyond the usual scope of merely compositorial correction, they sharpen and polish the prose in ways characteristic of Johnson's style, and they conform to his practice elsewhere (as in early reprints of the *Rambler*) of fine-tuning his writing in the aftermath of publication

[1] *Boswell's Life of Johnson*, ed. G. B. Hill, rev. L. F. Powell, 6 vols. (Oxford: Clarendon Press, 1934–64), iv, 119; i, 341.

[2] J. D. Fleeman, *A Bibliography of the Works of Samuel Johnson*, 2 vols. (Oxford: Clarendon Press, 2000), i, 785–90; see also Donald D. Eddy, 'The Publication Date of the First Edition of *Rasselas*', *Notes and Queries*, 9 (1962), 21–2. 'Corrected reimpression' is Fleeman's term; the second edition was announced as 'corrected' in newspaper advertisements (e.g. *Daily Advertiser*, 26 July 1759) but not on its title page.

[3] O. F. Emerson, 'The Text of Johnson's *Rasselas*', *Anglia*, 22 (1899), 499–509; Samuel Johnson, *The History of Rasselas, Prince of Abissinia*, ed. R. W. Chapman (Oxford: Clarendon Press, 1927), pp. xvii–xxi; see also Johnson, *Rasselas and Other Tales*, ed. Gwin J. Kolb (New Haven: Yale University Press, 1990), lxvii–lxx.

but leaving it unchanged when further separated in time from the original impulse of composition.

The present edition reprints the text established by Chapman, which incorporates Johnson's revisions to the second edition but also restores first-edition readings in a few cases of compositorial error and follows the third and later editions in correcting the sequence of chapter numbers (which goes awry in both editions of 1759 when two consecutives chapters are numbered XXVIII). In the present text, minor adjustments of house style have been made to the table of contents and the chapter headings.

One small mystery remains. Although the original manuscript of *Rasselas* does not survive, a copy of the first edition apparently presented to the novelist Samuel Richardson and bearing the ownership inscription of Richardson's daughter Anne contains eight handwritten emendations to the text, only the first two of which are observed in the second edition. Opinions have differed about the status of this copy (once owned by the collector Jerome Kern and now at the Beinecke Library, Yale University), but the most substantial of the changes recorded in it adds distinctively Johnsonian balance to a previously nondescript sentence (see below, 30.5–6), and collectively the corrections display several characteristic features of Johnson's handwriting, notably when compared with his style of mark-up in his proof sheets of *Taxation No Tyranny* (rescued by Boswell from a wastepaper basket and now in the Houghton Library, Harvard University) and his annotated copy of *A Dictionary of the English Language* (originally intended as printer's copy for the *Dictionary*'s fourth edition, and now in the British Library).[4] The handwriting is certainly not Richardson's, as has been suggested, though it was Richardson who docketed the copy as 'From the Author' on the front pastedown. The following table, keyed to page and line number in the present text, records the variants indicated in the Kern copy alongside the published readings of the first (1759a) and second (1759b) editions.

---

[4] The relevant pages are reproduced in *Samuel Johnson's Unpublished Revisions to the Dictionary of the English Language*, ed. Allen Reddick (Cambridge: Cambridge University Press, 2005).

7.15   pours *Kern, 1759b*] powers *1759a*
8.36   blissful *Kern, 1759b*] blisful *1759a*
8.36   these *1759a, 1759b*] those *Kern*
10.28   birds in *1759a, 1759b*] birds on *Kern*
11.4   drinks *1759a, 1759b*] drinks at *Kern*
30.6   bring *1759a, 1759b*] convey *Kern*
33.35   performance *1759a, 1759b*] performance *Kern*
71.11   fowl *1759a, 1759b*] fowls *Kern*

SELECT BIBLIOGRAPHY

Bibliography and Reference

Clifford, James L., and Greene, Donald J., *Samuel Johnson: A Survey and Bibliography of Critical Studies* (Minneapolis: University of Minnesota Press, 1970).

Clingham, Greg (ed.), *The Cambridge Companion to Samuel Johnson* (Cambridge: Cambridge University Press, 1997).

Greene, Donald J., and Vance, John A., *A Bibliography of Johnsonian Studies, 1970–1985* (Victoria: University of Victoria, 1987).

Fleeman, J. D., *A Bibliography of the Works of Samuel Johnson, Treating His Published Works from the Beginnings to 1984*, 2 vols. (Oxford: Clarendon Press, 2000); updated by Jim McLaverty at http://www.bibsocamer.org/BibSite/Fleeman/Fleeman-all.htm

Lynch, Jack, *A Bibliography of Johnson Studies, 1986–1998* (New York: AMS Press, 2000); updated at http://andromeda.rutgers.edu/~jlynch/Johnson/sjbib.html

Rogers, Pat, *The Samuel Johnson Encyclopedia* (Westport: Greenwood Press, 1996).

Biography

Bate, Walter Jackson, *Samuel Johnson* (New York: Harcourt Brace Jovanovich, 1977).

Clifford, James L., *Dictionary Johnson: Samuel Johnson's Middle Years* (New York: McGraw-Hill, 1979).

DeMaria, Robert, *The Life of Samuel Johnson: A Critical Biography* (Oxford: Blackwell, 1993).

Lipking, Lawrence, *Samuel Johnson: The Life of an Author* (Cambridge, Mass.: Harvard University Press, 1988).

Sources, Publication, Reception

Alkon, Paul, 'Illustrations of *Rasselas* and Reader-Response Criticism', in Donald Greene (ed.), *Samuel Johnson: Pictures and Words* (Los Angeles: William Andrews Clark Memorial Library, 1984), 3–62.

Boulton, James T. (ed.), *Johnson: The Critical Heritage* (London: RKP, 1971).

Eddy, Donald D., 'The Publication Date of the First Edition of *Rasselas*', *Notes and Queries*, 9 (1962), 21–2.

Eversole, Richard, 'Imlac and the Poets of Persia and Arabia', *Philological Quarterly*, 58 (1979), 155–70.

Folkenflik, Robert, 'The Tulip and Its Streaks: Contexts of *Rasselas* X', *Ariel*, 9 (1978), 57–71.

Hudson, Nicholas, 'Three Steps to Perfection: *Rasselas* and the Philosophy of Richard Hooker', *Eighteenth-Century Life*, 14 (1990), 29–39.

Jackson, H. J., *Marginalia: Readers Writing in Books* (New Haven: Yale University Press, 2001), ch. 4.

Kolb, Gwin J., 'The Early Reception of *Rasselas*', in Paul J. Korshin and Robert R. Allen (eds.), *Greene Centennial Studies* (Charlottesville: University Press of Virginia, 1984), 217–49.

—— 'The Intellectual Background of the Discourse on the Soul in *Rasselas*', *Philological Quarterly*, 54 (1975), 357–69.

—— 'Johnson's "Dissertation on Flying" and John Wilkins's *Mathematical Magick*', *Modern Philology*, 47 (1949), 24–31.

—— 'Rousseau and the Background of the Life Led According to Nature in Chapter 22 of *Rasselas*', *Modern Philology*, 73 (1976), S66–S73.

—— 'The Use of Stoical Doctrines in *Rasselas*, Chapter XVIII', *Modern Language Notes*, 68 (1953), 439–47.

Landa, Louis, 'Johnson's Feathered Man: "A Dissertation on the Art of Flying" Considered', in W. H. Bond (ed.), *Eighteenth-Century Studies in Honor of Donald F. Hyde* (New York: Grolier Club, 1970), pp. 161–78.

Lockhart, Donald M., '"The Fourth Son of the Mighty Emperor": The Ethiopian Background of Johnson's *Rasselas*', *PMLA* 78 (1963), 516–28.

Mace, Nancy A., 'What Was Johnson Paid for *Rasselas*?', *Modern Philology*, 91 (1994), 455–8.

Metzdorf, Robert F., 'The First American *Rasselas* and Its Imprint', *Papers of the Bibliographical Society of America*, 47 (1953), 374–6.

Preston, Thomas R., 'The Biblical Context of Johnson's *Rasselas*', *PMLA* 84 (1969), 274–81.

Richard, Jessica, '"I Am Equally Weary of Confinement": *Rasselas* and Women Writers from *Dinarbas* to *Jane Eyre*', *Tulsa Studies in Women's Literature*, 22 (2003), 335–56.

Uphaus, Robert W., 'Cornelia Knight's *Dinarbas*: A Sequel to Rasselas', *Philological Quarterly*, 65 (1986), 433–46.

Wasserman, Earl R., 'Johnson's *Rasselas*: Implicit Contexts', *Journal of English and Germanic Philology*, 74 (1975), 1–25.

Weitzman, Arthur J., 'More Light on *Rasselas*: The Background of the Egyptian Episodes', *Philological Quarterly*, 48 (1969), 42–58.

Rasselas *Criticism*

Baker, Sheridan, '*Rasselas*: Psychological Irony and Romance', *Philological Quarterly*, 45 (1966), 249–61.

Braverman, Richard, 'The Narrative Architecture of *Rasselas*', *The Age of Johnson*, 3 (1990), 91–111.

Damrosch, Leopold, 'Johnson's *Rasselas*: Limits of Wisdom, Limits of Art', in Douglas Lane Patey and Timothy Keegan (eds.), *Augustan Studies: Essays in Honor of Irvin Ehrenpreis* (Newark: University of Delaware Press, 1985), 205–14.

Ehrenpreis, Irvin, '*Rasselas* and some Meanings of "Structure" in Literary Criticism', *Novel*, 14 (1981), 101–17.

Folkenflik, Robert, '*Rasselas* and the Closed Field', *Huntington Library Quarterly*, 57 (1994), 337–52.

Hansen, Marlene R., 'Sex and Love, Marriage and Friendship: A Feminist Reading of the Quest for Happiness in *Rasselas*', *English Studies*, 66 (1985), 513–25.

Hardy, John, 'Hope and Fear in Johnson', *Essays in Criticism*, 26 (1976), 285–99.

Hilles, F. W., '*Rasselas* as "Uninstructive Tale"', in Mary Lascelles, James L. Clifford, J. D. Fleeman, and J. P. Hardy (eds.), *Johnson, Boswell, and Their Circle: Essays Presented to Lawrence Fitzroy Powell* (Oxford: Clarendon Press, 1965), 111–21.

Hudson, Nicholas, '"Open" and "Enclosed" Readings of *Rasselas*', *The Eighteenth Century: Theory and Interpretation*, 31 (1990), 47–67.

Jones, Emrys, 'The Artistic Form of *Rasselas*', *Review of English Studies*, 18 (1967), 387–401.

Justice, George, 'Imlac's Pedagogy', *The Age of Johnson*, 13 (2002), 1–29.

Kolb, Gwin J., 'The Structure of *Rasselas*', *PMLA* 66 (1951), 698–717.

Mayhew, Robert J., 'Nature and the Choice of Life in *Rasselas*', *Studies in English Literature 1500–1900*, 39 (1999), 539–56.

O'Flaherty, Patrick, 'Dr. Johnson as Equivocator: The Meaning of *Rasselas*', *Modern Language Quarterly*, 31 (1970), 195–208.

Scherwatzky, Steven, 'Johnson, *Rasselas*, and the Politics of Empire', *Eighteenth-Century Life*, 16 (1992), 103–13.

Smith, Duane H., 'Repetitive Patterns in Samuel Johnson's *Rasselas*', *Studies in English Literature 1500–1900*, 36 (1996), 623–39.

Smith, Frederik N., 'Johnson, Beckett, and "The Choice of Life"', *The Age of Johnson*, 9 (1998), 187–200.

Tomarken, Edward, *Johnson, Rasselas, and the Choice of Criticism* (Lexington: University Press of Kentucky, 1989).

Walker, Robert G., *Eighteenth-Century Arguments for Immortality and Johnson's 'Rasselas'* (Victoria, BC: University of Victoria, 1977).

Wallace, Tara Ghoshal, '"Guarded with Fragments": Body and Discourse in *Rasselas*', *South Central Review*, 9 (1992), 31–45.

Weinbrot, Howard, 'The Reader, the General, and the Particular: Johnson and Imlac in Chapter Ten of *Rasselas*', *Eighteenth-Century Studies*, 5 (1971), 80–96.

Wimsatt, W. K., 'In Praise of *Rasselas*: Four Notes (Converging)', in Maynard Mack and Ian Gregor (eds.), *Imagined Worlds: Essays on some English Novels and Novelists in Honour of John Butt* (London: Methuen, 1968), 111–36.

Background and General Criticism

Aravamudan, Srinivas, *Tropicopolitans: Colonialism and Agency, 1688–1804* (Durham, NC: Duke University Press, 1999), esp. ch. 5.

Ballaster, Ros, *Fabulous Orients: Fictions of the East in England, 1662–1785* (Oxford: Oxford University Press, 2005).

Curley, Thomas, *Samuel Johnson and the Age of Travel* (Athens, Ga.: University of Georgia Press, 1976), esp. ch. 5.

Fussell, Paul, *Samuel Johnson and the Life of Writing* (New York: Harcourt Brace Javanovich, 1971), esp. ch. 8.

Henson, Eithne, *'The Fictions of Romantic Chivalry': Samuel Johnson and Romance* (London: Associated University Presses, 1992), esp. ch. 4.

Hudson, Nicholas, *Samuel Johnson and Eighteenth-Century Thought* (Oxford: Clarendon Press, 1988).

—— *Samuel Johnson and the Making of Modern England* (Cambridge: Cambridge University Press, 2003).

Johnston, Freya, *Samuel Johnson and the Art of Sinking, 1709–1791* (Oxford: Oxford University Press, 2005).

Kemmerer, Kathleen Nulton, *'A Neutral Being between the Sexes': Samuel Johnson's Sexual Politics* (Lewisburg, Pa.: Bucknell University Press, 1998), esp. ch. 5.

Kenshur, Oscar, *Dilemmas of Enlightenment: Studies in the Rhetoric and Logic of Ideology* (Berkeley: University of California Press, 1993), esp. ch. 6.

McIntosh, Carey, *The Choice of Life: Samuel Johnson and the World of Fiction* (New Haven: Yale University Press, 1973), esp. ch. 6.

MacLean, Gerald, *Looking East: English Writing and the Ottoman Empire before 1800* (London: Palgrave Macmillan, 2007).

Makdisi, Saree, and Nussbaum, Felicity (eds.), *The Arabian Nights in Historical Context* (Oxford: Clarendon Press, 2008).

McMahon, Darrin M., *Happiness: A History* (New York: Grove Press, 2006), esp. ch. 4.

Parke, Catherine N., *Samuel Johnson and Biographical Thinking* (Columbus, Mo.: University of Missouri Press, 1991), esp. ch. 4.

Parker, Fred, *Scepticism and Literature: An Essay on Pope, Hume, Sterne, and Johnson* (Oxford: Oxford University Press, 2003), esp. ch. 6.

Porter, Roy, *Flesh in the Age of Reason: The Modern Foundations of Body and Soul* (London: Allen Lane, 2003), esp. ch. 10.

Potkay, Adam, *The Passion for Happiness: Samuel Johnson and David Hume* (Ithaca: Cornell University Press, 2000), esp. ch. 10.

Rothstein, Eric, *Systems of Order and Inquiry in Later Eighteenth-Century Fiction* (Berkeley: University of California Press, 1975), esp. ch. 1.

Watts, Carol, *The Cultural Work of Empire: The Seven Years War and the Imagining of the Shandean State* (Edinburgh: Edinburgh University Press, 2007), esp. ch. 1.

Weinbrot, Howard D., *Aspects of Samuel Johnson: Essays on His Arts, Mind, Afterlife, and Politics* (Newark: University of Delaware Press, 2005), esp. chs. 6 and 8.

Wiltshire, John, *Samuel Johnson in the Medical World* (Cambridge: Cambridge University Press, 1991), esp. ch. 5.

Wimsatt, W. K., *The Prose Style of Samuel Johnson* (New Haven: Yale University Press, 1941).

Yolton, John S., *Thinking Matter: Materialism in Eighteenth-Century Britain* (Minneapolis: University of Minnesota Press, 1983).

Further Reading in Oxford World's Classics

Arabian Nights' Entertainments, ed. Robert L. Mack.

Boswell, James, *Life of Johnson*, ed. R. W. Chapman and J. D. Fleeman, introduction by Pat Rogers.

Johnson, Samuel, *The Lives of the Poets*, text ed. Roger Lonsdale, selected with an introduction and notes by John Mullan.

—— *The Major Works*, ed. Donald Greene.

Sterne, Laurence, *Tristram Shandy*, ed. Ian Campbell Ross.

Voltaire, *Candide and Other Stories*, trans. and ed. Roger Pearson.

A CHRONOLOGY OF SAMUEL JOHNSON

1709   Samuel Johnson born (7 September, OS; 18, NS) at Lichfield, Staffordshire.

1712   Taken to London to be touched by Queen Anne for 'the Evil' (scrofula). Nathanael Johnson (brother) born.

1717   Enters Lichfield Grammar School.

1726   Visits his cousin, the Revd Cornelius Ford, at Stourbridge, Worcestershire; attends school there.

1728   Enters Pembroke College, Oxford, in October; leaves December 1729.

1731   Michael Johnson (father) dies.

1732   Teaches for some months at Market Bosworth, Leicestershire.

1733   At Birmingham. Translates Lobo's *Voyage to Abyssinia* (published 1735).

1735   Marries Elizabeth Jervis Porter (widow of Harry Porter, and mother of Jervis, Joseph, and Lucy Porter).

1736   Opens school at Edial, near Lichfield. Begins *Irene*.

1737   Nathanael Johnson dies. Moves to London (March) with David Garrick.

1738   Begins writing for Edward Cave's *Gentleman's Magazine*; publishes *London: A Poem, in Imitation of the Third Satire of Juvenal*.

1739   *Marmor Norfolciense, A Complete Vindication of the Licensers of the Stage* (anti-government pamphlets). 'Life of Boerhaave'; translation of Crousaz's *Commentary* on Pope's *Essay on Man*.

1740   Lives of Admiral Robert Blake, Sir Francis Drake, Jean-Philippe Barretier.

1741–4   'Life of Sydenham'. Contributions to *Harleian Miscellany* and catalogue of the Harleian library. 'Debates in the Senate of Lilliput' and other journalism for the *Gentleman's Magazine*. *Life of Savage*.

1745   Proposals (abortive) for an edition of Shakespeare. *Miscellaneous Observations on Macbeth*.

1746 Signs contract for *Dictionary*.

1749 *The Vanity of Human Wishes. Irene* performed and published.

1750 Begins *The Rambler* (to 1752).

1752 Elizabeth ('Tetty') Johnson (wife) dies.

1753 Contributes to *The Adventurer*.

1754 Publishes biography of Edward Cave.

1755 *Dictionary of the English Language* published; awarded honorary MA degree by Oxford University.

1758 Begins *The Idler* (to 1760).

1759 Sarah Johnson (mother) dies. *Rasselas*.

1762 Awarded annual pension of £300 by government.

1763 Meets James Boswell.

1764 Founds 'the Club': members include Sir Joshua Reynolds, Oliver Goldsmith, and Edmund Burke.

1765 Edition of Shakespeare published. Meets Henry and Hester Thrale. Honorary LL D, Trinity College, Dublin.

1766 Severe depression; recovers with help of Hester Thrale.

1770 *The False Alarm*.

1771 *Thoughts on Falkland's Islands*.

1773 Revised editions of *Dictionary* and Shakespeare published. Tours Scotland (August to November) with Boswell.

1774 Tours Wales with the Thrales. *The Patriot*.

1775 *Journey to the Western Islands of Scotland. Taxation No Tyranny*. Honorary DCL, Oxford. Visits France with the Thrales.

1777 Agreement with booksellers to write prefaces to works of English poets (*The Lives of the Poets*). Unsuccessful campaign to reprieve the Revd William Dodd, condemned to be hanged for forgery.

1779 Opening set of *Lives of the Poets*.

1781 Henry Thrale dies. Closing set of *Lives* published.

1782 'On the Death of Dr Robert Levet'.

1783 Stroke, temporary loss of speech. Recovers; during winter of 1783–4 ill and depressed.

1784 Breach with Hester Thrale on her marriage to Gabriel Piozzi. Dies 13 December. Buried in Westminster Abbey, 20 December.

THE

PRINCE

OF

ABISSINIA,

A

TALE.

IN TWO VOLUMES.

VOL. I.

LONDON:

Printed for R. and J. Dodsley, in Pall-Mall;
and W. Johnston, in Ludgate-Street.
MDCCLIX.

CONTENTS

I   Description of a palace in a valley   7

II   The discontent of Rasselas in the happy valley   9

III The wants of him that wants nothing   12

IV   The prince continues to grieve and muse   13

V   The prince meditates his escape   16

VI   A dissertation on the art of flying   17

VII The prince finds a man of learning   20

VIII The history of Imlac   21

IX   The history of Imlac continued   24

X   Imlac's history continued. A dissertation
     upon poetry   27

XI   Imlac's narrative continued. A hint on pilgrimage   29

XII The story of Imlac continued   32

XIII Rasselas discovers the means of escape   35

XIV Rasselas and Imlac receive an unexpected visit   37

XV   The prince and princess leave the valley,
     and see many wonders   38

XVI They enter Cairo, and find every man happy   40

XVII The prince associates with young
     men of spirit and gaiety   43

XVIII The prince finds a wise and happy man   44

XIX A glimpse of pastoral life   46

XX   The danger of prosperity   47

XXI	The happiness of solitude. The hermit's history	49
XXII	The happiness of a life led according to nature	51
XXIII	The prince and his sister divide between them the work of observation	53
XXIV	The prince examines the happiness of high stations	54
XXV	The princess persues her enquiry with more diligence than success	55
XXVI	The princess continues her remarks upon private life	57
XXVII	Disquisition upon greatness	59
XXVIII	Rasselas and Nekayah continue their conversation	61
XXIX	The debate on marriage continued	63
XXX	Imlac enters, and changes the conversation	66
XXXI	They visit the pyramids	69
XXXII	They enter the pyramid	70
XXXIII	The princess meets with an unexpected misfortune	72
XXXIV	They return to Cairo without Pekuah	73
XXXV	The princess languishes for want of Pekuah	75
XXXVI	Pekuah is still remembered. The progress of sorrow	78
XXXVII	The princess hears news of Pekuah	79
XXXVIII	The adventures of the lady Pekuah	80
XXXIX	The adventures of Pekuah continued	83
XL	The history of a man of learning	88

XLI The astronomer discovers the cause
of his uneasiness 89

XLII The opinion of the astronomer is
explained and justified 90

XLIII The astronomer leaves Imlac his directions 92

XLIV The dangerous prevalence of imagination 93

XLV They discourse with an old man 95

XLVI The princess and Pekuah visit the astronomer 97

XLVII The prince enters and brings a new topick 102

XLVIII Imlac discourses on the nature of the soul 105

XLIX The conclusion, in which nothing is concluded 108

THE

HISTORY

OF

RASSELAS,

PRINCE OF ABISSINIA.

CHAP. I

Description of a palace in a valley

hope, if you have heres a tale to get over it.

YE who listen with credulity to the <u>whispers of fancy</u>, and persue with eagerness the <u>phantoms of hope</u>; who expect that age will perform the promises of youth, and that the deficiencies of the present day will be supplied by the morrow; attend to the history of Rasselas prince of Abissinia.*

Rasselas was the fourth son of the mighty emperour,* in whose dominions the Father of waters begins his course;* whose bounty pours down the streams of plenty, and scatters over half the world the harvests of Egypt.

According to the custom which has descended from age to age among the monarchs of the torrid zone, Rasselas was confined in a private palace, with the other sons and daughters of Abissinian royalty, till the order of succession should call him to the throne.

The place, which the wisdom or policy of antiquity had destined for the residence of the Abissinian princes, was a spacious valley in the kingdom of Amhara, surrounded on every side by mountains, of which the summits overhang the middle part.* The only passage, by which it could be entered, was a cavern that passed under a rock, of which it has long been disputed whether it was the work of nature or of human industry. The outlet of the cavern was concealed by a thick wood, and the mouth which opened into the valley was closed with gates of iron, forged by the artificers of ancient days, so massy that no man could, without the help of engines, open or shut them.

From the mountains on every side, rivulets descended that filled all the valley with verdure and fertility, and formed a lake in the middle inhabited by fish of every species, and frequented by every fowl whom nature has taught to dip the wing in water. This lake discharged its superfluities by a stream which entered a dark cleft of the mountain on the northern side, and fell with dreadful noise from precipice to precipice till it was heard no more.

The sides of the mountains were covered with trees, the banks of the brooks were diversified with flowers; every blast shook spices from the rocks, and every month dropped fruits upon the ground. All animals that bite the grass, or brouse the shrub, whether wild or tame, wandered in this extensive circuit, secured from beasts of prey by the mountains which confined them. On one part were flocks and herds feeding in the pastures, on another all the beasts of chase frisking in the lawns; the sprightly kid was bounding on the rocks, the subtle monkey frolicking in the trees, and the solemn elephant reposing in the shade. All the diversities of the world were brought together, the blessings of nature were collected, and its evils extracted and excluded.

The valley, wide and fruitful, supplied its inhabitants with the necessaries of life, and all delights and superfluities were added* at the annual visit which the emperour paid his children,* when the iron gate was opened to the sound of musick; and during eight days every one that resided in the valley was required to propose whatever might contribute to make seclusion pleasant, to fill up the vacancies of attention, and lessen the tediousness of time. Every desire was immediately granted. All the artificers of pleasure were called to gladden the festivity; the musicians exerted the power of harmony, and the dancers shewed their activity before the princes, in hope that they should pass their lives in this blissful captivity, to which these only were admitted whose performance was thought able to add novelty to luxury. Such was the appearance of security and delight which this retirement afforded, that they to whom it was new always desired that it might be perpetual; and as those, on whom the iron gate had once closed, were never suffered to return, the effect of longer experience could not be known. Thus every year produced new schemes of delight, and new competitors for imprisonment.

The palace stood on an eminence raised about thirty paces above the surface of the lake. It was divided into many squares or courts, built with greater or less magnificence according to the rank of those for whom they were designed. The roofs were turned into arches of massy stone joined with a cement that grew harder by time, and the building stood from century to century, deriding the solstitial rains and equinoctial hurricanes, without need of reparation.

This house, which was so large as to be fully known to none but some ancient officers who successively inherited the secrets of the place, was built as if suspicion herself had dictated the plan. To every room there was an open and secret passage, every square had a communication with the rest, either from the upper stories by private galleries, or by subterranean passages from the lower apartments. Many of the columns had unsuspected cavities, in which a long race of monarchs had reposited their treasures. They then closed up the opening with marble, which was never to be removed but in the utmost exigencies of the kingdom; and recorded their accumulations in a book which was itself concealed in a tower not entered but by the emperour, attended by the prince who stood next in succession.

CHAP. II

The discontent of Rasselas in the happy valley

HERE the sons and daughters of Abissinia* lived only to know the soft vicissitudes of pleasure and repose, attended by all that were skilful to delight, and gratified with whatever the senses can enjoy. They wandered in gardens of fragrance, and slept in the fortresses of security. Every art was practised to make them pleased with their own condition. The sages who instructed them, told them of nothing but the miseries of publick life, and described all beyond the mountains as regions of calamity, where discord was always raging, and where man preyed upon man.*

To heighten their opinion of their own felicity, they were daily entertained with songs, the subject of which was the *happy valley*. Their appetites were excited by frequent enumerations of different enjoyments, and revelry and merriment was the business of every hour from the dawn of morning to the close of even.

These methods were generally successful; few of the Princes had ever wished to enlarge their bounds, but passed their lives in full conviction that they had all within their reach that art or nature could bestow, and pitied those whom fate had excluded from this seat of tranquility, as the sport of chance, and the slaves of misery.*

Thus they rose in the morning, and lay down at night, pleased with each other and with themselves, all but Rasselas, who, in the twenty-sixth year of his age, began to withdraw himself from their pastimes and assemblies, and to delight in solitary walks and silent meditation. He often sat before tables covered with luxury, and forgot to taste the dainties that were placed before him: he rose abruptly in the midst of the song, and hastily retired beyond the sound of musick. His attendants observed the change and endeavoured to renew his love of pleasure: he neglected their officiousness,* repulsed their invitations, and spent day after day on the banks of rivulets sheltered with trees, where he sometimes listened to the birds in the branches, sometimes observed the fish playing in the stream, and anon cast his eyes upon the pastures and mountains filled with animals, of which some were biting the herbage, and some sleeping among the bushes.

This singularity of his humour made him much observed. One of the Sages, in whose conversation he had formerly delighted, followed him secretly, in hope of discovering the cause of his disquiet. Rasselas, who knew not that any one was near him, having for some time fixed his eyes upon the goats that were brousing among the rocks, began to compare their condition with his own.

'What,' said he, 'makes the difference between man and all the rest of the animal creation?* Every beast that strays beside me has the same corporal necessities with myself; he is hungry and crops the grass, he is thirsty and drinks the stream, his thirst and hunger are appeased, he is satisfied and sleeps; he rises again and is hungry, he is again fed and is at rest. I am hungry and thirsty like him, but when thirst and hunger cease I am not at rest; I am, like him, pained with want, but am not, like him, satisfied with fulness. The intermediate hours are tedious and gloomy; I long again to be hungry that I may again quicken my attention.* The birds peck the berries or the corn, and fly away to the groves where they sit in seeming happiness on the branches, and waste their lives in tuning one unvaried series of sounds. I likewise can call the lutanist and the singer, but the sounds that pleased me yesterday weary me to day, and will grow yet more wearisome to morrow.* I can discover within me no power of perception which is not glutted with its proper pleasure, yet I do not feel myself delighted. Man has surely some latent sense for which this place affords no gratification, or he has some desires distinct from sense which must be satisfied before he can be happy.'*

After this he lifted up his head, and seeing the moon rising, walked towards the palace. As he passed through the fields, and saw the animals around him, 'Ye, said he, are happy, and need not envy me that walk thus among you, burthened with myself; nor do I, ye gentle beings, envy your felicity; for it is not the felicity of man.* I have many distresses from which ye are free; I fear pain when I do not feel it; I sometimes shrink at evils recollected, and sometimes start at evils anticipated: surely the equity of providence has ballanced peculiar sufferings with peculiar enjoyments.'

With observations like these the prince amused himself as he returned, uttering them with a plaintive voice, yet with a look that discovered him to feel some complacence in his own perspicacity, and to receive some solace of the miseries of life, from consciousness of the delicacy with which he felt, and the eloquence with which he bewailed them.* He mingled cheerfully in the diversions of the evening, and all rejoiced to find that his heart was lightened.

CHAP. III

The wants of him that wants nothing

ON the next day his old instructor, imagining that he had now made himself acquainted with his disease of mind,* was in hope of curing it by counsel, and officiously sought an opportunity of conference, which the prince, having long considered him as one whose intellects were exhausted, was not very willing to afford: 'Why, said he, does this man thus intrude upon me; shall I be never suffered to forget those lectures which pleased only while they were new, and to become new again must be forgotten?' He then walked into the wood, and composed himself to his usual meditations; when, before his thoughts had taken any settled form, he perceived his persuer at his side, and was at first prompted by his impatience to go hastily away; but, being unwilling to offend a man whom he had once reverenced and still loved, he invited him to sit down with him on the bank.

The old man, thus encouraged, began to lament the change which had been lately observed in the prince, and to enquire why he so often retired from the pleasures of the palace, to loneliness and silence. 'I fly from pleasure, said the prince, because pleasure has ceased to please; I am lonely because I am miserable, and am unwilling to cloud with my presence the happiness of others.' 'You, Sir, said the sage, are the first who has complained of misery in the *happy valley*. I hope to convince you that your complaints have no real cause. You are here in full possession of all that the emperour of Abissinia can bestow; here is neither labour to be endured nor danger to be dreaded, yet here is all that labour or danger can procure or purchase. Look round and tell me which of your wants is without supply: if you want nothing, how are you unhappy?'

'That I want nothing, said the prince, or that I know not what I want, is the cause of my complaint; if I had any known want, I should have a certain wish; that wish would excite endeavour, and I should not then repine to see the sun move so slowly towards the western mountain, or lament when the day breaks and sleep will no longer hide me from myself. When I see the kids and the lambs chasing one another, I fancy that I should be happy if I had something to persue. But, possessing all that I can want, I find one day and one hour exactly like another, except that the latter is still more tedious than the former. Let your experience inform me how the day may now seem as short as in my childhood, while nature was yet fresh, and every moment shewed me what I never had observed before.* I have already enjoyed too much; give me something to desire.'

The old man was surprized at this new species of affliction, and knew not what to reply, yet was unwilling to be silent. 'Sir, said he, if you had seen the miseries of the world, you would know how to value your present state.' 'Now, said the prince, you have given me something to desire; I shall long to see the miseries of the world, since the sight of them is necessary to happiness.'*

CHAP. IV

The prince continues to grieve and muse

AT this time the sound of musick proclaimed the hour of repast, and the conversation was concluded. The old man went away sufficiently discontented to find that his reasonings had produced the only conclusion which they were intended to prevent. But in the decline of life shame and grief are of short duration; whether it be that we bear easily what we have born long, or that, finding ourselves in age less regarded, we less regard others; or, that we look with slight regard upon afflictions, to which we know that the hand of death is about to put an end.

The prince, whose views were extended to a wider space, could not speedily quiet his emotions. He had been before terrified at the length of life which nature promised him, because he considered that in a long time much must be endured; he now rejoiced in his youth, because in many years much might be done.

This first beam of hope, that had been ever darted into his mind, rekindled youth in his cheeks, and doubled the lustre of his eyes. He was fired with the desire of doing something, though he knew not yet with distinctness, either end or means.

He was now no longer gloomy and unsocial; but, considering himself as master of a secret stock of happiness, which he could enjoy only by concealing it, he affected to be busy in all schemes of diversion, and endeavoured to make others pleased with the state of which he himself was weary. But pleasures never can be so multiplied or continued, as not to leave much of life unemployed; there were many hours, both of the night and day, which he could spend without suspicion in solitary thought. The load of life was much lightened: he went eagerly into the assemblies, because he supposed the frequency of his presence necessary to the success of his purposes; he retired gladly to privacy, because he had now a subject of thought.

His chief amusement was to picture to himself that world which he had never seen; to place himself in various conditions; to be entangled in imaginary difficulties, and to be engaged in wild adventures: but his benevolence always terminated his projects in the relief of distress, the detection of fraud, the defeat of oppression, and the diffusion of happiness.

Thus passed twenty months of the life of Rasselas. He busied himself so intensely in visionary bustle, that he forgot his real solitude; and, amidst hourly preparations for the various incidents of human affairs, neglected to consider by what means he should mingle with mankind.

One day, as he was sitting on a bank, he feigned to himself an orphan virgin robbed of her little portion by a treacherous lover, and crying after him for restitution and redress. So strongly was the image impressed upon his mind, that he started up in the maid's defence, and run* forward to seize the plunderer with all the eagerness of real persuit. Fear naturally quickens the flight of guilt. Rasselas could not catch the fugitive with his utmost efforts; but, resolving to weary, by perseverance, him whom he could not surpass in speed, he pressed on till the foot of the mountain stopped his course.

Here he recollected himself, and smiled at his own useless impetuosity. Then raising his eyes to the mountain, 'This, said he, is the fatal obstacle that hinders at once the enjoyment of pleasure, and the exercise of virtue. How long is it that my hopes and wishes have flown beyond this boundary of my life, which yet I never have attempted to surmount!'

Struck with this reflection, he sat down to muse, and remembered, that since he first resolved to escape from his confinement, the sun had passed twice over him in his annual course. He now felt a degree of regret with which he had never been before acquainted. He considered how much might have been done in the time which had passed, and left nothing real behind it.* He compared twenty months with the life of man. 'In life, said he, is not to be counted the ignorance of infancy, or imbecility of age. We are long before we are able to think, and we soon cease from the power of acting. The true period of human existence may be reasonably estimated as forty years, of which I have mused away the four and twentieth part. What I have lost was certain, for I have certainly possessed it; but of twenty months to come who can assure me?'

The consciousness of his own folly pierced him deeply, and he was long before he could be reconciled to himself. 'The rest of my time, said he, has been lost by the crime or folly of my ancestors, and the absurd institutions of my country; I remember it with disgust, yet without remorse: but the months that have passed since new light darted into my soul, since I formed a scheme of reasonable felicity, have been squandered by my own fault. I have lost that which can never be restored: I have seen the sun rise and set for twenty months, an idle gazer on the light of heaven: In this time the birds have left the nest of their mother, and committed themselves to the woods and to the skies: the kid has forsaken the teat, and learned by degrees to climb the rocks in quest of independant sustenance. I only have made no advances, but am still helpless and ignorant. The moon by more than twenty changes, admonished me of the flux of life; the stream that rolled before my feet upbraided my inactivity. I sat feasting on intellectual luxury, regardless alike of the examples of the earth, and the instructions of the planets. Twenty months are past, who shall restore them!'

These sorrowful meditations fastened upon his mind; he past four months in resolving to lose no more time in idle resolves, and was awakened to more vigorous exertion by hearing a maid, who had broken a porcelain cup, remark, that what cannot be repaired is not to be regretted.*

This was obvious; and Rasselas reproached himself that he had not discovered it, having not known, or not considered, how many useful hints are obtained by chance, and how often the mind, hurried by her own ardour to distant views, neglects the truths that lie open before her. He, for a few hours, regretted his regret,* and from that time bent his whole mind upon the means of escaping from the valley of happiness.

CHAP. V

The prince meditates his escape

HE now found that it would be very difficult to effect that which it was very easy to suppose effected. When he looked round about him, he saw himself confined by the bars of nature which had never yet been broken, and by the gate, through which none that once had passed it were ever able to return. He was now impatient as an eagle in a grate.* He passed week after week in clambering the mountains, to see if there was any aperture which the bushes might conceal, but found all the summits inaccessible by their prominence. The iron gate he despaired to open; for it was not only secured with all the power of art, but was always watched by successive sentinels, and was by its position exposed to the perpetual observation of all the inhabitants.

He then examined the cavern through which the waters of the lake were discharged; and, looking down at a time when the sun shone strongly upon its mouth, he discovered it to be full of broken rocks, which, though they permitted the stream to flow through many narrow passages, would stop any body of solid bulk. He returned discouraged and dejected; but, having now known the blessing of hope,* resolved never to despair.

In these fruitless searches he spent ten months. The time, however, passed chearfully away: in the morning he rose with new hope, in the evening applauded his own diligence, and in the night slept sound after his fatigue. He met a thousand amusements which beguiled his labour, and diversified his thoughts. He discerned the various instincts of animals, and properties of plants, and found the place replete with wonders, of which he purposed to solace himself with the contemplation, if he should never be able to accomplish his flight; rejoicing that his endeavours, though yet unsucessful, had supplied him with a source of inexhaustible enquiry.

But his original curiosity was not yet abated; he resolved to obtain some knowledge of the ways of men. His wish still continued, but his hope grew less. He ceased to survey any longer the walls of his prison, and spared to search by new toils for interstices which he knew could not be found, yet determined to keep his design always in view, and lay hold on any expedient that time should offer.

CHAP. VI

*A dissertation on the art of flying**

AMONG the artists that had been allured into the happy valley, to labour for the accommodation and pleasure of its inhabitants, was a man eminent for his knowledge of the mechanick powers, who had contrived many engines both of use and recreation. By a wheel, which the stream turned, he forced the water into a tower, whence it was distributed to all the apartments of the palace. He erected a pavillion in the garden, around which he kept the air always cool by artificial showers. One of the groves, appropriated to the ladies, was ventilated by fans, to which the rivulet that run through it gave a constant motion; and instruments of soft musick were placed at proper distances, of which some played by the impulse of the wind, and some by the power of the stream.

This artist was sometimes visited by Rasselas, who was pleased with every kind of knowledge, imagining that the time would come when all his acquisitions should be of use to him in the open world. He came one day to amuse himself in his usual manner, and found the master busy in building a sailing chariot:* he saw that the design was practicable upon a level surface, and with expressions of great esteem solicited its completion. The workman was pleased to find himself so much regarded by the prince, and resolved to gain yet higher honours. 'Sir, said he, you have seen but a small part of what the mechanick sciences can perform. I have been long of opinion, that, instead of the tardy conveyance of ships and chariots, man might use the swifter migration of wings; that the fields of air are open to knowledge, and that only ignorance and idleness need crawl upon the ground.'

This hint rekindled the prince's desire of passing the mountains; having seen what the mechanist had already performed, he was willing to fancy that he could do more; yet resolved to enquire further before he suffered hope to afflict him by disappointment. 'I am afraid, said he to the artist, that your imagination prevails over your skill, and that you now tell me rather what you wish than what you know. Every animal has his element assigned him; the birds have the air, and man and beasts the earth.' 'So, replied the mechanist, fishes have the water, in which yet beasts can swim by nature, and men by art. He that can swim needs not despair to fly: to swim is to fly in a grosser fluid, and to fly is to swim in a subtler. We are only to proportion our power of resistance to the different density of the matter through which we are to pass. You will be necessarily upborn by the air, if you can renew any impulse upon it, faster than the air can recede from the pressure.'

'But the exercise of swimming, said the prince, is very laborious; the strongest limbs are soon wearied; I am afraid the act of flying will be yet more violent, and wings will be of no great use, unless we can fly further than we can swim.'

'The labour of rising from the ground, said the artist, will be great, as we see it in the heavier domestick fowls; but, as we mount higher, the earth's attraction, and the body's gravity, will be gradually diminished, till we shall arrive at a region where the man will float in the air without any tendency to fall: no care will then be necessary, but to move forwards, which the gentlest

inha
sively,
parallel.*
moving scene of lan
with equal security the marts
mountains infested by barbarians, and fr...
by plenty, and lulled by peace! How easily shall we the
the Nile through all his passage; pass over to distant regions,
and examine the face of nature from one extremity of the earth to
the other!'

'All this, said the prince, is much to be desired, but I am afraid
that no man will be able to breathe in these regions of speculation
and tranquility. I have been told, that respiration is difficult upon
lofty mountains, yet from these precipices, though so high as to
produce great tenuity* of the air, it is very easy to fall: therefore I
suspect, that from any height, where life can be supported, there
may be danger of too quick descent.'

'Nothing, replied the artist, will ever be attempted, if all possible objections must be first overcome.* If you will favour my
project I will try the first flight at my own hazard. I have considered the structure of all volant* animals, and find the folding
continuity of the bat's wings most easily accommodated to the
human form.* Upon this model I shall begin my task to morrow,
and in a year expect to tower into the air beyond the malice or
persuit of man. But I will work only on this condition, that the art
shall not be divulged, and that you shall not require me to make
wings for any but ourselves.'

'Why, said Rasselas, should you envy others so great an advantage? All skill ought to be exerted for universal good; every man
has owed much to others, and ought to repay the kindness that he
has received.'

'If men were all virtuous, returned the artist, I should with
great alacrity teach them all to fly. But what would be the security
of the good, if the bad could at pleasure invade them from the sky?

that
rinces,
en descent
on the coast of the

secrecy, and waited for the performance,
holly hopeless of success. He visited the work from time
to time, observed its progress, and remarked many ingenious
contrivances to facilitate motion, and unite levity with strength.
The artist was every day more certain that he should leave vultures and eagles behind him, and the contagion of his confidence
seized upon the prince.

In a year the wings were finished, and, on a morning appointed,
the maker appeared furnished for flight on a little promontory: he
waved his pinions a while to gather air, then leaped from his stand,
and in an instant dropped into the lake.* His wings, which were of
no use in the air, sustained him in the water, and the prince drew
him to land, half dead with terrour and vexation.

CHAP. VII

The prince finds a man of learning

THE prince was not much afflicted by this disaster, having
suffered himself to hope for a happier event, only because he had
no other means of escape in view. He still persisted in his design
to leave the happy valley by the first opportunity.

His imagination was now at a stand; he had no prospect of
entering into the world; and, notwithstanding all his endeavours
to support himself, discontent by degrees preyed upon him, and
he began again to lose his thoughts in sadness, when the rainy
season,* which in these countries is periodical, made it inconvenient to wander in the woods.

The rain continued longer and with more violence than had been ever known: the clouds broke on the surrounding mountains, and the torrents streamed into the plain on every side, till the cavern was too narrow to discharge the water. The lake overflowed its banks, and all the level of the valley was covered with the inundation. The eminence, on which the palace was built, and some other spots of rising ground, were all that the eye could now discover. The herds and flocks left the pastures, and both the wild beasts and the tame retreated to the mountains.

This inundation confined all the princes to domestick amusements, and the attention of Rasselas was particularly seized by a poem, which Imlac* rehearsed* upon the various conditions of humanity. He commanded the poet to attend him in his apartment, and recite his verses a second time; then entering into familiar talk, he thought himself happy in having found a man who knew the world so well, and could so skilfully paint the scenes of life. He asked a thousand questions about things, to which, though common to all other mortals, his confinement from childhood had kept him a stranger. The poet pitied his ignorance, and loved his curiosity, and entertained him from day to day with novelty and instruction, so that the prince regretted the necessity of sleep, and longed till the morning should renew his pleasure.

As they were sitting together, the prince commanded Imlac to relate his history, and to tell by what accident he was forced, or by what motive induced, to close his life in the happy valley. As he was going to begin his narrative, Rasselas was called to a concert, and obliged to restrain his curiosity till the evening.

CHAP. VIII

The history of Imlac

THE close of the day is, in the regions of the torrid zone, the only season of diversion and entertainment, and it was therefore mid-night before the musick ceased, and the princesses retired.

Rasselas then called for his companion and required him to begin the story of his life.

'Sir, said Imlac, my history will not be long: the life that is devoted to knowledge passes silently away, and is very little diversified by events. To talk in publick, to think in solitude, to read and to hear, to inquire, and answer inquiries, is the business of a scholar.* He wanders about the world without pomp or terrour, and is neither known nor valued but by men like himself.

'I was born in the kingdom of Goiama, at no great distance from the fountain of the Nile.* My father was a wealthy merchant, who traded between the inland countries of Africk and the ports of the red sea. He was honest, frugal and diligent, but of mean sentiments, and narrow comprehension: he desired only to be rich, and to conceal his riches, lest he should be spoiled by the governours of the province.'*

'Surely, said the prince, my father must be negligent of his charge, if any man in his dominions dares take that which belongs to another. Does he not know that kings are accountable for injustice permitted as well as done? If I were emperour, not the meanest of my subjects should be oppressed with impunity. My blood boils when I am told that a merchant durst not enjoy his honest gains for fear of losing them by the rapacity of power. Name the governour who robbed the people, that I may declare his crimes to the emperour.'

'Sir, said Imlac, your ardour is the natural effect of virtue animated by youth: the time will come when you will acquit your father, and perhaps hear with less impatience of the governour. Oppression is, in the Abissinian dominions, neither frequent nor tolerated; but no form of government has been yet discovered, by which cruelty can be wholly prevented. Subordination* supposes power on one part and subjection on the other; and if power be in the hands of men, it will sometimes be abused. The vigilance of the supreme magistrate may do much, but much will still remain undone. He can never know all the crimes that are committed, and can seldom punish all that he knows.'

'This, said the prince, I do not understand, but I had rather hear thee than dispute. Continue thy narration.'

'My father, proceeded Imlac, originally intended that I should have no other education, than such as might qualify me for commerce; and discovering in me great strength of memory, and quickness of apprehension, often declared his hope that I should be some time the richest man in Abissinia.'

'Why, said the prince, did thy father desire the increase of his wealth, when it was already greater than he durst discover or enjoy? I am unwilling to doubt thy veracity, yet inconsistencies cannot both be true.'

'Inconsistencies, answered Imlac, cannot both be right, but, imputed to man, they may both be true. Yet diversity is not inconsistency. My father might expect a time of greater security. However, some desire is necessary to keep life in motion, and he, whose real wants are supplied, must admit those of fancy.'

'This, said the prince, I can in some measure conceive. I repent that I interrupted thee.'

'With this hope, proceeded Imlac, he sent me to school; but when I had once found the delight of knowledge, and felt the pleasure of intelligence and the pride of invention, I began silently to despise riches, and determined to disappoint the purpose of my father, whose grossness of conception raised my pity. I was twenty years old before his tenderness would expose me to the fatigue of travel, in which time I had been instructed, by successive masters, in all the literature of my native country. As every hour taught me something new, I lived in a continual course of gratifications; but, as I advanced towards manhood, I lost much of the reverence with which I had been used to look on my instructors; because, when the lesson was ended, I did not find them wiser or better than common men.

'At length my father resolved to initiate me in commerce, and, opening one of his subterranean treasuries, counted out ten thousand pieces of gold. This, young man, said he, is the stock with which you must negociate. I began with less than the fifth part, and you see how diligence and parsimony have increased it. This is your own to waste or to improve.* If you squander it by negligence or caprice, you must wait for my death before you will be rich: if, in four years, you double your stock, we will thenceforward let subordination cease, and live together as friends and partners; for he shall always be equal with me, who is equally skilled in the art of growing rich.

'We laid our money upon camels, concealed in bales of cheap goods, and travelled to the shore of the red sea. When I cast my eye on the expanse of waters my heart bounded like that of a prisoner escaped. I felt an unextinguishable curiosity kindle in my mind, and resolved to snatch this opportunity of seeing the manners of other nations, and of learning sciences unknown in Abissinia.

'I remembered that my father had obliged me to the improvement of my stock, not by a promise which I ought not to violate, but by a penalty which I was at liberty to incur; and therefore determined to gratify my predominant desire, and by drinking at the fountains of knowledge, to quench the thirst of curiosity.

'As I was supposed to trade without connexion with my father, it was easy for me to become acquainted with the master of a ship, and procure a passage to some other country. I had no motives of choice to regulate my voyage; it was sufficient for me that, wherever I wandered, I should see a country which I had not seen before. I therefore entered a ship bound for Surat,* having left a letter for my father declaring my intention.

CHAP. IX

The history of Imlac continued

'WHEN I first entered upon the world of waters,* and lost sight of land, I looked round about me with pleasing terrour,* and thinking my soul enlarged by the boundless prospect, imagined that I could gaze round for ever without satiety; but, in a short time, I grew weary of looking on barren uniformity, where I could only see again what I had already seen. I then descended into the ship, and doubted for a while whether all my future pleasures would not end like this in disgust and disappointment. Yet, surely, said I, the ocean and the land are very different; the only variety of water is rest and motion, but the earth has mountains and vallies, desarts and cities: it is inhabited by men of different customs and contrary opinions; and I may hope to find variety in life, though I should miss it in nature.

'With this thought I quieted my mind; and amused myself during the voyage, sometimes by learning from the sailors the art of navigation, which I have never practised, and sometimes by forming schemes for my conduct in different situations, in not one of which I have been ever placed.

'I was almost weary of my naval amusements when we landed safely at Surat. I secured my money, and purchasing some commodities for show, joined myself to a caravan that was passing into the inland country. My companions, for some reason or other, conjecturing that I was rich, and, by my inquiries and admiration, finding that I was ignorant, considered me as a novice whom they had a right to cheat, and who was to learn at the usual expence the art of fraud. They exposed me to the theft of servants, and the exaction of officers, and saw me plundered upon false pretences, without any advantage to themselves, but that of rejoicing in the superiority of their own knowledge.'

'Stop a moment, said the prince. Is there such depravity in man, as that he should injure another without benefit to himself?* I can easily conceive that all are pleased with superiority; but your ignorance was merely accidental, which, being neither your crime nor your folly, could afford them no reason to applaud themselves; and the knowledge which they had, and which you wanted, they might as effectually have shown by warning, as betraying you.'

'Pride, said Imlac, is seldom delicate, it will please itself with very mean advantages; and envy feels not its own happiness, but when it may be compared with the misery of others. They were my enemies because they grieved to think me rich, and my oppressors because they delighted to find me weak.'

'Proceed, said the prince: I doubt not of the facts which you relate, but imagine that you impute them to mistaken motives.'

'In this company, said Imlac, I arrived at Agra, the capital of Indostan, the city in which the great Mogul commonly resides.*

I applied myself to the language of the country, and in a few months was able to converse with the learned men; some of whom I found morose and reserved, and others easy and communicative; some were unwilling to teach another what they had with difficulty learned themselves; and some shewed that the end of their studies was to gain the dignity of instructing.*

'To the tutor of the young princes I recommended myself so much, that I was presented to the emperour as a man of uncommon knowledge. The emperour asked me many questions concerning my country and my travels; and though I cannot now recollect any thing that he uttered above the power of a common man, he dismissed me astonished at his wisdom, and enamoured of his goodness.

'My credit was now so high, that the merchants, with whom I had travelled, applied to me for recommendations to the ladies of the court. I was surprised at their confidence of solicitation, and gently reproached them with their practices on the road. They heard me with cold indifference, and shewed no tokens of shame or sorrow.

'They then urged their request with the offer of a bribe; but what I would not do for kindness I would not do for money; and refused them, not because they had injured me, but because I would not enable them to injure others; for I knew they would have made use of my credit to cheat those who should buy their wares.

'Having resided at Agra till there was no more to be learned, I travelled into Persia, where I saw many remains of ancient magnificence, and observed many new accommodations of life. The Persians are a nation eminently social,* and their assemblies afforded me daily opportunities of remarking characters and manners, and of tracing human nature through all its variations.

'From Persia I passed into Arabia, where I saw a nation at once pastoral and warlike; who live without any settled habitation; whose only wealth is their flocks and herds; and who have yet carried on, through all ages, an hereditary war with all mankind,* though they neither covet nor envy their possessions.

CHAP. X

Imlac's history continued. A dissertation upon poetry

'WHEREVER I went, I found that Poetry was considered as the highest learning,* and regarded with a veneration somewhat approaching to that which man would pay to the Angelick Nature. And it yet fills me with wonder, that, in almost all countries, the most ancient poets are considered as the best:* whether it be that every other kind of knowledge is an acquisition gradually attained, and poetry is a gift conferred at once; or that the first poetry of every nation surprised them as a novelty, and retained the credit by consent which it received by accident at first: or whether, as the province of poetry is to describe Nature and Passion, which are always the same,* the first writers took possession of the most striking objects for description, and the most probable occurrences for fiction, and left nothing to those that followed them, but transcription of the same events, and new combinations of the same images. Whatever be the reason, it is commonly observed that the early writers are in possession of nature, and their followers of art: that the first excel in strength and invention, and the latter in elegance and refinement.

'I was desirous to add my name to this illustrious fraternity. I read all the poets of Persia and Arabia, and was able to repeat by memory the volumes that are suspended in the mosque of Mecca.* But I soon found that no man was ever great by imitation. My desire of excellence impelled me to transfer my attention to nature and to life. Nature was to be my subject, and men to be my auditors: I could never describe what I had not seen: I could not hope to move those with delight or terrour, whose interests and opinions I did not understand.

'Being now resolved to be a poet, I saw every thing with a new purpose; my sphere of attention was suddenly magnified: no kind of knowledge was to be overlooked. I ranged mountains and deserts for images and resemblances, and pictured upon my mind every tree of the forest and flower of the valley. I observed with equal care the crags of the rock and the pinnacles of the palace.

Sometimes I wandered along the mazes of the rivulet, and sometimes watched the changes of the summer clouds. To a poet nothing can be useless. Whatever is beautiful, and whatever is dreadful, must be familiar to his imagination: he must be conversant with all that is awfully vast or elegantly little. The plants of the garden, the animals of the wood, the minerals of the earth, and meteors of the sky, must all concur to store his mind with inexhaustible variety:* for every idea* is useful for the inforcement or decoration of moral or religious truth; and he, who knows most, will have most power of diversifying his scenes, and of gratifying his reader with remote allusions and unexpected instruction.

'All the appearances of nature I was therefore careful to study, and every country which I have surveyed has contributed something to my poetical powers.'

'In so wide a survey, said the prince, you must surely have left much unobserved. I have lived, till now, within the circuit of these mountains, and yet cannot walk abroad without the sight of something which I had never beheld before, or never heeded.'

'The business of a poet, said Imlac, is to examine, not the individual, but the species;* to remark general properties and large appearances: he does not number the streaks of the tulip,* or describe the different shades in the verdure of the forest. He is to exhibit in his portraits of nature such prominent and striking features, as recal the original to every mind; and must neglect the minuter discriminations, which one may have remarked, and another have neglected, for those characteristicks which are alike obvious to vigilance and carelesness.

'But the knowledge of nature is only half the task of a poet; he must be acquainted likewise with all the modes of life. His character requires that he estimate the happiness and misery of every condition; observe the power of all the passions in all their combinations, and trace the changes of the human mind as they are modified by various institutions and accidental influences of climate or custom, from the spriteliness of infancy to the despondence of decrepitude. He must divest himself of the prejudices of his age or country; he must consider right and wrong in their abstracted and invariable state; he must disregard present laws and opinions, and rise to general and transcendental truths, which will always be the same: he must therefore content himself with the slow progress of his name; contemn the applause of his own time, and commit his claims to the justice of posterity. He must write as the interpreter of nature, and the legislator of mankind,* and consider himself as presiding over the thoughts and manners of future generations; as a being superiour to time and place.

'His labour is not yet at an end: he must know many languages and many sciences; and, that his stile may be worthy of his thoughts, must, by incessant practice, familiarize to himself every delicacy of speech and grace of harmony.'

CHAP. XI

Imlac's narrative continued. A hint on pilgrimage

IMLAC now felt the enthusiastic fit, and was proceeding to aggrandize his own profession, when the prince cried out, 'Enough! Thou hast convinced me, that no human being can ever be a poet. Proceed with thy narration.'

'To be a poet, said Imlac, is indeed very difficult.' 'So difficult, returned the prince, that I will at present hear no more of his labours. Tell me whither you went when you had seen Persia.'

'From Persia, said the poet, I travelled through Syria, and for three years resided in Palestine, where I conversed with great numbers of the northern and western nations of Europe; the nations which are now in possession of all power and all knowledge; whose armies are irresistible, and whose fleets command the remotest parts of the globe.* When I compared these men with the natives of our own kingdom, and those that surround us, they appeared almost another order of beings. In their countries it is difficult to wish for any thing that may not be obtained: a thousand arts, of which we never heard, are continually labouring for their convenience and pleasure; and whatever their own climate has denied them is supplied by their commerce.'

'By what means, said the prince, are the Europeans thus powerful? or why, since they can so easily visit Asia and Africa for trade or conquest, cannot the Asiaticks and Africans invade their coasts, plant colonies in their ports, and give laws to their natural princes? The same wind that carries them back would bring us thither.'

'They are more powerful, Sir, than we, answered Imlac, because they are wiser; knowledge will always predominate over ignorance, as man governs the other animals. But why their knowledge is more than ours, I know not what reason can be given, but the unsearchable will of the Supreme Being.'*

'When, said the prince with a sigh, shall I be able to visit Palestine, and mingle with this mighty confluence of nations? Till that happy moment shall arrive, let me fill up the time with such representations as thou canst give me. I am not ignorant of the motive that assembles such numbers in that place, and cannot but consider it as the center of wisdom and piety, to which the best and wisest men of every land must be continually resorting.'*

'There are some nations, said Imlac, that send few visitants to Palestine; for many numerous and learned sects in Europe, concur to censure pilgrimage as superstitious, or deride it as ridiculous.'

'You know, said the prince, how little my life has made me acquainted with diversity of opinions: it will be too long to hear the arguments on both sides; you, that have considered them, tell me the result.'

'Pilgrimage, said Imlac, like many other acts of piety, may be reasonable or superstitious, according to the principles upon which it is performed. Long journies in search of truth are not commanded. Truth, such as is necessary to the regulation of life, is always found where it is honestly sought. Change of place is no natural cause of the increase of piety, for it inevitably produces dissipation of mind. Yet, since men go every day to view the fields where great actions have been performed, and return with stronger impressions of the event, curiosity of the same kind may naturally dispose us to view that country whence our religion had its beginning; and I believe no man surveys those awful scenes without some confirmation of holy resolutions.* That the Supreme

Being may be more easily propitiated in one place than in another, is the dream of idle superstition; but that some places may operate upon our own minds in an uncommon manner, is an opinion which hourly experience will justify. He who supposes that his vices may be more successfully combated in Palestine, will, perhaps, find himself mistaken, yet he may go thither without folly: he who thinks they will be more freely pardoned, dishonours at once his reason and religion.'

'These, said the prince, are European distinctions. I will consider them another time. What have you found to be the effect of knowledge? Are those nations happier than we?' (NATIONS: Europeans)

'There is so much infelicity, said the poet, in the world, that scarce any man has leisure from his own distresses to estimate the comparative happiness of others. Knowledge is certainly one of the means of pleasure, as is confessed by the natural desire which every mind feels of increasing its ideas.* Ignorance is mere privation, by which nothing can be produced: it is a vacuity in which the soul sits motionless and torpid for want of attraction; and, without knowing why, we always rejoice when we learn, and grieve when we forget. I am therefore inclined to conclude, that, if nothing counteracts the natural consequence of learning, we grow more happy as our minds take a wider range.*

'In enumerating the particular comforts of life we shall find many advantages on the side of the Europeans. They cure wounds and diseases with which we languish and perish. We suffer inclemencies of weather which they can obviate. They have engines for the despatch of many laborious works, which we must perform by manual industry. There is such communication between distant places, that one friend can hardly be said to be absent from another. Their policy removes all publick inconveniencies: they have roads cut through their mountains, and bridges laid upon their rivers. And, if we descend to the privacies of life, their habitations are more commodious, and their possessions are more secure.'

'They are surely happy, said the prince, who have all these conveniencies, of which I envy none so much as the facility with which separated friends interchange their thoughts.'

★ 'The Europeans, answered Imlac, are less unhappy than we, but they are not happy. Human life is every where a state in which much is to be endured, and little to be enjoyed.'* ↙

[handwritten: A life of pain]
[handwritten: sounds like a little joy out of a lot of sufferin]

CHAP. XII

The story of Imlac continued

'I AM not yet willing, said the prince, to suppose that happiness is so parsimoniously distributed to mortals; nor can believe but that, if I had the choice of life,* I should be able to fill every day with pleasure. I would injure no man, and should provoke no resentment: I would relieve every distress, and should enjoy the benedictions of gratitude. I would choose my friends among the wise, and my wife among the virtuous; and therefore should be in no danger from treachery, or unkindness. My children should, by my care, be learned and pious, and would repay to my age what their childhood had received. What would dare to molest him who might call on every side to thousands enriched by his bounty, or assisted by his power? And why should not life glide quietly away in the soft reciprocation of protection and reverence?* All this may be done without the help of European refinements, which appear by their effects to be rather specious than useful. Let us leave them and persue our journey.'

★ *[handwritten vertical: The Misery of the World]* 'From Palestine, said Imlac, I passed through many regions of Asia; in the more civilized kingdoms as a trader, and among the Barbarians of the mountains as a pilgrim. At last I began to long for my native country, that I might repose after my travels, and fatigues, in the places where I had spent my earliest years, and gladden my old companions with the recital of my adventures. Often did I figure to myself those, with whom I had sported away the gay hours of dawning life, sitting round me in its evening, wondering at my tales, and listening to my counsels.*

'When this thought had taken possession of my mind, I considered every moment as wasted which did not bring me nearer to Abissinia. I hastened into Egypt, and, notwithstanding my impatience, was detained ten months in the contemplation of its ancient magnificence, and in enquiries after the remains of its ancient learning.* I found in Cairo a mixture of all nations;* some brought thither by the love of knowledge, some by the hope of gain, and many by the desire of living after their own manner without observation, and of lying hid in the obscurity of multitudes: for, in a city, populous as Cairo, it is possible to obtain at the same time the gratifications of society, and the secrecy of solitude.

'From Cairo I travelled to Suez,* and embarked on the Red sea, passing along the coast till I arrived at the port from which I had departed twenty years before. Here I joined myself to a caravan and re-entered my native country.

'I now expected the caresses of my kinsmen, and the congratulations of my friends, and was not without hope that my father, whatever value he had set upon riches, would own with gladness and pride a son who was able to add to the felicity and honour of the nation. But I was soon convinced that my thoughts were vain. My father had been dead fourteen years, having divided his wealth among my brothers, who were removed to some other provinces. Of my companions the greater part was in the grave, of the rest some could with difficulty remember me, and some considered me as one corrupted by foreign manners.*

'A man used to vicissitudes is not easily dejected. I forgot, after a time, my disappointment, and endeavoured to recommend myself to the nobles of the kingdom: they admitted me to their tables, heard my story, and dismissed me. I opened a school, and was prohibited to teach. I then resolved to sit down in the quiet of domestick life, and addressed a lady that was fond of my conversation, but rejected my suit, because my father was a merchant.*

'Wearied at last with solicitation and repulses, I resolved to hide myself for ever from the world, and depend no longer on the opinion or caprice of others. I waited for the time when the gate of the *happy valley* should open, that I might bid farewell to hope and fear: the day came; my performance was distinguished with favour, and I resigned myself with joy to perpetual confinement.'

'Hast thou here found happiness at last? said Rasselas. Tell me without reserve; art thou content with thy condition? or, dost thou wish to be again wandering and inquiring? All the inhabitants of this valley celebrate their lot, and, at the annual visit of the emperour, invite others to partake of their felicity.'

'Great prince, said Imlac, I shall speak the truth: I know not one of all your attendants who does not lament the hour when he entered this retreat. I am less unhappy than the rest, because I have a mind replete with images, which I can vary and combine at pleasure.* I can amuse my solitude by the renovation of the knowledge which begins to fade from my memory, and by recollection of the accidents of my past life. Yet all this ends in the sorrowful consideration, that my acquirements are now useless, and that none of my pleasures can be again enjoyed. The rest, whose minds have no impression but of the present moment, are either corroded by malignant passions, or sit stupid in the gloom of perpetual vacancy.'

'What passions can infest those, said the prince, who have no rivals? We are in a place where impotence precludes malice, and where all envy is repressed by community of enjoyments.'

'There may be community, said Imlac, of material possessions, but there can never be community of love or of esteem. It must happen that one will please more than another; he that knows himself despised will always be envious; and still more envious and malevolent, if he is condemned to live in the presence of those who despise him. The invitations, by which they allure others to a state which they feel to be wretched, proceed from the natural malignity of hopeless misery. They are weary of themselves, and of each other, and expect to find relief in new companions. They envy the liberty which their folly has forfeited, and would gladly see all mankind imprisoned like themselves.

'From this crime, however, I am wholly free. No man can say that he is wretched by my persuasion. I look with pity on the crowds who are annually soliciting admission to captivity, and wish that it were lawful for me to warn them of their danger.'

'My dear Imlac, said the prince, I will open to thee my whole heart. I have long meditated an escape from the happy valley.

I have examined the mountains on every side, but find myself insuperably barred: teach me the way to break my prison; thou shalt be the companion of my flight, the guide of my rambles, the partner of my fortune, and my sole director in the *choice of life*.'

'Sir, answered the poet, your escape will be difficult, and, perhaps, you may soon repent your curiosity. The world, which you figure to yourself smooth and quiet as the lake in the valley, you will find a sea foaming with tempests, and boiling with whirlpools: you will be sometimes overwhelmed by the waves of violence, and sometimes dashed against the rocks of treachery. Amidst wrongs and frauds, competitions and anxieties, you will wish a thousand times for these seats of quiet, and willingly quit hope to be free from fear.'

'Do not seek to deter me from my purpose, said the prince: I am impatient to see what thou hast seen; and, since thou art thyself weary of the valley, it is evident, that thy former state was better than this. Whatever be the consequence of my experiment, I am resolved to judge with my own eyes of the various conditions of men, and then to make deliberately my *choice of life*.'

'I am afraid, said Imlac, you are hindered by stronger restraints than my persuasions; yet, if your determination is fixed, I do not counsel you to despair. Few things are impossible to diligence and skill.'

CHAP. XIII

Rasselas discovers the means of escape

THE prince now dismissed his favourite to rest, but the narrative of wonders and novelties filled his mind with perturbation. He revolved all that he had heard, and prepared innumerable questions for the morning.

Much of his uneasiness was now removed. He had a friend to whom he could impart his thoughts, and whose experience could assist him in his designs. His heart was no longer condemned to swell with silent vexation. He thought that even the *happy valley* might be endured with such a companion, and that, if they could range the world together, he should have nothing further to desire.

In a few days the water was discharged, and the ground dried. The prince and Imlac then walked out together to converse without the notice of the rest. The prince, whose thoughts were always on the wing, as he passed by the gate, said, with a countenance of sorrow,* 'Why art thou so strong, and why is man so weak?'

'Man is not weak, answered his companion; knowledge is more than equivalent to force. The master of mechanicks laughs at strength.* I can burst the gate, but cannot do it secretly. Some other expedient must be tried.'

As they were walking on the side of the mountain, they observed that the conies, which the rain had driven from their burrows, had taken shelter among the bushes, and formed holes behind them, tending upwards in an oblique line. 'It has been the opinion of antiquity, said Imlac, that human reason borrowed many arts from the instinct of animals;* let us, therefore, not think ourselves degraded by learning from the coney. We may escape by piercing the mountain in the same direction. We will begin where the summit hangs over the middle part, and labour upward till we shall issue out beyond the prominence.'

The eyes of the prince, when he heard this proposal, sparkled with joy. The execution was easy, and the success certain.

No time was now lost. They hastened early in the morning to chuse a place proper for their mine. They clambered with great fatigue among crags and brambles, and returned without having discovered any part that favoured their design. The second and the third day were spent in the same manner, and with the same frustration. But, on the fourth, they found a small cavern, concealed by a thicket, where they resolved to make their experiment.

Imlac procured instruments proper to hew stone and remove earth, and they fell to their work on the next day with more eagerness than vigour. They were presently exhausted by their efforts, and sat down to pant upon the grass. The prince, for a moment, appeared to be discouraged. 'Sir, said his companion, practice will enable us to continue our labour for a longer time; mark, however, how far we have advanced, and you will find that our toil will some time have an end. Great works are performed, not by strength, but perseverance:* yonder palace was raised by single stones, yet you see its height and spaciousness. He that shall walk with vigour three hours a day will pass in seven years a space equal to the circumference of the globe.'

They returned to their work day after day, and, in a short time, found a fissure in the rock, which enabled them to pass far with very little obstruction. This Rasselas considered as a good omen. 'Do not disturb your mind, said Imlac, with other hopes or fears than reason may suggest: if you are pleased with prognosticks of good, you will be terrified likewise with tokens of evil, and your whole life will be a prey to superstition. Whatever facilitates our work is more than an omen, it is a cause of success. This is one of those pleasing surprises which often happen to active resolution. Many things difficult to design prove easy to performance.'

CHAP. XIV

Rasselas and Imlac receive an unexpected visit

THEY had now wrought their way to the middle, and solaced their toil with the approach of liberty, when the prince, coming down to refresh himself with air, found his sister Nekayah standing before the mouth of the cavity. He started and stood confused, afraid to tell his design, and yet hopeless to conceal it. A few moments determined him to repose on her fidelity, and secure her secrecy by a declaration without reserve.

'Do not imagine, said the princess, that I came hither as a spy: I had long observed from my window, that you and Imlac directed your walk every day towards the same point, but I did not suppose you had any better reason for the preference than a cooler shade, or more fragrant bank; nor followed you with any other design than to partake of your conversation. Since then not suspicion but fondness has detected you, let me not lose the

advantage of my discovery. I am equally weary of confinement
with yourself, and not less desirous of knowing what is done or
suffered in the world. Permit me to fly with you from this tasteless
tranquility, which will yet grow more loathsome when you have
left me. You may deny me to accompany you, but cannot hinder
me from following.'

The prince, who loved Nekayah above his other sisters, had no
inclination to refuse her request, and grieved that he had lost an
opportunity of shewing his confidence by a voluntary communication. It was therefore agreed that she should leave the valley
with them; and that, in the mean time, she should watch, lest any
other straggler should, by chance or curiosity, follow them to the
mountain.

At length their labour was at an end; they saw light beyond the
prominence, and, issuing to the top of the mountain, beheld the
Nile, yet a narrow current, wandering beneath them.

The prince looked round with rapture, anticipated all the
pleasures of travel, and in thought was already transported
beyond his father's dominions. Imlac, though very joyful at his
escape, had less expectation of pleasure in the world, which he
had before tried, and of which he had been weary.

Rasselas was so much delighted with a wider horizon, that he
could not soon be persuaded to return into the valley. He
informed his sister that the way was open, and that nothing now
remained but to prepare for their departure.

CHAP. XV

*The prince and princess leave the valley,
and see many wonders*

THE prince and princess had jewels sufficient to make them rich
whenever they came into a place of commerce, which, by Imlac's
direction, they hid in their cloaths, and, on the night of the next
full moon, all left the valley. The princess was followed only by a
single favourite,* who did not know whither she was going.

They clambered through the cavity, and began to go down on the other side. The princess and her maid turned their eyes towards every part, and, seeing nothing to bound their prospect, considered themselves as in danger of being lost in a dreary vacuity. They stopped and trembled. 'I am almost afraid, said the princess, to begin a journey of which I cannot perceive an end, and to venture into this immense plain where I may be approached on every side by men whom I never saw.' The prince felt nearly the same emotions, though he thought it more manly to conceal them.

Imlac smiled at their terrours, and encouraged them to proceed; but the princess continued irresolute till she had been imperceptibly drawn forward too far to return.

In the morning they found some shepherds in the field, who set milk and fruits before them. The princess wondered that she did not see a palace ready for her reception, and a table spread with delicacies;* but, being faint and hungry, she drank the milk and eat* the fruits, and thought them of a higher flavour than the products of the valley.

They travelled forward by easy journeys, being all unaccustomed to toil or difficulty, and knowing, that though they might be missed, they could not be persued. In a few days they came into a more populous region, where Imlac was diverted with the admiration which his companions expressed at the diversity of manners, stations and employments.

Their dress was such as might not bring upon them the suspicion of having any thing to conceal, yet the prince, wherever he came, expected to be obeyed, and the princess was frighted, because those that came into her presence did not prostrate themselves before her. Imlac was forced to observe them with great vigilance, lest they should betray their rank by their unusual behaviour, and detained them several weeks in the first village to accustom them to the sight of common mortals.

By degrees the royal wanderers were taught to understand that they had for a time laid aside their dignity, and were to expect only such regard as liberality and courtesy could procure. And Imlac, having, by many admonitions, prepared them to endure the tumults of a port, and the ruggedness of the commercial race,* brought them down to the sea-coast.

The prince and his sister, to whom every thing was new, were gratified equally at all places, and therefore remained for some months at the port without any inclination to pass further. Imlac was content with their stay, because he did not think it safe to expose them, unpractised in the world, to the hazards of a foreign country.

At last he began to fear lest they should be discovered, and proposed to fix a day for their departure. They had no pretensions to judge for themselves, and referred the whole scheme to his direction. He therefore took passage in a ship to Suez; and, when the time came, with great difficulty prevailed on the princess to enter the vessel. They had a quick and prosperous voyage, and from Suez travelled by land to Cairo.

CHAP. XVI

They enter Cairo, and find every man happy

As they approached the city, which filled the strangers with astonishment, 'This, said Imlac to the prince, is the place where travellers and merchants assemble from all the corners of the earth. You will here find men of every character, and every occupation. Commerce is here honourable: I will act as a merchant, and you shall live as strangers, who have no other end of travel than curiosity; it will soon be observed that we are rich; our reputation will procure us access to all whom we shall desire to know; you will see all the conditions of humanity, and enable yourself at leisure to make your *choice of life*.'

They now entered the town, stunned by the noise, and offended by the crowds. Instruction had not yet so prevailed over habit, but that they wondered to see themselves pass undistinguished along the street, and met by the lowest of the people without reverence or notice. The princess could not at first bear the thought of being levelled with the vulgar, and, for some days, continued in her chamber, where she was served by her favourite Pekuah as in the palace of the valley.

Imlac, who understood traffick, sold part of the jewels the next day, and hired a house, which he adorned with such magnificence, that he was immediately considered as a merchant of great wealth. His politeness attracted many acquaintance, and his generosity made him courted by many dependants. His table was crowded by men of every nation, who all admired his knowledge, and solicited his favour. His companions, not being able to mix in the conversation, could make no discovery of their ignorance or surprise, and were gradually initiated in the world as they gained knowledge of the language.

The prince had, by frequent lectures, been taught the use and nature of money;* but the ladies could not, for a long time, comprehend what the merchants did with small pieces of gold and silver, or why things of so little use should be received as equivalent to the necessaries of life.

They studied the language two years, while Imlac was preparing to set before them the various ranks and conditions of mankind. He grew acquainted with all who had any thing uncommon in their fortune or conduct. He frequented the voluptuous and the frugal, the idle and the busy, the merchants and the men of learning.

The prince, being now able to converse with fluency, and having learned the caution necessary to be observed in his intercourse with strangers, began to accompany Imlac to places of resort, and to enter into all assemblies, that he might make his *choice of life*.

For some time he thought choice needless, because all appeared to him equally happy. Wherever he went he met gayety and kindness, and heard the song of joy, or the laugh of carelesness. He began to believe that the world overflowed with universal plenty, and that nothing was withheld either from want or merit; that every hand showered liberality, and every heart melted with benevolence: 'and who then, says he, will be suffered to be wretched?'

Imlac permitted the pleasing delusion, and was unwilling to crush the hope of inexperience; till one day, having sat a while silent, 'I know not, said the prince, what can be the reason that

I am more unhappy than any of our friends. I see them perpetually and unalterably chearful, but feel my own mind restless and uneasy. I am unsatisfied with those pleasures which I seem most to court; I live in the crowds of jollity, not so much to enjoy company as to shun myself,* and am only loud and merry to conceal my sadness.'

(Is Johnson saying this or is Imlac being bitter?)

'Every man, said Imlac, may, by examining his own mind, guess what passes in the minds of others: when you feel that your own gaiety is counterfeit, it may justly lead you to suspect that of your companions not to be sincere. Envy is commonly reciprocal. We are long before we are convinced that happiness is never to be found, and each believes it possessed by others, to keep alive the hope of obtaining it for himself. In the assembly, where you passed the last night, there appeared such spriteliness of air, and volatility of fancy, as might have suited beings of an higher order, formed to inhabit serener regions inaccessible to care or sorrow: yet, believe me, prince, there was not one who did not dread the moment when solitude should deliver him to the tyranny of reflection.'

the miseries of the world

'This, said the prince, may be true of others, since it is true of me; yet, whatever be the general infelicity of man, one condition is more happy than another, and wisdom surely directs us to take the least evil in the *choice of life*.'

'The causes of good and evil, answered Imlac, are so various and uncertain, so often entangled with each other, so diversified by various relations, and so much subject to accidents which cannot be foreseen, that he who would fix his condition upon incontestable reasons of preference, must live and die inquiring and deliberating.'*

'But surely, said Rasselas, the wise men, to whom we listen with reverence and wonder, chose that mode of life for themselves which they thought most likely to make them happy.'

'Very few, said the poet, live by choice. Every man is placed in his present condition by causes which acted without his foresight, and with which he did not always willingly co-operate;* and therefore you will rarely meet one who does not think the lot of his neighbour better than his own.'

'I am pleased to think, said the prince, that my birth has given me at least one advantage over others, by enabling me to determine for myself. I have here the world before me;* I will review it at leisure: surely happiness is somewhere to be found.'

CHAP. XVII

The prince associates with young men of spirit and gaiety

RASSELAS rose next day, and resolved to begin his experiments upon life. 'Youth, cried he, is the time of gladness: I will join myself to the young men, whose only business is to gratify their desires, and whose time is all spent in a succession of enjoyments.'

To such societies he was readily admitted, but a few days brought him back weary and disgusted. Their mirth was without images, their laughter without motive; their pleasures were gross and sensual, in which the mind had no part; their conduct was at once wild and mean; they laughed at order and at law, but the frown of power dejected, and the eye of wisdom abashed them.

The prince soon concluded, that he should never be happy in a course of life of which he was ashamed. He thought it unsuitable to a reasonable being to act without a plan, and to be sad or chearful only by chance. 'Happiness, said he, must be something solid and permanent, without fear and without uncertainty.*

But his young companions had gained so much of his regard by their frankness and courtesy, that he could not leave them without warning and remonstrance. 'My friends, said he, I have seriously considered our manners and our prospects, and find that we have mistaken our own interest. The first years of man must make provision for the last. He that never thinks never can be wise. Perpetual levity must end in ignorance; and intemperance, though it may fire the spirits for an hour, will make life short or miserable. Let us consider that youth is of no long duration, and that in maturer age, when the enchantments of fancy shall cease, and phantoms of delight dance no more about us, we shall have no comforts but the esteem of wise men, and the means of doing good. Let us, therefore, stop, while to stop is in our power: let us live as men who are sometime to grow old, and to whom it will be the most dreadful of all evils not to count their past years but by follies, and to be reminded of their former luxuriance of health only by the maladies which riot has produced.'

They stared a while in silence one upon another, and, at last, drove him away by a general chorus of continued laughter.

The consciousness that his sentiments were just, and his intentions kind, was scarcely sufficient to support him against the horrour of derision. But he recovered his tranquility, and persued his search.

CHAP. XVIII

The prince finds a wise and happy man

As he was one day walking in the street, he saw a spacious building which all were, by the open doors, invited to enter: he followed the stream of people, and found it a hall or school of declamation, in which professors read lectures to their auditory. He fixed his eye upon a sage raised above the rest, who discoursed with great energy on the government of the passions.* His look was venerable, his action graceful, his pronunciation clear, and his diction elegant. He shewed, with great strength of sentiment, and variety of illustration, that human nature is degraded and debased, when the lower faculties predominate over the higher; that when fancy, the parent of passion, usurps the dominion of the mind, nothing ensues but the natural effect of unlawful government, perturbation and confusion; that she betrays the fortresses of the intellect to rebels, and excites her children to sedition against reason their lawful sovereign. He compared reason to the sun, of which the light is constant, uniform, and lasting; and fancy to a meteor, of bright but transitory lustre, irregular in its motion, and delusive in its direction.

He then communicated the various precepts given from time to time for the conquest of passion, and displayed the happiness of those who had obtained the important victory, after which man is no longer the slave of fear, nor the fool of hope; is no more emaciated by envy, inflamed by anger, emasculated by tenderness, or depressed by grief; but walks on calmly through the tumults or the privacies of life, as the sun persues alike his course through the calm or the stormy sky.

He enumerated many examples of heroes immovable by pain or pleasure, who looked with indifference on those modes or accidents to which the vulgar give the names of good and evil. He exhorted his hearers to lay aside their prejudices, and arm themselves against the shafts of malice or misfortune, by invulnerable patience; concluding, that this state only was happiness, and that this happiness was in every one's power.

Rasselas listened to him with the veneration due to the instructions of a superior being, and, waiting for him at the door, humbly implored the liberty of visiting so great a master of true wisdom. The lecturer hesitated a moment, when Rasselas put a purse of gold into his hand, which he received with a mixture of joy and wonder.

'I have found, said the prince, at his return to Imlac, a man who can teach all that is necessary to be known, who, from the unshaken throne of rational fortitude, looks down on the scenes of life changing beneath him. He speaks, and attention watches his lips. He reasons, and conviction closes his periods. This man shall be my future guide: I will learn his doctrines, and imitate his life.'

'Be not too hasty, said Imlac, to trust, or to admire, the teachers of morality: they discourse like angels, but they live like men.'

Rasselas, who could not conceive how any man could reason so forcibly without feeling the cogency of his own arguments, paid his visit in a few days, and was denied admission. He had now learned the power of money, and made his way by a piece of gold to the inner apartment, where he found the philosopher in a room half darkened, with his eyes misty, and his face pale. 'Sir, said he, you are come at a time when all human friendship is useless; what I suffer cannot be remedied, what I have lost cannot be supplied. My daughter, my only daughter, from whose tenderness I expected all the comforts of my age, died last night of a fever.*

My views, my purposes, my hopes are at an end: I am now a lonely being disunited from society.'

'Sir, said the prince, mortality is an event by which a wise man can never be surprised: we know that death is always near, and it should therefore always be expected.' 'Young man, answered the philosopher, you speak like one that has never felt the pangs of separation.' 'Have you then forgot the precepts, said Rasselas, which you so powerfully enforced? Has wisdom no strength to arm the heart against calamity?* Consider, that external things are naturally variable, but truth and reason are always the same.' 'What comfort, said the mourner, can truth and reason afford me? of what effect are they now, but to tell me, that my daughter will not be restored?'

The prince, whose humanity would not suffer him to insult misery with reproof, went away convinced of the emptiness of rhetorical sound, and the inefficacy of polished periods and studied sentences.

CHAP. XIX

A glimpse of pastoral life

HE was still eager upon the same enquiry; and, having heard of a hermit, that lived near the lowest cataract of the Nile,* and filled the whole country with the fame of his sanctity, resolved to visit his retreat, and enquire whether that felicity, which publick life could not afford, was to be found in solitude; and whether a man, whose age and virtue made him venerable, could teach any peculiar art of shunning evils, or enduring them.

Imlac and the princess agreed to accompany him, and, after the necessary preparations, they began their journey. Their way lay through fields, where shepherds tended their flocks, and the lambs were playing upon the pasture. 'This, said the poet, is the life which has been often celebrated for its innocence and quiet: let us pass the heat of the day among the shepherds tents, and know whether all our searches are not to terminate in pastoral simplicity.'*

The proposal pleased them, and they induced the shepherds, by small presents and familiar questions, to tell their opinion of their own state: they were so rude and ignorant, so little able to compare the good with the evil of the occupation, and so indistinct in their narratives and descriptions, that very little could be learned from them. But it was evident that their hearts were cankered with discontent; that they considered themselves as condemned to labour for the luxury of the rich, and looked up with stupid malevolence toward those that were placed above them.

The princess pronounced with vehemence, that she would never suffer these envious savages to be her companions, and that she should not soon be desirous of seeing any more specimens of rustick happiness; but could not believe that all the accounts of primeval pleasures were fabulous, and was yet in doubt whether life had any thing that could be justly preferred to the placid gratifications of fields and woods. She hoped that the time would come, when with a few virtuous and elegant companions, she should gather flowers planted by her own hand, fondle the lambs of her own ewe, and listen, without care, among brooks and breezes, to one of her maidens reading in the shade.

CHAP. XX

The danger of prosperity

ON the next day they continued their journey, till the heat compelled them to look round for shelter. At a small distance they saw a thick wood, which they no sooner entered than they perceived that they were approaching the habitations of men. The shrubs were diligently cut away to open walks where the shades were darkest; the boughs of opposite trees were artificially interwoven; seats of flowery turf were raised in vacant spaces, and a rivulet, that wantoned along the side of a winding path, had its banks sometimes opened into small basons, and its stream sometimes obstructed by little mounds of stone heaped together to increase its murmurs.

They passed slowly through the wood, delighted with such unexpected accommodations, and entertained each other with conjecturing what, or who, he could be, that, in those rude and unfrequented regions, had leisure and art for such harmless luxury.*

As they advanced, they heard the sound of musick, and saw youths and virgins dancing in the grove; and, going still further, beheld a stately palace built upon a hill surrounded with woods. The laws of eastern hospitality allowed them to enter, and the master welcomed them like a man liberal and wealthy.*

He was skilful enough in appearances soon to discern that they were no common guests, and spread his table with magnificence. The eloquence of Imlac caught his attention, and the lofty courtesy of the princess excited his respect. When they offered to depart he entreated their stay, and was the next day still more unwilling to dismiss them than before. They were easily persuaded to stop, and civility grew up in time to freedom and confidence.

The prince now saw all the domesticks chearful, and all the face of nature smiling round the place, and could not forbear to hope that he should find here what he was seeking; but when he was congratulating the master upon his possessions, he answered with a sigh, 'My condition has indeed the appearance of happiness, but appearances are delusive. My prosperity puts my life in danger; the Bassa* of Egypt is my enemy, incensed only by my wealth and popularity. I have been hitherto protected against him by the princes of the country; but, as the favour of the great is uncertain, I know not how soon my defenders may be persuaded to share the plunder with the Bassa. I have sent my treasures into a distant country, and, upon the first alarm, am prepared to follow them. Then will my enemies riot in my mansion, and enjoy the gardens which I have planted.'

They all joined in lamenting his danger, and deprecating his exile; and the princess was so much disturbed with the tumult of grief and indignation, that she retired to her apartment. They continued with their kind inviter a few days longer, and then went forward to find the hermit.

CHAP. XXI

The happiness of solitude. The hermit's history

THEY came on the third day, by the direction of the peasants, to the hermit's cell: it was a cavern in the side of the mountain, over-shadowed with palm-trees; at such a distance from the cataract, that nothing more was heard than a gentle uniform murmur, such as composed the mind to pensive meditation, especially when it was assisted by the wind whistling among the branches. The first rude essay of nature had been so much improved by human labour, that the cave contained several apartments, appropriated to different uses, and often afforded lodging to travellers, whom darkness or tempests happened to overtake.

The hermit sat on a bench at the door, to enjoy the coolness of the evening. On one side lay a book with pens and papers, on the other mechanical instruments of various kinds. As they approached him unregarded, the princess observed that he had not the countenance of a man that had found, or could teach, the way to happiness.

They saluted him with great respect, which he repaid like a man not unaccustomed to the forms of courts. 'My children, said he, if you have lost your way, you shall be willingly supplied with such conveniencies for the night as this cavern will afford. I have all that nature requires, and you will not expect delicacies in a hermit's cell.'

They thanked him, and, entering, were pleased with the neatness and regularity of the place. The hermit set flesh and wine before them, though he fed only upon fruits and water. His discourse was chearful without levity, and pious without enthusiasm. He soon gained the esteem of his guests, and the princess repented of her hasty censure.

At last Imlac began thus: 'I do not now wonder that your reputation is so far extended; we have heard at Cairo of your wisdom, and came hither to implore your direction for this young man and maiden in the *choice of life*.'

'To him that lives well, answered the hermit, every form of life is good; nor can I give any other rule for choice, than to remove from all apparent evil.'

'He will remove most certainly from evil, said the prince, who shall devote himself to that solitude which you have recommended by your example.'

'I have indeed lived fifteen years in solitude, said the hermit, but have no desire that my example should gain any imitators. In my youth I professed arms, and was raised by degrees to the highest military rank. I have traversed wide countries at the head of my troops, and seen many battles and sieges. At last, being disgusted by the preferment of a younger officer, and feeling that my vigour was beginning to decay, I resolved to close my life in peace, having found the world full of snares, discord, and misery. I had once escaped from the persuit of the enemy by the shelter of this cavern, and therefore chose it for my final residence. I employed artificers to form it into chambers, and stored it with all that I was likely to want.

'For some time after my retreat, I rejoiced like a tempest-beaten sailor at his entrance into the harbour, being delighted with the sudden change of the noise and hurry of war, to stillness and repose. When the pleasure of novelty went away, I employed my hours in examining the plants which grow in the valley, and the minerals which I collected from the rocks. But that enquiry is now grown tasteless and irksome. I have been for some time unsettled and distracted: my mind is disturbed with a thousand perplexities of doubt, and vanities of imagination, which hourly prevail upon me, because I have no opportunities of relaxation or diversion.* I am sometimes ashamed to think that I could not secure myself from vice, but by retiring from the exercise of virtue, and begin to suspect that I was rather impelled by resentment, than led by devotion, into solitude. My fancy riots in scenes of folly, and I lament that I have lost so much, and have gained so little. In solitude, if I escape the example of bad men, I want likewise the counsel and conversation of the good. I have been long comparing the evils with the advantages of society, and resolve to return into the world to morrow. The life of a solitary man will be certainly miserable, but not certainly devout.'

They heard his resolution with surprise, but, after a short pause, offered to conduct him to Cairo. He dug up a considerable treasure which he had hid among the rocks, and accompanied them to the city, on which, as he approached it, he gazed with rapture.

CHAP. XXII

The happiness of a life led according to nature*

RASSELAS went often to an assembly of learned men, who met at stated times to unbend their minds, and compare their opinions. Their manners were somewhat coarse, but their conversation was instructive, and their disputations acute, though sometimes too violent, and often continued till neither controvertist remembered upon what question they began. Some faults were almost general among them: every one was desirous to dictate to the rest, and every one was pleased to hear the genius or knowledge of another depreciated.

In this assembly Rasselas was relating his interview with the hermit, and the wonder with which he heard him censure a course of life which he had so deliberately chosen, and so laudably followed. The sentiments of the hearers were various. Some were of opinion, that the folly of his choice had been justly punished by condemnation to perpetual perseverance. One of the youngest among them, with great vehemence, pronounced him an hypocrite. Some talked of the right of society to the labour of individuals, and considered retirement as a desertion of duty. Others readily allowed, that there was a time when the claims of the publick were satisfied, and when a man might properly sequester himself, to review his life, and purify his heart.*

One, who appeared more affected with the narrative than the rest, thought it likely, that the hermit would, in a few years, go back to his retreat, and, perhaps, if shame did not restrain, or death intercept him, return once more from his retreat into the world: 'For the hope of happiness, said he, is so strongly impressed, that the longest experience is not able to efface it. Of the present state, whatever it be, we feel, and are forced to confess, the misery, yet, when the same state is again at a distance, imagination paints it as desirable. But the time will surely come, when desire will be no longer our torment, and no man shall be wretched but by his own fault.'*

'This, said a philosopher,* who had heard him with tokens of great impatience, is the present condition of a wise man. The time is already come, when none are wretched but by their own fault. Nothing is more idle, than to inquire after happiness, which nature has kindly placed within our reach.* The way to be happy is to live according to nature, in obedience to that universal and unalterable law with which every heart is originally impressed; which is not written on it by precept, but engraven by destiny, not instilled by education, but infused at our nativity.* He that lives according to nature will suffer nothing from the delusions of hope, or importunities of desire: he will receive and reject with equability of temper; and act or suffer as the reason of things shall alternately prescribe.* Other men may amuse themselves with subtle definitions, or intricate raciocination. Let them learn to be wise by easier means: let them observe the hind of the forest, and the linnet of the grove: let them consider the life of animals, whose motions are regulated by instinct; they obey their guide and are happy. Let us therefore, at length, cease to dispute, and learn to live; throw away the incumbrance of precepts, which they who utter them with so much pride and pomp do not understand, and carry with us this simple and intelligible maxim, That deviation from nature is deviation from happiness.'*

When he had spoken, he looked round him with a placid air, and enjoyed the consciousness of his own beneficence. 'Sir, said the prince, with great modesty, as I, like all the rest of mankind, am desirous of felicity, my closest attention has been fixed upon your discourse: I doubt not the truth of a position which a man so learned has so confidently advanced. Let me only know what it is to live according to nature.'

'When I find young men so humble and so docile, said the philosopher, I can deny them no information which my studies have enabled me to afford. To live according to nature, is to act always with due regard to the fitness arising from the relations and qualities of causes and effects; to concur with the great and unchangeable scheme of universal felicity; to co-operate with the general disposition and tendency of the present system of things.'*

The prince soon found that this was one of the sages whom he should understand less as he heard him longer.* He therefore bowed and was silent, and the philosopher, supposing him satisfied, and the rest vanquished, rose up and departed with the air of a man that had co-operated with the present system.

CHAP. XXIII

*The prince and his sister divide between them
the work of observation*

RASSELAS returned home full of reflexions, doubtful how to direct his future steps. Of the way to happiness he found the learned and simple equally ignorant; but, as he was yet young,* he flattered himself that he had time remaining for more experiments, and further enquiries. He communicated to Imlac his observations and his doubts, but was answered by him with new doubts, and remarks that gave him no comfort. He therefore discoursed more frequently and freely with his sister, who had yet the same hope with himself, and always assisted him to give some reason why, though he had been hitherto frustrated, he might succeed at last.

'We have hitherto, said she, known but little of the world: we have never yet been either great or mean. In our own country, though we had royalty, we had no power, and in this we have not yet seen the private recesses of domestick peace. Imlac favours not our search, lest we should in time find him mistaken. We will divide the task between us: you shall try what is to be found in the splendour of courts, and I will range the shades of humbler life.

Perhaps command and authority may be the supreme blessings, as they afford most opportunities of doing good: or, perhaps, what this world can give may be found in the modest habitations of middle fortune;* too low for great designs, and too high for penury and distress.'

CHAP. XXIV

The prince examines the happiness of high stations

Rasselas applauded the design, and appeared next day with a splendid retinue at the court of the Bassa. He was soon distinguished for his magnificence, and admitted, as a prince whose curiosity had brought him from distant countries, to an intimacy with the great officers, and frequent conversation with the Bassa himself.

He was at first inclined to believe, that the man must be pleased with his own condition, whom all approached with reverence, and heard with obedience, and who had the power to extend his edicts to a whole kingdom. 'There can be no pleasure, said he, equal to that of feeling at once the joy of thousands all made happy by wise administration. Yet, since, by the law of subordination, this sublime delight can be in one nation but the lot of one,* it is surely reasonable to think that there is some satisfaction more popular and accessible, and that millions can hardly be subjected to the will of a single man, only to fill his particular breast with incommunicable content.'

These thoughts were often in his mind, and he found no solution of the difficulty. But as presents and civilities gained him more familiarity, he found that almost every man who stood high in employment hated all the rest, and was hated by them, and that their lives were a continual succession of plots and detections, stratagems and escapes, faction and treachery. Many of those, who surrounded the Bassa, were sent only to watch and report his conduct; every tongue was muttering censure and every eye was searching for a fault.

At last the letters of revocation arrived, the Bassa was carried in chains to Constantinople,* and his name was mentioned no more.

'What are we now to think of the prerogatives of power, said Rasselas to his sister; is it without any efficacy to good? or, is the subordinate degree only dangerous, and the supreme safe and glorious? Is the Sultan the only happy man in his dominions? or, is the Sultan himself subject to the torments of suspicion, and the dread of enemies?'

In a short time the second Bassa was deposed. The Sultan, that had advanced him, was murdered by the Janisaries,* and his successor had other views and different favourites.

CHAP. XXV

The princess persues her enquiry with more diligence than success

THE princess, in the mean time, insinuated herself into many families; for there are few doors, through which liberality, joined with good humour, cannot find its way. The daughters of many houses were airy and chearful, but Nekayah had been too long accustomed to the conversation of Imlac and her brother to be much pleased with childish levity and prattle which had no meaning. She found their thoughts narrow, their wishes low, and their merriment often artificial. Their pleasures, poor as they were, could not be preserved pure, but were embittered by petty competitions and worthless emulation. They were always jealous of the beauty of each other; of a quality to which solicitude can add nothing, and from which detraction can take nothing away. Many were in love with triflers like themselves, and many fancied that they were in love when in truth they were only idle. Their affection was seldom fixed on sense or virtue, and therefore seldom ended but in vexation. Their grief, however, like their joy, was transient; every thing floated in their mind unconnected with the past or future, so that one desire easily gave way to another, as a second stone cast into the water effaces and confounds the circles of the first.

With these girls she played as with inoffensive animals, and found them proud of her countenance, and weary of her company.

But her purpose was to examine more deeply, and her affability easily persuaded the hearts that were swelling with sorrow to discharge their secrets in her ear: and those whom hope flattered, or prosperity delighted, often courted her to partake their pleasures.

The princess and her brother commonly met in the evening in a private summer-house on the bank of the Nile, and related to each other the occurrences of the day. As they were sitting together, the princess cast her eyes upon the river that flowed before her. 'Answer, said she, great father of waters,* thou that rollest thy floods through eighty nations, to the invocations of the daughter of thy native king. Tell me if thou waterest, through all thy course, a single habitation from which thou dost not hear the murmurs of complaint?'

'You are then, said Rasselas, not more successful in private houses than I have been in courts.' 'I have, since the last partition of our provinces, said the princess, enabled myself to enter familiarly into many families, where there was the fairest show of prosperity and peace, and know not one house that is not haunted by some fury* that destroys its quiet.

'I did not seek ease among the poor, because I concluded that there it could not be found.* But I saw many poor whom I had supposed to live in affluence. Poverty has, in large cities, very different appearances: it is often concealed in splendour, and often in extravagance. It is the care of a very great part of mankind to conceal their indigence from the rest:* they support themselves by temporary expedients, and every day is lost in contriving for the morrow.

'This, however, was an evil, which, though frequent, I saw with less pain, because I could relieve it. Yet some have refused my bounties; more offended with my quickness to detect their wants, than pleased with my readiness to succour them: and others, whose exigencies compelled them to admit my kindness, have never been able to forgive their benefactress.* Many, however, have been sincerely grateful without the ostentation of gratitude, or the hope of other favours.'

CHAP. XXVI

The princess continues her remarks upon private life

NEKAYAH perceiving her brother's attention fixed, proceeded in her narrative.

'In families, where there is or is not poverty, there is commonly discord: if a kingdom be, as Imlac tells us, a great family, a family likewise is a little kingdom, torn with factions and exposed to revolutions.* An unpractised observer expects the love of parents and children to be constant and equal; but this kindness seldom continues beyond the years of infancy: in a short time the children become rivals to their parents. Benefits are allayed by reproaches, and gratitude debased by envy.

'Parents and children seldom act in concert: each child endeavours to appropriate the esteem or fondness of the parents,* and the parents, with yet less temptation, betray each other to their children; thus some place their confidence in the father, and some in the mother, and, by degrees, the house is filled with artifices and feuds.

'The opinions of children and parents, of the young and the old, are naturally opposite, by the contrary effects of hope and despondence, of expectation and experience, without crime or folly on either side. The colours of life in youth and age appear different, as the face of nature in spring and winter.* And how can children credit the assertions of parents, which their own eyes show them to be false?

'Few parents act in such a manner as much to enforce their maxims by the credit of their lives. The old man trusts wholly to slow contrivance and gradual progression: the youth expects to force his way by genius, vigour, and precipitance. The old man pays regard to riches, and the youth reverences virtue. The old man deifies prudence: the youth commits himself to magnanimity

and chance. The young man, who intends no ill, believes that
none is intended, and therefore acts with openness and candour:
but his father, having suffered the injuries of fraud, is impelled to
suspect, and too often allured to practice it. Age looks with anger
on the temerity of youth, and youth with contempt on the scrupulosity* of age. Thus parents and children, for the greatest part,
live on to love less and less: and, if those whom nature has thus
closely united are the torments of each other, where shall we look
for tenderness and consolation?'

'Surely, said the prince, you must have been unfortunate in
your choice of acquaintance: I am unwilling to believe, that the
most tender of all relations is thus impeded in its effects by natural necessity.'

'Domestick discord, answered she, is not inevitably and fatally
necessary; but yet is not easily avoided. We seldom see that a
whole family is virtuous: the good and evil cannot well agree; and
the evil can yet less agree with one another: even the virtuous fall
sometimes to variance, when their virtues are of different kinds,
and tending to extremes. In general, those parents have most
reverence who most deserve it: for he that lives well cannot be
despised.

'Many other evils infest private life. Some are the slaves of
servants whom they have trusted with their affairs. Some are
kept in continual anxiety to the caprice of rich relations, whom
they cannot please, and dare not offend. Some husbands are
imperious, and some wives perverse: and, as it is always more easy
to do evil than good, though the wisdom or virtue of one can very
rarely make many happy, the folly or vice of one may often make
many miserable.'

'If such be the general effect of marriage, said the prince,
I shall, for the future, think it dangerous to connect my interest
with that of another, lest I should be unhappy by my partner's
fault.'

'I have met, said the princess, with many who live single for
that reason; but I never found that their prudence ought to raise
envy. They dream away their time without friendship, without
fondness, and are driven to rid themselves of the day, for which

they have no use, by childish amusements, or vicious delights. They act as beings under the constant sense of some known inferiority, that fills their minds with rancour, and their tongues with censure. They are peevish at home, and malevolent abroad; and, as the out-laws of human nature, make it their business and their pleasure to disturb that society which debars them from its privileges. To live without feeling or exciting sympathy, to be fortunate without adding to the felicity of others, or afflicted without tasting the balm of pity, is a state more gloomy than solitude: it is not retreat but exclusion from mankind. Marriage has many pains, but celibacy has no pleasures.'*

'What then is to be done? said Rasselas; the more we enquire, the less we can resolve. Surely he is most likely to please himself that has no other inclination to regard.'

CHAP. XXVII

Disquisition upon greatness

THE conversation had a short pause. The prince having considered his sister's observations, told her, that she had surveyed life with prejudice, and supposed misery where she did not find it. 'Your narrative, says he, throws yet a darker gloom upon the prospects of futurity: the predictions of Imlac were but faint sketches of the evils painted by Nekayah. I have been lately convinced that quiet is not the daughter of grandeur, or of power: that her presence is not to be bought by wealth, nor enforced by conquest. It is evident, that as any man acts in a wider compass, he must be more exposed to opposition from enmity or miscarriage from chance; whoever has many to please or to govern, must use the ministry of many agents, some of whom will be wicked, and some ignorant; by some he will be misled, and by others betrayed. If he gratifies one he will offend another: those that are not favoured will think themselves injured; and, since favours can be conferred but upon few, the greater number will be always discontented.'*

'The discontent, said the princess, which is thus unreasonable, I hope that I shall always have spirit to despise, and you, power to repress.'

'Discontent, answered Rasselas, will not always be without reason under the most just or vigilant administration of publick affairs. None, however attentive, can always discover that merit which indigence or faction may happen to obscure; and none, however powerful, can always reward it. Yet, he that sees inferiour desert advanced above him, will naturally impute that preference to partiality or caprice; and, indeed, it can scarcely be hoped that any man, however magnanimous by nature, or exalted by condition, will be able to persist for ever in fixed and inexorable justice of distribution: he will sometimes indulge his own affections, and sometimes those of his favourites; he will permit some to please him who can never serve him; he will discover in those whom he loves qualities which in reality they do not possess; and to those, from whom he receives pleasure, he will in his turn endeavour to give it. Thus will recommendations sometimes prevail which were purchased by money, or by the more destructive bribery of flattery and servility.*

'He that has much to do will do something wrong, and of that wrong must suffer the consequences; and, if it were possible that he should always act rightly, yet when such numbers are to judge of his conduct, the bad will censure and obstruct him by malevolence, and the good sometimes by mistake.

'The highest stations cannot therefore hope to be the abodes of happiness, which I would willingly believe to have fled from thrones and palaces to seats of humble privacy and placid obscurity. For what can hinder the satisfaction, or intercept the expectations, of him whose abilities are adequate to his employments, who sees with his own eyes the whole circuit of his influence, who chooses by his own knowledge all whom he trusts, and whom none are tempted to deceive by hope or fear? Surely he has nothing to do but to love and to be loved, to be virtuous and to be happy.'

'Whether perfect happiness would be procured by perfect goodness, said Nekayah, this world will never afford an opportunity of deciding. But this, at least, may be maintained, that we do not always find visible happiness in proportion to visible virtue. All natural and almost all political evils, are incident alike to the bad and good:* they are confounded in the misery of a famine, and not much distinguished in the fury of a faction; they sink together in a tempest, and are driven together from their country by invaders. All that virtue can afford is quietness of conscience, a steady prospect of a happier state; this may enable us to endure calamity with patience; but remember that patience must suppose pain.'*

CHAP. XXVIII

Rasselas and Nekayah continue their conversation

'DEAR princess, said Rasselas, you fall into the common errours of exaggeratory declamation, by producing, in a familiar disquisition, examples of national calamities, and scenes of extensive misery, which are found in books rather than in the world, and which, as they are horrid, are ordained to be rare. Let us not imagine evils which we do not feel, nor injure life by misrepresentations. I cannot bear that querulous eloquence which threatens every city with a siege like that of Jerusalem,* that makes famine attend on every flight of locusts, and suspends pestilence on the wing of every blast that issues from the south.

'On necessary and inevitable evils, which overwhelm kingdoms at once, all disputation is vain: when they happen they must be endured. But it is evident, that these bursts of universal distress are more dreaded than felt: thousands and ten thousands flourish in youth, and wither in age, without the knowledge of any other than domestick evils, and share the same pleasures and vexations whether their kings are mild or cruel, whether the armies of their country persue their enemies, or retreat before them. While courts are disturbed with intestine competitions, and ambassadours are negotiating in foreign countries, the smith still plies his anvil, and the husbandman drives his plow forward; the necessaries of life are required and obtained, and the successive business of the seasons continues to make its wonted revolutions.*

'Let us cease to consider what, perhaps, may never happen, and what, when it shall happen, will laugh at human speculation. We will not endeavour to modify the motions of the elements, or to fix the destiny of kingdoms. It is our business to consider what beings like us may perform; each labouring for his own happiness, by promoting within his circle, however narrow, the happiness of others.

'Marriage is evidently the dictate of nature; men and women were made to be companions of each other, and therefore I cannot be persuaded but that marriage is one of the means of happiness.'

'I know not, said the princess, whether marriage be more than one of the innumerable modes of human misery. When I see and reckon the various forms of connubial infelicity,* the unexpected causes of lasting discord, the diversities of temper, the oppositions of opinion, the rude collisions of contrary desire where both are urged by violent impulses, the obstinate contests of disagreeing virtues, where both are supported by consciousness of good intention, I am sometimes disposed to think with the severer casuists of most nations, that marriage is rather permitted than approved, and that none, but by the instigation of a passion too much indulged, entangle themselves with indissoluble compacts.'

'You seem to forget, replied Rasselas, that you have, even now, represented celibacy as less happy than marriage. Both conditions may be bad, but they cannot both be worst. Thus it happens when wrong opinions are entertained, that they mutually destroy each other, and leave the mind open to truth.'

'I did not expect, answered the princess, to hear that imputed to falshood which is the consequence only of frailty. To the mind, as to the eye, it is difficult to compare with exactness objects vast in their extent, and various in their parts. Where we see or conceive the whole at once we readily note the discriminations and decide the preference: but of two systems, of which neither can be surveyed by any human being in its full compass of magnitude and multiplicity of complication, where is the wonder, that judging of the whole by parts, I am alternately affected by one and the other as either presses on my memory or fancy?* We differ from ourselves just as we differ from each other, when we see only part of the question, as in the multifarious relations of politicks and morality: but when we perceive the whole at once, as in numerical computations, all agree in one judgment, and none ever varies his opinion.'

'Let us not add, said the prince, to the other evils of life, the bitterness of controversy, nor endeavour to vie with each other in subtilties of argument. We are employed in a search, of which both are equally to enjoy the success, or suffer by the miscarriage. It is therefore fit that we assist each other. You surely conclude too hastily from the infelicity of marriage against its institution; will not the misery of life prove equally that life cannot be the gift of heaven? The world must be peopled by marriage, or peopled without it.'

'How the world is to be peopled, returned Nekayah, is not my care, and needs not be yours. I see no danger that the present generation should omit to leave successors behind them: we are not now enquiring for the world, but for ourselves.'

CHAP. XXIX

The debate on marriage continued

'THE good of the whole, says Rasselas, is the same with the good of all its parts. If marriage be best for mankind it must be evidently best for individuals, or a permanent and necessary duty must be the cause of evil, and some must be inevitably sacrificed to the convenience of others. In the estimate which you have made of the two states, it appears that the incommodities of a single life are, in a great measure, necessary and certain, but those of the conjugal state accidental and avoidable.

'I cannot forbear to flatter myself that prudence and benevolence will make marriage happy. The general folly of mankind is the cause of general complaint. What can be expected but

disappointment and repentance from a choice made in the imma-
turity of youth, in the ardour of desire, without judgment, without
foresight, without enquiry after conformity of opinions, similarity
of manners, rectitude of judgment, or purity of sentiment.

'Such is the common process of marriage. A youth and maiden
meeting by chance, or brought together by artifice, exchange
glances, reciprocate civilities, go home, and dream of one another.
Having little to divert attention, or diversify thought, they find
themselves uneasy when they are apart, and therefore conclude
that they shall be happy together. They marry, and discover what
nothing but voluntary blindness had before concealed; they wear
out life in altercations, and charge nature with cruelty.

'From those early marriages proceeds likewise the rivalry of
parents and children: the son is eager to enjoy the world before
the father is willing to forsake it, and there is hardly room at once
for two generations. The daughter begins to bloom before the
mother can be content to fade, and neither can forbear to wish for
the absence of the other.

'Surely all these evils may be avoided by that deliberation and
delay which prudence prescribes to irrevocable choice. In the
variety and jollity of youthful pleasures life may be well enough
supported without the help of a partner. Longer time will increase
experience, and wider views will allow better opportunities of
enquiry and selection: one advantage, at least, will be certain; the
parents will be visibly older than their children.'

'What reason cannot collect, said Nekayah, and what experiment has not yet taught, can be known only from the report of
others. I have been told that late marriages are not eminently
happy. This is a question too important to be neglected, and
I have often proposed it to those, whose accuracy of remark, and
comprehensiveness of knowledge, made their suffrages worthy of
regard. They have generally determined, that it is dangerous for
a man and woman to suspend their fate upon each other, at a
time when opinions are fixed, and habits are established; when
friendships have been contracted on both sides, when life has
been planned into method, and the mind has long enjoyed the
contemplation of its own prospects.

'It is scarcely possible that two travelling through the world under the conduct of chance, should have been both directed to the same path, and it will not often happen that either will quit the track which custom has made pleasing. When the desultory levity of youth has settled into regularity, it is soon succeeded by pride ashamed to yield, or obstinacy delighting to contend. And even though mutual esteem produces mutual desire to please, time itself, as it modifies unchangeably the external mien, determines likewise the direction of the passions, and gives an inflexible rigidity to the manners. Long customs are not easily broken: he that attempts to change the course of his own life, very often labours in vain;* and how shall we do that for others which we are seldom able to do for ourselves?'

'But surely, interposed the prince, you suppose the chief motive of choice forgotten or neglected. Whenever I shall seek a wife, it shall be my first question, whether she be willing to be led by reason?'

'Thus it is, said Nekayah, that philosophers are deceived. There are a thousand familiar disputes which reason never can decide; questions that elude investigation, and make logick ridiculous; cases where something must be done, and where little can be said. Consider the state of mankind, and enquire how few can be supposed to act upon any occasions, whether small or great, with all the reasons of action present to their minds. Wretched would be the pair above all names of wretchedness, who should be doomed to adjust by reason every morning all the minute detail of a domestick day.

'Those who marry at an advanced age, will probably escape the encroachments of their children; but, in diminution of this advantage, they will be likely to leave them, ignorant and helpless, to a guardian's mercy: or, if that should not happen, they must at least go out of the world before they see those whom they love best either wise or great.

'From their children, if they have less to fear, they have less also to hope, and they lose, without equivalent the joys of early love, and the convenience of uniting with manners pliant, and minds susceptible of new impressions, which might wear away their dissimilitudes by long cohabitation, as soft bodies, by continual attrition, conform their surfaces to each other.

'I believe it will be found that those who marry late are best pleased with their children, and those who marry early with their partners.'

'The union of these two affections, said Rasselas, would produce all that could be wished. Perhaps there is a time when marriage might unite them, a time neither too early for the father, nor too late for the husband.'

'Every hour, answered the princess, confirms my prejudice in favour of the position so often uttered by the mouth of Imlac, "That nature sets her gifts on the right hand and on the left." Those conditions, which flatter hope and attract desire, are so constituted, that, as we approach one, we recede from another. There are goods so opposed that we cannot seize both, but, by too much prudence, may pass between them as too great a distance to reach either. This is often the fate of long consideration; he does nothing who endeavours to do more than is allowed to humanity. Flatter not yourself with contrarieties of pleasure. Of the blessings set before you make your choice, and be content. No man can taste the fruits of autumn while he is delighting his scent with the flowers of the spring: no man can, at the same time, fill his cup from the source and from the mouth of the Nile.'*

CHAP. XXX

Imlac enters, and changes the conversation

HERE Imlac entered, and interrupted them. 'Imlac, said Rasselas, I have been taking from the princess the dismal history of private life, and am almost discouraged from further search.'

'It seems to me, said Imlac, that while you are making the choice of life, you neglect to live. You wander about a single city, which, however large and diversified, can now afford few novelties, and forget that you are in a country, famous among the earliest monarchies for the power and wisdom of its inhabitants;

a country where the sciences first dawned that illuminate the world, and beyond which the arts cannot be traced of civil society or domestick life.*

'The old Egyptians have left behind them monuments of industry and power before which all European magnificence is confessed to fade away. The ruins of their architecture are the schools of modern builders, and from the wonders which time has spared we may conjecture, though uncertainly, what it has destroyed.'

'My curiosity, said Rasselas, does not very strongly lead me to survey piles of stone, or mounds of earth; my business is with man.* I came hither not to measure fragments of temples, or trace choaked aqueducts, but to look upon the various scenes of the present world.'

'The things that are now before us, said the princess, require attention, and deserve it.* What have I to do with the heroes or the monuments of ancient times? with times which never can return, and heroes, whose form of life was different from all that the present condition of mankind requires or allows.'

'To know any thing, returned the poet, we must know its effects; to see men we must see their works, that we may learn what reason has dictated, or passion has incited, and find what are the most powerful motives of action. To judge rightly of the present we must oppose it to the past; for all judgment is comparative, and of the future nothing can be known. The truth is, that no mind is much employed upon the present: recollection and anticipation fill up almost all our moments.* Our passions are joy and grief, love and hatred, hope and fear. Of joy and grief the past is the object, and the future of hope and fear; even love and hatred respect the past, for the cause must have been before the effect.

'The present state of things is the consequence of the former, and it is natural to inquire what were the sources of the good that we enjoy, or of the evil that we suffer. If we act only for ourselves, to neglect the study of history is not prudent: if we are entrusted with the care of others, it is not just. Ignorance, when it is voluntary, is criminal; and he may properly be charged with evil who refused to learn how he might prevent it.

'There is no part of history so generally useful as that which relates the progress of the human mind, the gradual improvement of reason, the successive advances of science, the vicissitudes of learning and ignorance, which are the light and darkness of thinking beings, the extinction and resuscitation of arts, and all the revolutions of the intellectual world.* If accounts of battles and invasions are peculiarly the business of princes, the useful or elegant arts are not to be neglected; those who have kingdoms to govern, have understandings to cultivate.

'Example is always more efficacious than precept.* A soldier is formed in war, and a painter must copy pictures. In this, contemplative life has the advantage: great actions are seldom seen, but the labours of art are always at hand for those who desire to know what art has been able to perform.

'When the eye or the imagination is struck with any uncommon work the next transition of an active mind is to the means by which it was performed.* Here begins the true use of such contemplation; we enlarge our comprehension by new ideas, and perhaps recover some art lost to mankind, or learn what is less perfectly known in our own country. At least we compare our own with former times, and either rejoice at our improvements, or, what is the first motion towards good, discover our defects.'

'I am willing, said the prince, to see all that can deserve my search.' 'And I, said the princess, shall rejoice to learn something of the manners of antiquity.'

'The most pompous monument of Egyptian greatness, and one of the most bulky works of manual industry, said Imlac, are the pyramids; fabricks raised before the time of history, and of which the earliest narratives afford us only uncertain traditions.* Of these the greatest is still standing, very little injured by time.'

'Let us visit them to morrow, said Nekayah. I have often heard of the pyramids, and shall not rest, till I have seen them within and without with my own eyes.'

CHAP. XXXI

They visit the pyramids

THE resolution being thus taken, they set out the next day. They laid tents upon their camels, being resolved to stay among the pyramids till their curiosity was fully satisfied. They travelled gently, turned aside to every thing remarkable, stopped from time to time and conversed with the inhabitants, and observed the various appearances of towns ruined and inhabited, of wild and cultivated nature.

When they came to the great pyramid they were astonished at the extent of the base, and the height of the top. Imlac explained to them the principles upon which the pyramidal form was chosen for a fabrick intended to co-extend its duration with that of the world: he showed that its gradual diminution gave it such stability, as defeated all the common attacks of the elements, and could scarcely be overthrown by earthquakes themselves, the least resistible of natural violence. A concussion that should shatter the pyramid would threaten the dissolution of the continent.*

They measured all its dimensions, and pitched their tents at its foot. Next day they prepared to enter its interiour apartments, and having hired the common guides climbed up to the first passage, when the favourite of the princess, looking into the cavity, stepped back and trembled. 'Pekuah, said the princess, of what art thou afraid?' 'Of the narrow entrance, answered the lady, and of the dreadful gloom.* I dare not enter a place which must surely be inhabited by unquiet souls. The original possessors of these dreadful vaults will start up before us, and, perhaps, shut us in for ever.' She spoke, and threw her arms round the neck of her mistress.

'If all your fear be of apparitions, said the prince, I will promise you safety: there is no danger from the dead; he that is once buried will be seen no more.'

'That the dead are seen no more, said Imlac, I will not undertake to maintain against the concurrent and unvaried testimony of all ages, and of all nations. There is no people, rude or learned,

among whom apparitions of the dead are not related and believed.*
This opinion, which, perhaps, prevails as far as human nature is
diffused, could become universal only by its truth: those, that
never heard of one another, would not have agreed in a tale which
nothing but experience can make credible. That it is doubted by
single cavillers can very little weaken the general evidence, and
some who deny it with their tongues confess it by their fears.

'Yet I do not mean to add new terrours to those which have
already seized upon Pekuah. There can be no reason why spectres
should haunt the pyramid more than other places, or why they
should have power or will to hurt innocence and purity. Our
entrance is no violation of their privileges; we can take nothing
from them, how then can we offend them?'

'My dear Pekuah, said the princess, I will always go before you,
and Imlac shall follow you. Remember that you are the companion of the princess of Abissinia.'

'If the princess is pleased that her servant should die, returned
the lady, let her command some death less dreadful than
enclosure in this horrid cavern. You know I dare not disobey you:
I must go if you command me; but, if I once enter, I never shall
come back.'

The princess saw that her fear was too strong for expostulation
or reproof, and embracing her, told her that she should stay in the
tent till their return. Pekuah was yet not satisfied, but entreated
the princess not to persue so dreadful a purpose, as that of entering the recesses of the pyramid. 'Though I cannot teach courage,
said Nekayah, I must not learn cowardise; nor leave at last undone
what I came hither only to do.'

CHAP. XXXII

They enter the pyramid

PEKUAH descended to the tents, and the rest entered the pyramid:
they passed through the galleries, surveyed the vaults of marble,
and examined the chest in which the body of the founder is

supposed to have been reposited.* They then sat down in one of the most spacious chambers to rest a while before they attempted to return.

'We have now, said Imlac, gratified our minds with an exact view of the greatest work of man, except the wall of China.'*

'Of the wall it is very easy to assign the motives. It secured a wealthy and timorous nation from the incursions of Barbarians, whose unskilfulness in arts made it easier for them to supply their wants by rapine than by industry, and who from time to time poured in upon the habitations of peaceful commerce, as vultures descend upon domestick fowl. Their celerity and fierceness made the wall necessary, and their ignorance made it efficacious.

'But for the pyramids no reason has ever been given adequate to the cost and labour of the work. The narrowness of the chambers proves that it could afford no retreat from enemies, and treasures might have been reposited at far less expence with equal security. It seems to have been erected only in compliance with that hunger of imagination which preys incessantly upon life, and must be always appeased by some employment. Those who have already all that they can enjoy, must enlarge their desires. He that has built for use, till use is supplied, must begin to build for vanity, and extend his plan to the utmost power of human performance, that he may not be soon reduced to form another wish.

'I consider this mighty structure as a monument of the insufficiency of human enjoyments.* A king, whose power is unlimited, and whose treasures surmount all real and imaginary wants, is compelled to solace, by the erection of a pyramid, the satiety of dominion and tastelesness of pleasures, and to amuse the tediousness of declining life, by seeing thousands labouring without end, and one stone, for no purpose, laid upon another. Whoever thou art, that, not content with a moderate condition, imaginest happiness in royal magnificence, and dreamest that command or riches can feed the appetite of novelty with perpetual gratifications, survey the pyramids, and confess thy folly!'*

CHAP. XXXIII

The princess meets with an unexpected misfortune

THEY rose up, and returned through the cavity at which they had entered, and the princess prepared for her favourite a long narrative of dark labyrinths, and costly rooms, and of the different impressions which the varieties of the way had made upon her. But, when they came to their train, they found every one silent and dejected: the men discovered shame and fear in their countenances, and the women were weeping in the tents.

What had happened they did not try to conjecture, but immediately enquired. 'You had scarcely entered into the pyramid, said one of the attendants, when a troop of Arabs rushed upon us: we were too few to resist them, and too slow to escape. They were about to search the tents, set us on our camels, and drive us along before them, when the approach of some Turkish horsemen put them to flight; but they seized the lady Pekuah with her two maids, and carried them away: the Turks are now persuing them by our instigation, but I fear they will not be able to overtake them.'

The princess was overpowered with surprise and grief. Rasselas, in the first heat of his resentment, ordered his servants to follow him, and prepared to persue the robbers with his sabre in his hand. 'Sir, said Imlac, what can you hope from violence or valour? the Arabs are mounted on horses trained to battle and retreat; we have only beasts of burden. By leaving our present station we may lose the princess, but cannot hope to regain Pekuah.'

In a short time the Turks returned, having not been able to reach the enemy. The princess burst out into new lamentations, and Rasselas could scarcely forbear to reproach them with cowardice; but Imlac was of opinion, that the escape of the Arabs was no addition to their misfortune, for, perhaps, they would have killed their captives rather than have resigned them.

CHAP. XXXIV

They return to Cairo without Pekuah

THERE was nothing to be hoped from longer stay. They returned to Cairo repenting of their curiosity, censuring the negligence of the government, lamenting their own rashness which had neglected to procure a guard, imagining many expedients by which the loss of Pekuah might have been prevented, and resolving to do something for her recovery, though none could find any thing proper to be done.

Nekayah retired to her chamber, where her women attempted to comfort her, by telling her that all had their troubles, and that lady Pekuah had enjoyed much happiness in the world for a long time, and might reasonably expect a change of fortune. They hoped that some good would befal her wheresoever she was, and that their mistress would find another friend who might supply her place.

The princess made them no answer, and they continued the form of condolence, not much grieved in their hearts that the favourite was lost.

Next day the prince presented to the Bassa a memorial of the wrong which he had suffered, and a petition for redress.* The Bassa threatened to punish the robbers, but did not attempt to catch them, nor, indeed, could any account or description be given by which he might direct the persuit.

It soon appeared that nothing would be done by authority. Governors, being accustomed to hear of more crimes than they can punish, and more wrongs than they can redress, set themselves at ease by indiscriminate negligence, and presently forget the request when they lose sight of the petitioner.

Imlac then endeavoured to gain some intelligence by private agents. He found many who pretended to an exact knowledge of all the haunts of the Arabs, and to regular correspondence with their chiefs, and who readily undertook the recovery of Pekuah. Of these, some were furnished with money for their journey, and came back no more; some were liberally paid for accounts which a few days discovered to be false. But the princess would not suffer any means, however improbable, to be left untried. While she was doing something she kept her hope alive. As one expedient failed, another was suggested; when one messenger returned unsuccessful, another was despatched to a different quarter.

Two months had now passed, and of Pekuah nothing had been heard; the hopes which they had endeavoured to raise in each other grew more languid, and the princess, when she saw nothing more to be tried, sunk* down inconsolable in hopeless dejection. A thousand times she reproached herself with the easy compliance by which she permitted her favourite to stay behind her. 'Had not my fondness, said she, lessened my authority, Pekuah had not dared to talk of her terrours. She ought to have feared me more than spectres. A severe look would have overpowered her; a peremptory command would have compelled obedience. Why did foolish indulgence prevail upon me? Why did I not speak and refuse to hear?'

'Great princess, said Imlac, do not reproach yourself for your virtue, or consider that as blameable by which evil has accidentally been caused. Your tenderness for the timidity of Pekuah was generous and kind. When we act according to our duty, we commit the event to him by whose laws our actions are governed, and who will suffer none to be finally punished for obedience. When, in prospect of some good, whether natural or moral, we break the rules prescribed us, we withdraw from the direction of superiour wisdom, and take all consequences upon ourselves. Man cannot so far know the connexion of causes and events, as that he may venture to do wrong in order to do right. When we persue our end by lawful means, we may always console our miscarriage by the hope of future recompense. When we consult only our own policy, and attempt to find a nearer way to good, by overleaping the settled boundaries of right and wrong, we cannot be happy even by success, because we cannot escape the consciousness of our fault; but, if we miscarry, the disappointment is irremediably embittered. How comfortless is the sorrow of him, who feels at once the pangs of guilt, and the vexation of calamity which guilt has brought upon him?

'Consider, princess, what would have been your condition, if the lady Pekuah had entreated to accompany you, and, being compelled to stay in the tents, had been carried away; or how would you have born the thought, if you had forced her into the pyramid, and she had died before you in agonies of terrour.'

'Had either happened, said Nekayah, I could not have endured life till now: I should have been tortured to madness by the remembrance of such cruelty, or must have pined away in abhorrence of myself.'

'This at least, said Imlac, is the present reward of virtuous conduct, that no unlucky consequence can oblige us to repent it.'

CHAP. XXXV

The princess languishes for want of Pekuah

NEKAYAH, being thus reconciled to herself, found that no evil is insupportable but that which is accompanied with consciousness of wrong. She was, from that time, delivered from the violence of tempestuous sorrow, and sunk into silent pensiveness and gloomy tranquillity. She sat from morning to evening recollecting all that had been done or said by her Pekuah, treasured up with care every trifle on which Pekuah had set an accidental value, and which might recal to mind any little incident or careless conversation. The sentiments of her, whom she now expected to see no more, were treasured in her memory as rules of life, and she deliberated to no other end than to conjecture on any occasion what would have been the opinion and counsel of Pekuah.

The women, by whom she was attended, knew nothing of her real condition, and therefore she could not talk to them but with caution and reserve. She began to remit her curiosity, having no great care to collect notions which she had no convenience of uttering. Rasselas endeavoured first to comfort and afterwards to divert her; he hired musicians, to whom she seemed to listen, but did not hear them, and procured masters to instruct her in various arts, whose lectures, when they visited her again, were again to be repeated. She had lost her taste of pleasure and her ambition of excellence. And her mind, though forced into short excursions, always recurred to the image of her friend.

Imlac was every morning earnestly enjoined to renew his enquiries, and was asked every night whether he had yet heard of Pekuah, till not being able to return the princess the answer that she desired, he was less and less willing to come into her presence. She observed his backwardness, and commanded him to attend her. 'You are not, said she, to confound impatience with resentment, or to suppose that I charge you with negligence, because I repine at your unsuccessfulness. I do not much wonder at your absence; I know that the unhappy are never pleasing, and that all naturally avoid the contagion of misery. To hear complaints is wearisome alike to the wretched and the happy; for who would cloud by adventitious grief the short gleams of gaiety which life allows us? or who, that is struggling under his own evils, will add to them the miseries of another?

'The time is at hand, when none shall be disturbed any longer by the sighs of Nekayah: my search after happiness is now at an end. I am resolved to retire from the world with all its flatteries and deceits, and will hide myself in solitude, without any other care than to compose my thoughts, and regulate my hours by a constant succession of innocent occupations, till, with a mind purified from all earthly desires, I shall enter into that state, to which all are hastening, and in which I hope again to enjoy the friendship of Pekuah.'

'Do not entangle your mind, said Imlac, by irrevocable determinations,* nor increase the burthen of life by a voluntary accumulation of misery: the weariness of retirement will continue or increase when the loss of Pekuah is forgotten. That you have been deprived of one pleasure is no very good reason for rejection of the rest.'

'Since Pekuah was taken from me, said the princess, I have no pleasure to reject or to retain. She that has no one to love or trust has little to hope. She wants the radical principle of happiness. We may, perhaps, allow that what satisfaction this world can afford, must arise from the conjunction of wealth, knowledge and goodness: wealth is nothing but as it is bestowed, and knowledge nothing but as it is communicated: they must therefore be imparted to others, and to whom could I now delight to impart them? Goodness affords the only comfort which can be enjoyed without a partner, and goodness may be practised in retirement.'

'How far solitude may admit goodness, or advance it, I shall not, replied Imlac, dispute at present. Remember the confession of the pious hermit. You will wish to return into the world, when the image of your companion has left your thoughts.' 'That time, said Nekayah, will never come. The generous frankness, the modest obsequiousness, and the faithful secrecy of my dear Pekuah, will always be more missed, as I shall live longer to see vice and folly.'

'The state of a mind oppressed with a sudden calamity, said Imlac, is like that of the fabulous inhabitants of the new created earth, who, when the first night came upon them, supposed that day never would return.* When the clouds of sorrow gather over us, we see nothing beyond them, nor can imagine how they will be dispelled: yet a new day succeeded to the night, and sorrow is never long without a dawn of ease. But they who restrain themselves from receiving comfort, do as the savages would have done, had they put out their eyes when it was dark. Our minds, like our bodies, are in continual flux; something is hourly lost, and something acquired. To lose much at once is inconvenient to either, but while the vital powers remain uninjured, nature will find the means of reparation. Distance has the same effect on the mind as on the eye, and while we glide along the stream of time, whatever we leave behind us is always lessening, and that which we approach increasing in magnitude. Do not suffer life to stagnate; it will grow muddy for want of motion: commit yourself again to the current of the world;* Pekuah will vanish by degrees; you will meet in your way some other favourite, or learn to diffuse yourself in general conversation.'

'At least, said the prince, do not despair before all remedies have been tried: the enquiry after the unfortunate lady is still continued, and shall be carried on with yet greater diligence, on condition that you will promise to wait a year for the event, without any unalterable resolution.'

Nekayah thought this a reasonable demand, and made the promise to her brother, who had been advised by Imlac to require it. Imlac had, indeed, no great hope of regaining Pekuah, but he supposed, that if he could secure the interval of a year, the princess would be then in no danger of a cloister.

CHAP. XXXVI

Pekuah is still remembered. The progress of sorrow

NEKAYAH, seeing that nothing was omitted for the recovery of her favourite, and having, by her promise, set her intention of retirement at a distance, began imperceptibly to return to common cares and common pleasures. She rejoiced without her own consent at the suspension of her sorrows,* and sometimes caught herself with indignation in the act of turning away her mind from the remembrance of her, whom yet she resolved never to forget.

She then appointed a certain hour of the day for meditation on the merits and fondness of Pekuah, and for some weeks retired constantly at the time fixed, and returned with her eyes swollen and her countenance clouded. By degrees she grew less scrupulous, and suffered any important and pressing avocation to delay the tribute of daily tears. She then yielded to less occasions; sometimes forgot what she was indeed afraid to remember, and, at last, wholly released herself from the duty of periodical affliction.

Her real love of Pekuah was yet not diminished. A thousand occurrences brought her back to memory, and a thousand wants, which nothing but the confidence of friendship can supply, made her frequently regretted. She, therefore, solicited Imlac never to desist from enquiry, and to leave no art of intelligence untried, that, at least, she might have the comfort of knowing that she did not suffer by negligence or sluggishness. 'Yet what, said she, is to be expected from our persuit of happiness, when we find the state of life to be such, that happiness itself is the cause of misery?

Why should we endeavour to attain that, of which the possession cannot be secured? I shall henceforward fear to yield my heart to excellence, however bright, or to fondness, however tender, lest I should lose again what I have lost in Pekuah.'*

CHAP. XXXVII

The Princess hears news of Pekuah

IN seven months, one of the messengers, who had been sent away upon the day when the promise was drawn from the princess, returned, after many unsuccessful rambles, from the borders of Nubia,* with an account that Pekuah was in the hands of an Arab chief, who possessed a castle or fortress on the extremity of Egypt. The Arab, whose revenue was plunder, was willing to restore her, with her two attendants, for two hundred ounces of gold.

The price was no subject of debate. The princess was in extasies when she heard that her favourite was alive, and might so cheaply be ransomed. She could not think of delaying for a moment Pekuah's happiness or her own, but entreated her brother to send back the messenger with the sum required. Imlac, being consulted, was not very confident of the veracity of the relator, and was still more doubtful of the Arab's faith, who might, if he were too liberally trusted, detain at once the money and the captives. He thought it dangerous to put themselves in the power of the Arab, by going into his district, and could not expect that the Rover would so much expose himself as to come into the lower country,* where he might be seized by the forces of the Bassa.

It is difficult to negotiate where neither will trust. But Imlac, after some deliberation, directed the messenger to propose that Pekuah should be conducted by ten horsemen to the monastery of St. Anthony,* which is situated in the deserts of Upper-Egypt, where she should be met by the same number, and her ransome should be paid.

That no time might be lost, as they expected that the proposal would not be refused, they immediately began their journey to the monastery; and, when they arrived, Imlac went forward with the former messenger to the Arab's fortress. Rasselas was desirous to go with them, but neither his sister nor Imlac would consent. The Arab, according to the custom of his nation, observed the laws of hospitality with great exactness to those who put themselves into his power,* and, in a few days, brought Pekuah with her maids, by easy journeys, to their place appointed, where receiving the stipulated price, he restored her with great respect to liberty and her friends, and undertook to conduct them back towards Cairo beyond all danger of robbery or violence.

The princess and her favourite embraced each other with transport too violent to be expressed, and went out together to pour the tears of tenderness in secret, and exchange professions of kindness and gratitude. After a few hours they returned into the refectory of the convent, where, in the presence of the prior and his brethren, the prince required of Pekuah the history of her adventures.

CHAP. XXXVIII

The adventures of the lady Pekuah

'AT what time, and in what manner, I was forced away, said Pekuah, your servants have told you. The suddenness of the event struck me with surprise, and I was at first rather stupified than agitated with any passion of either fear or sorrow. My confusion was encreased by the speed and tumult of our flight while we were followed by the Turks, who, as it seemed, soon despaired to overtake us, or were afraid of those whom they made a shew of menacing.

'When the Arabs saw themselves out of danger they slackened their course, and, as I was less harassed by external violence, I began to feel more uneasiness in my mind. After some time we stopped near a spring shaded with trees in a pleasant meadow,

where we were set upon the ground, and offered such refresh-
ments as our masters were partaking. I was suffered to sit with my
maids apart from the rest, and none attempted to comfort or
insult us. Here I first began to feel the full weight of my misery.
The girls sat weeping in silence, and from time to time looked on
me for succour. I knew not to what condition we were doomed,
nor could conjecture where would be the place of our captivity, or
whence to draw any hope of deliverance. I was in the hands of
robbers and savages, and had no reason to suppose that their pity
was more than their justice, or that they would forbear the gratification of any ardour of desire, or caprice of cruelty. I, however,
kissed my maids, and endeavoured to pacify them by remarking,
that we were yet treated with decency, and that, since we were
now carried beyond persuit, there was no danger of violence to
our lives.

'When we were to be set again on horseback, my maids clung
round me, and refused to be parted, but I commanded them not
to irritate those who had us in their power. We travelled the
remaining part of the day through an unfrequented and pathless
country, and came by moonlight to the side of a hill, where the
rest of the troop was stationed. Their tents were pitched, and
their fires kindled, and our chief was welcomed as a man much
beloved by his dependants.

'We were received into a large tent, where we found women
who had attended their husbands in the expedition. They set
before us the supper which they had provided, and I eat it rather
to encourage my maids than to comply with any appetite of my
own. When the meat was taken away they spread the carpets for
repose. I was weary, and hoped to find in sleep that remission of
distress which nature seldom denies. Ordering myself therefore
to be undrest, I observed that the women looked very earnestly
upon me, not expecting, I suppose, to see me so submissively
attended. When my upper vest was taken off, they were apparently struck with the splendour of my cloaths, and one of them
timorously laid her hand upon the embroidery.* She then went
out, and, in a short time, came back with another woman, who
seemed to be of higher rank, and greater authority. She did, at her

entrance, the usual act of reverence, and, taking me by the hand, placed me in a smaller tent, spread with finer carpets, where I spent the night quietly with my maids.

'In the morning, as I was sitting on the grass, the chief of the troop came towards me. I rose up to receive him, and he bowed with great respect. 'Illustrious lady, said he, my fortune is better than I had presumed to hope; I am told by my women, that I have a princess in my camp.' Sir, answered I, your women have deceived themselves and you; I am not a princess, but an unhappy stranger who intended soon to have left this country, in which I am now to be imprisoned for ever. 'Whoever, or whencesoever, you are, returned the Arab, your dress, and that of your servants, show your rank to be high, and your wealth to be great. Why should you, who can so easily procure your ransome, think yourself in danger of perpetual captivity? The purpose of my incursions is to encrease my riches, or more properly to gather tribute. The sons of Ishmael are the natural and hereditary lords of this part of the continent, which is usurped by late invaders, and lowborn tyrants, from whom we are compelled to take by the sword what is denied to justice.* The violence of war admits no distinction; the lance that is lifted at guilt and power will sometimes fall on innocence and gentleness.'

'How little, said I, did I expect that yesterday it should have fallen upon me.'

'Misfortunes, answered the Arab, should always be expected. If the eye of hostility could learn reverence or pity, excellence like yours had been exempt from injury. But the angels of affliction spread their toils alike for the virtuous and the wicked, for the mighty and the mean. Do not be disconsolate; I am not one of the lawless and cruel rovers of the desart; I know the rules of civil life: I will fix your ransome, give a passport to your messenger, and perform my stipulation with nice punctuality.'

'You will easily believe that I was pleased with his courtesy; and finding that his predominant passion was desire of money, I began now to think my danger less, for I knew that no sum would be thought too great for the release of Pekuah. I told him that he should have no reason to charge me with ingratitude, if I was used with kindness, and that any ransome, which could be expected for a maid of common rank, would be paid, but that he must not persist to rate me as a princess. He said, he would consider what he should demand, and then, smiling, bowed and retired.

'Soon after the women came about me, each contending to be more officious than the other, and my maids themselves were served with reverence. We travelled onward by short journeys. On the fourth day the chief told me, that my ransome must be two hundred ounces of gold, which I not only promised him, but told him, that I would add fifty more, if I and my maids were honourably treated.

'I never knew the power of gold before. From that time I was the leader of the troop. The march of every day was longer or shorter as I commanded, and the tents were pitched where I chose to rest. We now had camels and other conveniencies for travel, my own women were always at my side, and I amused myself with observing the manners of the vagrant nations, and with viewing remains of ancient edifices with which these deserted countries appear to have been, in some distant age, lavishly embellished.

'The chief of the band was a man far from illiterate: he was able to travel by the stars or the compass, and had marked in his erratick expeditions such places as are most worthy the notice of a passenger. He observed to me, that buildings are always best preserved in places little frequented, and difficult of access: for, when once a country declines from its primitive splendour, the more inhabitants are left, the quicker ruin will be made. Walls supply stones more easily than quarries, and palaces and temples will be demolished to make stables of granate, and cottages of porphyry.*

CHAP. XXXIX

The adventures of Pekuah continued

'WE wandered about in this manner for some weeks, whether, as our chief pretended, for my gratification, or, as I rather suspected, for some convenience of his own. I endeavoured to appear contented where sullenness and resentment would have been of no use, and that endeavour conduced much to the calmness of my mind; but my heart was always with Nekayah, and the troubles of the night much overbalanced the amusements of the day. My women, who threw all their cares upon their mistress, set their minds at ease from the time when they saw me treated with respect, and gave themselves up to the incidental alleviations of our fatigue without solicitude or sorrow. I was pleased with their pleasure, and animated with their confidence. My condition had lost much of its terrour, since I found that the Arab ranged the country merely to get riches. Avarice is an uniform and tractable vice: other intellectual distempers are different in different constitutions of mind; that which sooths the pride of one will offend the pride of another; but to the favour of the covetous there is a ready way, bring money and nothing is denied.

'At last we came to the dwelling of our chief, a strong and spacious house built with stone in an island of the Nile, which lies, as I was told, under the tropick. 'Lady, said the Arab, you shall rest after your journey a few weeks in this place, where you are to consider yourself as sovereign. My occupation is war: I have therefore chosen this obscure residence, from which I can issue unexpected, and to which I can retire unpersued. You may now repose in security: here are few pleasures, but here is no danger.' He then led me into the inner apartments, and seating me on the richest couch, bowed to the ground. His women, who considered me as a rival, looked on me with malignity; but being soon informed that I was a great lady detained only for my ransome, they began to vie with each other in obsequiousness and reverence.

'Being again comforted with new assurances of speedy liberty, I was for some days diverted from impatience by the novelty of the place. The turrets overlooked the country to a great distance, and afforded a view of many windings of the stream. In the day I wandered from one place to another as the course of the sun varied the splendour of the prospect, and saw many things which I had never seen before. The crocodiles and river-horses* are common in this unpeopled region, and I often looked upon them with terrour, though I knew that they could not hurt me. For some time I expected to see mermaids and tritons, which, as Imlac has told me, the European travellers have stationed in the Nile, but no such beings ever appeared, and the Arab, when I enquired after them, laughed at my credulity.*

'At night the Arab always attended me to a tower set apart for celestial observations, where he endeavoured to teach me the names and courses of the stars.* I had no great inclination to this study, but an appearance of attention was necessary to please my instructor, who valued himself for his skill, and, in a little while, I found some employment requisite to beguile the tediousness of time, which was to be passed always amidst the same objects. I was weary of looking in the morning on things from which I had turned away weary in the evening: I therefore was at last willing to observe the stars rather than do nothing, but could not always compose my thoughts, and was very often thinking on Nekayah when others imagined me contemplating the sky. Soon after the Arab went upon another expedition, and then my only pleasure was to talk with my maids about the accident by which we were carried away, and the happiness that we should all enjoy at the end of our captivity.'

'There were women in your Arab's fortress, said the princess, why did you not make them your companions, enjoy their conversation, and partake their diversions? In a place where they found business or amusement, why should you alone sit corroded with idle melancholy? or why could not you bear for a few months that condition to which they were condemned for life?'

'The diversions of the women, answered Pekuah, were only childish play, by which the mind accustomed to stronger operations could not be kept busy. I could do all which they delighted in doing by powers merely sensitive, while my intellectual faculties were flown to Cairo. They ran from room to room as a bird hops from wire to wire in his cage. They danced for the sake of motion, as lambs frisk in a meadow. One sometimes pretended to be hurt that the rest might be alarmed, or hid herself that another might seek her. Part of their time passed in watching the progress of light bodies that floated on the river, and part in marking the various forms into which clouds broke in the sky.

'Their business was only needlework, in which I and my maids sometimes helped them; but you know that the mind will easily straggle from the fingers, nor will you suspect that captivity and absence from Nekayah could receive solace from silken flowers.

'Nor was much satisfaction to be hoped from their conversation: for of what could they be expected to talk? They had seen nothing; for they had lived from early youth in that narrow spot: of what they had not seen they could have no knowledge, for they could not read. They had no ideas but of the few things that were within their view, and had hardly names for any thing but their cloaths and their food. As I bore a superiour character, I was often called to terminate their quarrels, which I decided as equitably as I could. If it could have amused me to hear the complaints of each against the rest, I might have been often detained by long stories, but the motives of their animosity were so small that I could not listen without intercepting the tale.'*

'How, said Rasselas, can the Arab, whom you represented as a man of more than common accomplishments, take any pleasure in his seraglio, when it is filled only with women like these. Are they exquisitely beautiful?'

'They do not, said Pekuah, want that unaffecting and ignoble beauty which may subsist without spriteliness or sublimity, without energy of thought or dignity of virtue. But to a man like the Arab such beauty was only a flower casually plucked and carelessly thrown away. Whatever pleasures he might find among them, they were not those of friendship or society. When they were playing about him he looked on them with inattentive superiority: when they vied for his regard he sometimes turned away disgusted. As they had no knowledge, their talk could take nothing from the tediousness of life:* as they had no choice, their fondness, or appearance of fondness, excited in him neither pride nor gratitude; he was not exalted in his own esteem by the smiles of a woman who saw no other man, nor was much obliged by that regard, of which he could never know the sincerity, and which he might often perceive to be exerted not so much to delight him as to pain a rival. That which he gave, and they received, as love, was only a careless distribution of superfluous time, such love as man can bestow upon that which he despises, such as has neither hope nor fear, neither joy nor sorrow.'

'You have reason, lady, to think yourself happy, said Imlac, that you have been thus easily dismissed. How could a mind, hungry for knowledge, be willing, in an intellectual famine, to lose such a banquet as Pekuah's conversation?'

'I am inclined to believe, answered Pekuah, that he was for some time in suspense; for, notwithstanding his promise, whenever I proposed to dispatch a messenger to Cairo, he found some excuse for delay. While I was detained in his house he made many incursions into the neighbouring countries, and, perhaps, he would have refused to discharge me, had his plunder been equal to his wishes. He returned always courteous, related his adventures, delighted to hear my observations, and endeavoured to advance my acquaintance with the stars. When I importuned him to send away my letters, he soothed me with professions of honour and sincerity; and, when I could be no longer decently denied, put his troop again in motion, and left me to govern in his absence. I was much afflicted by this studied procrastination, and was sometimes afraid that I should be forgotten; that you would leave Cairo, and I must end my days in an island of the Nile.

'I grew at last hopeless and dejected, and cared so little to entertain him, that he for a while more frequently talked with my maids. That he should fall in love with them, or with me, might have been equally fatal, and I was not much pleased with the growing friendship. My anxiety was not long; for, as I recovered some degree of chearfulness, he returned to me, and I could not forbear to despise my former uneasiness.

'He still delayed to send for my ransome, and would, perhaps, never have determined, had not your agent found his way to him. The gold, which he would not fetch, he could not reject when it was offered. He hastened to prepare for our journey hither, like a man delivered from the pain of an intestine conflict. I took leave of my companions in the house, who dismissed me with cold indifference.'

Nekayah, having heard her favourite's relation, rose and embraced her, and Rasselas gave her an hundred ounces of gold, which she presented to the Arab for the fifty that were promised.

CHAP. XL

The history of a man of learning

THEY returned to Cairo, and were so well pleased at finding themselves together, that none of them went much abroad. The prince began to love learning, and one day declared to Imlac, that he intended to devote himself to science, and pass the rest of his days in literary solitude.

'Before you make your final choice, answered Imlac, you ought to examine its hazards, and converse with some of those who are grown old in the company of themselves. I have just left the observatory of one of the most learned astronomers in the world, who has spent forty years in unwearied attention to the motions and appearances of the celestial bodies, and has drawn out his soul in endless calculations.* He admits a few friends once a month to hear his deductions and enjoy his discoveries. I was introduced as a man of knowledge worthy of his notice. Men of various ideas and fluent conversation are commonly welcome to those whose thoughts have been long fixed upon a single point, and who find the images of other things stealing away. I delighted him with my remarks, he smiled at the narrative of my travels, and was glad to forget the constellations, and descend for a moment into the lower world.

'On the next day of vacation I renewed my visit, and was so fortunate as to please him again. He relaxed from that time the severity of his rule, and permitted me to enter at my own choice. I found him always busy, and always glad to be relieved. As each knew much which the other was desirous of learning, we exchanged our notions with great delight. I perceived that I had every day more of his confidence, and always found new cause of admiration in the profundity of his mind. His comprehension is vast, his memory capacious and retentive, his discourse is methodical, and his expression clear.

'His integrity and benevolence are equal to his learning. His deepest researches and most favourite studies are willingly interrupted for any opportunity of doing good by his counsel or his riches. To his closest retreat, at his most busy moments, all are admitted that want his assistance: 'For though I exclude idleness and pleasure, I will never, says he, bar my doors against charity. To man is permitted the contemplation of the skies, but the practice of virtue is commanded.'*

'Surely, said the princess, this man is happy.'

'I visited him, said Imlac, with more and more frequency, and was every time more enamoured of his conversation: he was sublime without haughtiness, courteous without formality, and communicative without ostentation. I was at first, great princess, of your opinion, thought him the happiest of mankind, and often congratulated him on the blessing that he enjoyed. He seemed to hear nothing with indifference but the praises of his condition, to which he always returned a general answer, and diverted the conversation to some other topick.

'Amidst this willingness to be pleased, and labour to please, I had quickly reason to imagine that some painful sentiment pressed upon his mind. He often looked up earnestly towards the sun, and let his voice fall in the midst of his discourse. He would sometimes, when we were alone, gaze upon me in silence with the air of a man who longed to speak what he was yet resolved to suppress. He would often send for me with vehement injunctions of haste, though, when I came to him, he had nothing extraordinary to say. And sometimes, when I was leaving him, would call me back, pause a few moments and then dismiss me.

CHAP. XLI

The astronomer discovers the cause of his uneasiness

'At last the time came when the secret burst his reserve. We were sitting together last night in the turret of his house, watching the emersion of a satellite of Jupiter. A sudden tempest clouded the sky, and disappointed our observation. We sat a while silent in the dark, and then he addressed himself to me in these words: 'Imlac, I have long considered thy friendship as the greatest blessing of my life. Integrity without knowledge is weak and useless, and knowledge without integrity is dangerous and dreadful. I have found in thee all the qualities requisite for trust, benevolence, experience, and fortitude. I have long discharged an office which I must soon quit at the call of nature, and shall rejoice in the hour of imbecility and pain to devolve it upon thee.'

'I thought myself honoured by this testimony, and protested that whatever could conduce to his happiness would add likewise to mine.'

'Hear, Imlac, what thou wilt not without difficulty credit. I have possessed for five years the regulation of weather, and the distribution of the seasons: the sun has listened to my dictates, and passed from tropick to tropick by my direction; the clouds, at my call, have poured their waters, and the Nile has overflowed at my command; I have restrained the rage of the dog-star, and mitigated the fervours of the crab.* The winds alone, of all the elemental powers, have hitherto refused my authority, and multitudes have perished by equinoctial tempests which I found myself unable to prohibit or restrain. I have administered this great office with exact justice, and made to the different nations of the earth an impartial dividend of rain and sunshine. What must have been the misery of half the globe, if I had limited the clouds to particular regions, or confined the sun to either side of the equator?'

CHAP. XLII

The opinion of the astronomer is explained and justified

'I SUPPOSE he discovered in me, through the obscurity of the room, some tokens of amazement and doubt, for, after a short pause, he proceeded thus:

'Not to be easily credited will neither surprise nor offend me; for I am, probably, the first of human beings to whom this trust has been imparted. Nor do I know whether to deem this distinction as reward or punishment; since I have possessed it I have been far less happy than before, and nothing but the consciousness of good intention could have enabled me to support the weariness of unremitted vigilance.'

'How long, Sir, said I, has this great office been in your hands?'

'About ten years ago, said he, my daily observations of the changes of the sky led me to consider, whether, if I had the power of the seasons, I could confer greater plenty upon the inhabitants of the earth. This contemplation fastened on my mind, and I sat days and nights in imaginary dominion, pouring upon this country and that the showers of fertility, and seconding every fall of rain with a due proportion of sunshine. I had yet only the will to do good, and did not imagine that I should ever have the power.

'One day as I was looking on the fields withering with heat, I felt in my mind a sudden wish that I could send rain on the southern mountains, and raise the Nile to an inundation.* In the hurry of my imagination I commanded rain to fall, and, by comparing the time of my command, with that of the inundation, I found that the clouds had listned to my lips.'

'Might not some other cause, said I, produce this concurrence? the Nile does not always rise on the same day.'

'Do not believe, said he with impatience, that such objections could escape me: I reasoned long against my own conviction, and laboured against truth with the utmost obstinacy. I sometimes suspected myself of madness, and should not have dared to impart this secret but to a man like you, capable of distinguishing the wonderful from the impossible, and the incredible from the false.'

'Why, Sir, said I, do you call that incredible, which you know, or think you know, to be true?'

'Because, said he, I cannot prove it by any external evidence; and I know too well the laws of demonstration to think that my conviction ought to influence another, who cannot, like me, be conscious of its force. I, therefore, shall not attempt to gain credit by disputation. It is sufficient that I feel this power, that I have long possessed, and every day exerted it. But the life of man is short, the infirmities of age increase upon me, and the time will soon come when the regulator of the year must mingle with the dust. The care of appointing a successor has long disturbed me; the night and the day have been spent in comparisons of all the characters which have come to my knowledge, and I have yet found none so worthy as thyself.

CHAP. XLIII

The astronomer leaves Imlac his directions

'HEAR therefore, what I shall impart, with attention, such as the welfare of a world requires. If the task of a king be considered as difficult, who has the care only of a few millions, to whom he cannot do much good or harm, what must be the anxiety of him, on whom depend the action of the elements, and the great gifts of light and heat!—Hear me therefore with attention.

'I have diligently considered the position of the earth and sun, and formed innumerable schemes in which I changed their situation. I have sometimes turned aside the axis of the earth, and sometimes varied the ecliptick of the sun: but I have found it impossible to make a disposition by which the world may be advantaged;* what one region gains, another loses by any imaginable alteration, even without considering the distant parts of the solar system with which we are unacquainted. Do not, therefore, in thy administration of the year, indulge thy pride by innovation; do not please thyself with thinking that thou canst make thyself renowned to all future ages, by disordering the seasons. The memory of mischief is no desirable fame. Much less will it become thee to let kindness or interest prevail. Never rob other countries of rain to pour it on thine own. For us the Nile is sufficient.'*

'I promised that when I possessed the power, I would use it with inflexible integrity, and he dismissed me, pressing my hand.' 'My heart, said he, will be now at rest, and my benevolence will no more destroy my quiet: I have found a man of wisdom and virtue, to whom I can chearfully bequeath the inheritance of the sun.'

The prince heard this narration with very serious regard, but the princess smiled, and Pekuah convulsed herself with laughter. 'Ladies, said Imlac, to mock the heaviest of human afflictions is neither charitable nor wise. Few can attain this man's knowledge, and few practise his virtues; but all may suffer his calamity. Of the uncertainties of our present state, the most dreadful and alarming is the uncertain continuance of reason.'*

The princess was recollected,* and the favourite was abashed. Rasselas, more deeply affected, enquired of Imlac, whether he thought such maladies of the mind frequent, and how they were contracted.

CHAP. XLIV

The dangerous prevalence of imagination

'Disorders of intellect, answered Imlac, happen much more often than superficial observers will easily believe. Perhaps, if we speak with rigorous exactness, no human mind is in its right state. There is no man whose imagination does not sometimes predominate over his reason, who can regulate his attention wholly by his will, and whose ideas will come and go at his command.* No man will be found in whose mind airy notions do not sometimes tyrannise, and force him to hope or fear beyond the limits of sober probability. All power of fancy over reason is a degree of insanity; but while this power is such as we can controul and repress, it is not visible to others, nor considered as any depravation of the mental faculties: it is not pronounced madness but when it comes ungovernable, and apparently influences speech or action.*

'To indulge the power of fiction, and send imagination out upon the wing, is often the sport of those who delight too much in silent speculation. When we are alone we are not always busy; the labour of excogitation is too violent to last long; the ardour of enquiry will sometimes give way to idleness or satiety.* He who has nothing external that can divert him, must find pleasure in his own thoughts, and must conceive himself what he is not; for who

is pleased with what he is? He then expatiates in boundless futurity, and culls from all imaginable conditions that which for the
present moment he should most desire, amuses his desires with
impossible enjoyments, and confers upon his pride unattainable
dominion. The mind dances from scene to scene, unites all pleasures in all combinations, and riots in delights which nature and
fortune, with all their bounty, cannot bestow.*

'In time some particular train of ideas fixes the attention, all
other intellectual gratifications are rejected, the mind, in weariness or leisure, recurs constantly to the favourite conception, and
feasts on the luscious falsehood whenever she is offended with the
bitterness of truth.* By degrees the reign of fancy is confirmed;
she grows first imperious, and in time despotick. Then fictions
begin to operate as realities, false opinions fasten upon the mind,
and life passes in dreams of rapture or of anguish.*

'This, Sir, is one of the dangers of solitude, which the hermit
has confessed not always to promote goodness, and the astronomer's misery has proved to be not always propitious to wisdom.'

'I will no more, said the favourite, imagine myself the queen of
Abissinia. I have often spent the hours, which the princess gave
to my own disposal, in adjusting ceremonies and regulating the
court; I have repressed the pride of the powerful, and granted the
petitions of the poor; I have built new palaces in more happy situations, planted groves upon the tops of mountains, and have
exulted in the beneficence of royalty, till, when the princess
entered, I had almost forgotten to bow down before her.'

'And I, said the princess, will not allow myself any more to play
the shepherdess in my waking dreams. I have often soothed my
thoughts with the quiet and innocence of pastoral employments,
till I have in my chamber heard the winds whistle, and the
sheep bleat; sometimes freed the lamb entangled in the thicket,
and sometimes with my crook encountered the wolf. I have a
dress like that of the village maids, which I put on to help my
imagination, and a pipe on which I play softly, and suppose
myself followed by my flocks.'

'I will confess, said the prince, an indulgence of fantastick
delight more dangerous than yours. I have frequently endeavoured

to image the possibility of a perfect government,* by which all wrong should be restrained, all vice reformed, and all the subjects preserved in tranquility and innocence. This thought produced innumerable schemes of reformation, and dictated many useful regulations and salutary edicts. This has been the sport and some-times the labour of my solitude; and I start, when I think with how little anguish I once supposed the death of my father and my brothers.'

'Such, says Imlac, are the effects of visionary schemes: when we first form them we know them to be absurd, but familiarise them by degrees, and in time lose sight of their folly.'*

CHAP. XLV

They discourse with an old man

THE evening was now far past, and they rose to return home. As they walked along the bank of the Nile, delighted with the beams of the moon quivering on the water, they saw at a small distance an old man, whom the prince had often heard in the assembly of the sages. 'Yonder, said he, is one whose years have calmed his passions, but not clouded his reason: let us close the disquisitions of the night, by enquiring what are his sentiments of his own state, that we may know whether youth alone is to struggle with vexation, and whether any better hope remains for the latter part of life.'

Here the sage approached and saluted them. They invited him to join their walk, and prattled a while as acquaintance that had unexpectedly met one another. The old man was chearful and talkative, and the way seemed short in his company. He was pleased to find himself not disregarded, accompanied them to their house, and, at the prince's request, entered with them. They placed him in the seat of honour, and set wine and conserves before him.

'Sir, said the princess, an evening walk must give to a man of learning, like you, pleasures which ignorance and youth can hardly conceive. You know the qualities and the causes of all that you behold, the laws by which the river flows, the periods in which the planets perform their revolutions. Every thing must supply you with contemplation, and renew the consciousness of your own dignity.'

'Lady, answered he, let the gay and the vigorous expect pleasure in their excursions, it is enough that age can obtain ease.* To me the world has lost its novelty: I look round, and see what I remember to have seen in happier days. I rest against a tree, and consider, that in the same shade I once disputed upon the annual overflow of the Nile with a friend who is now silent in the grave. I cast my eyes upwards, fix them on the changing moon, and think with pain on the vicissitudes of life.* I have ceased to take much delight in physical truth; for what have I to do with those things which I am soon to leave?'

'You may at least recreate yourself, said Imlac, with the recollection of an honourable and useful life, and enjoy the praise which all agree to give you.'

'Praise, said the sage, with a sigh, is to an old man an empty sound. I have neither mother to be delighted with the reputation of her son, nor wife to partake the honours of her husband. I have outlived my friends and my rivals.* Nothing is now of much importance; for I cannot extend my interest beyond myself. Youth is delighted with applause, because it is considered as the earnest of some future good, and because the prospect of life is far extended: but to me, who am now declining to decrepitude, there is little to be feared from the malevolence of men, and yet less to be hoped from their affection or esteem. Something they may yet take away, but they can give me nothing. Riches would now be useless, and high employment would be pain. My retrospect of life recalls to my view many opportunities of good neglected, much time squandered upon trifles, and more lost in idleness and vacancy. I leave many great designs unattempted, and many great attempts unfinished.* My mind is burthened with no heavy crime, and therefore I compose myself to tranquility; endeavour to abstract my thoughts from hopes and cares, which, though reason knows them to be vain, still try to keep their old possession of the heart; expect, with serene humility, that hour which nature cannot long delay; and hope to possess in a better state that happiness which here I could not find,* and that virtue which here I have not attained.'

He rose and went away, leaving his audience not much elated with the hope of long life. The prince consoled himself with remarking, that it was not reasonable to be disappointed by this account; for age had never been considered as the season of felicity, and, if it was possible to be easy in decline and weakness, it was likely that the days of vigour and alacrity might be happy: that the moon of life might be bright, if the evening could be calm.

The princess suspected that age was querulous and malignant,* and delighted to repress the expectations of those who had newly entered the world. She had seen the possessors of estates look with envy on their heirs, and known many who enjoy pleasure no longer than they can confine it to themselves.

Pekuah conjectured, that the man was older than he appeared, and was willing to impute his complaints to delirious dejection; or else supposed that he had been unfortunate, and was therefore discontented: 'For nothing, said she, is more common than to call our own condition, the condition of life.'

Imlac, who had no desire to see them depressed, smiled at the comforts which they could so readily procure to themselves, and remembered, that at the same age, he was equally confident of unmingled prosperity, and equally fertile of consolatory expedients. He forbore to force upon them unwelcome knowledge, which time itself would too soon impress. The princess and her lady retired; the madness of the astronomer hung upon their minds, and they desired Imlac to enter upon his office, and delay next morning the rising of the sun.

CHAP. XLVI

The princess and Pekuah visit the astronomer

THE princess and Pekuah having talked in private of Imlac's astronomer, thought his character at once so amiable and so strange, that they could not be satisfied without a nearer knowledge, and Imlac was requested to find the means of bringing them together.

This was somewhat difficult; the philosopher had never received any visits from women, though he lived in a city that had in it many Europeans who followed the manners of their own countries, and many from other parts of the world that lived there with European liberty.* The ladies would not be refused, and several schemes were proposed for the accomplishment of their design. It was proposed to introduce them as strangers in distress, to whom the sage was always accessible; but, after some deliberation, it appeared, that by this artifice, no acquaintance could be formed, for their conversation would be short, and they could not decently importune him often. 'This, said Rasselas, is true; but I have yet a stronger objection against the misrepresentation of your state. I have always considered it as treason against the great republick of human nature, to make any man's virtues the means of deceiving him, whether on great or little occasions. All imposture weakens confidence and chills benevolence.* When the sage finds that you are not what you seemed, he will feel the resentment natural to a man who, conscious of great abilities, discovers that he has been tricked by understandings meaner than his own, and, perhaps, the distrust, which he can never afterwards wholly lay aside, may stop the voice of counsel, and close the hand of charity; and where will you find the power of restoring his benefactions to mankind, or his peace to himself?'

To this no reply was attempted, and Imlac began to hope that their curiosity would subside; but, next day, Pekuah told him, she had now found an honest pretence for a visit to the astronomer, for she would solicite permission to continue under him the studies in which she had been initiated by the Arab, and the princess might go with her either as a fellow-student, or because a woman could not decently come alone. 'I am afraid, said Imlac, that he will be soon weary of your company: men advanced far in knowledge do not love to repeat the elements of their art, and I am not certain that even of the elements, as he will deliver them connected with inferences, and mingled with reflections, you are a very capable auditress.' 'That, said Pekuah, must be my care: I ask of you only to take me thither. My knowledge is, perhaps, more than you imagine it, and by concurring always with his opinions I shall make him think it greater than it is.'

The astronomer, in pursuance of this resolution, was told, that a foreign lady, travelling in search of knowledge, had heard of his reputation, and was desirous to become his scholar. The uncommonness of the proposal raised at once his surprize and curiosity, and when, after a short deliberation, he consented to admit her, he could not stay without impatience till the next day.

The ladies dressed themselves magnificently, and were attended by Imlac to the astronomer, who was pleased to see himself approached with respect by persons of so splendid an appearance. In the exchange of the first civilities he was timorous and bashful; but when the talk became regular, he recollected his powers, and justified the character which Imlac had given. Enquiring of Pekuah what could have turned her inclination towards astronomy, he received from her a history of her adventure at the pyramid, and of the time passed in the Arab's island. She told her tale with ease and elegance, and her conversation took possession of his heart. The discourse was then turned to astronomy: Pekuah displayed what she knew: he looked upon her as a prodigy of genius, and intreated her not to desist from a study which she had so happily begun.

They came again and again, and were every time more welcome than before. The sage endeavoured to amuse them, that they might prolong their visits, for he found his thoughts grow brighter in their company; the clouds of solicitude vanished by degrees, as he forced himself to entertain them, and he grieved when he was left at their departure to his old employment of regulating the seasons.

The princess and her favourite had now watched his lips for several months, and could not catch a single word from which they could judge whether he continued, or not, in the opinion of his preternatural commission. They often contrived to bring him to an open declaration, but he easily eluded all their attacks, and on which side soever they pressed him escaped from them to some other topick.

As their familiarity increased they invited him often to the house of Imlac, where they distinguished him by extraordinary respect. He began gradually to delight in sublunary pleasures. He came early and departed late; laboured to recommend himself by assiduity and compliance; excited their curiosity after new arts, that they might still want his assistance; and when they made any excursion of pleasure or enquiry, entreated to attend them.

By long experience of his integrity and wisdom, the prince and his sister were convinced that he might be trusted without danger; and lest he should draw any false hopes from the civilities which he received, discovered to him their condition, with the motives of their journey, and required his opinion on the choice of life.

'Of the various conditions which the world spreads before you, which you shall prefer, said the sage, I am not able to instruct you. I can only tell that I have chosen wrong. I have passed my time in study without experience; in the attainment of sciences which can, for the most part, be but remotely useful to mankind.* I have purchased knowledge at the expence of all the common comforts of life: I have missed the endearing elegance of female friendship, and the happy commerce of domestick tenderness. If I have obtained any prerogatives above other students, they have been accompanied with fear, disquiet, and scrupulosity; but even of these prerogatives, whatever they were, I have, since my thoughts have been diversified by more intercourse with the world, begun to question the reality. When I have been for a few days lost in pleasing dissipation, I am always tempted to think that my enquiries have ended in errour, and that I have suffered much, and suffered it in vain.'

Imlac was delighted to find that the sage's understanding was breaking through its mists, and resolved to detain him from the planets till he should forget his task of ruling them, and reason should recover its original influence.

From this time the astronomer was received into familiar friendship, and partook of all their projects and pleasures: his respect kept him attentive, and the activity of Rasselas did not leave much time unengaged. Something was always to be done;

the day was spent in making observations which furnished talk for the evening, and the evening was closed with a scheme for the morrow.

The sage confessed to Imlac, that since he had mingled in the gay tumults of life, and divided his hours by a succession of amusements, he found the conviction of his authority over the skies fade gradually from his mind, and began to trust less to an opinion which he never could prove to others, and which he now found subject to variation from causes in which reason had no part. 'If I am accidentally left alone for a few hours, said he, my inveterate persuasion rushes upon my soul, and my thoughts are chained down by some irresistible violence, but they are soon disentangled by the prince's conversation, and instantaneously released at the entrance of Pekuah. I am like a man habitually afraid of spectres, who is set at ease by a lamp, and wonders at the dread which harrassed him in the dark, yet, if his lamp be extinguished, feels again the terrours which he knows that when it is light he shall feel no more. But I am sometimes afraid lest I indulge my quiet by criminal negligence, and voluntarily forget the great charge with which I am intrusted. If I favour myself in a known errour, or am determined by my own ease in a doubtful question of this importance, how dreadful is my crime!'

'No disease of the imagination, answered Imlac, is so difficult of cure, as that which is complicated with the dread of guilt: fancy and conscience then act interchangeably upon us, and so often shift their places, that the illusions of one are not distinguished from the dictates of the other. If fancy presents images not moral or religious, the mind drives them away when they give it pain, but when melancholick notions take the form of duty, they lay hold on the faculties without opposition, because we are afraid to exclude or banish them. For this reason the superstitious are often melancholy, and the melancholy almost always superstitious.

'But do not let the suggestions of timidity overpower your better reason: the danger of neglect can be but as the probability of the obligation, which when you consider it with freedom, you find very little, and that little growing every day less. Open your heart to the influence of the light, which, from time to time, breaks in upon you: when scruples importune you, which you in your lucid moments know to be vain, do not stand to parley, but fly to business or to Pekuah,* and keep this thought always prevalent, that you are only one atom of the mass of humanity, and have neither such virtue nor vice, as that you should be singled out for supernatural favours or afflictions.'

CHAP. XLVII

The prince enters and brings a new topick

'ALL this, said the astronomer, I have often thought, but my reason has been so long subjugated by an uncontrolable and overwhelming idea, that it durst not confide in its own decisions. I now see how fatally I betrayed my quiet, by suffering chimeras to prey upon me in secret; but melancholy shrinks from communication, and I never found a man before, to whom I could impart my troubles, though I had been certain of relief. I rejoice to find my own sentiments confirmed by yours, who are not easily deceived, and can have no motive or purpose to deceive. I hope that time and variety will dissipate the gloom that has so long surrounded me,* and the latter part of my days will be spent in peace.'

'Your learning and virtue, said Imlac, may justly give you hopes.'

Rasselas then entered with the princess and Pekuah, and enquired whether they had contrived any new diversion for the next day. 'Such, said Nekayah, is the state of life, that none are happy but by the anticipation of change: the change itself is nothing; when we have made it, the next wish is to change again.* The world is not yet exhausted; let me see something to morrow which I never saw before.'

'Variety, said Rasselas, is so necessary to content,* that even the happy valley disgusted me by the recurrence of its luxuries; yet I could not forbear to reproach myself with impatience, when

I saw the monks of St. Anthony support without complaint, a life, not of uniform delight, but uniform hardship.'*

'Those men, answered Imlac, are less wretched in their silent convent than the Abissinian princes in their prison of pleasure. Whatever is done by the monks is incited by an adequate and reasonable motive. Their labour supplies them with necessaries; it therefore cannot be omitted, and is certainly rewarded. Their devotion prepares them for another state, and reminds them of its approach, while it fits them for it. Their time is regularly distributed; one duty succeeds another, so that they are not left open to the distraction of unguided choice, nor lost in the shades of listless inactivity. There is a certain task to be performed at an appropriated hour; and their toils are cheerful, because they consider them as acts of piety, by which they are always advancing towards endless felicity.'*

'Do you think, said Nekayah, that the monastick rule is a more holy and less imperfect state than any other? May not he equally hope for future happiness who converses openly with mankind, who succours the distressed by his charity, instructs the ignorant by his learning, and contributes by his industry to the general system of life; even though he should omit some of the mortifications which are practised in the cloister, and allow himself such harmless delights as his condition may place within his reach?'

'This, said Imlac, is a question which has long divided the wise, and perplexed the good. I am afraid to decide on either part. He that lives well in the world is better than he that lives well in a monastery. But, perhaps, every one is not able to stem the temptations of publick life; and, if he cannot conquer, he may properly retreat.* Some have little power to do good, and have likewise little strength to resist evil. Many weary of their conflicts with adversity, and are willing to eject those passions which have long busied them in vain. And many are dismissed by age and diseases from the more laborious duties of society.* In monasteries the weak and timorous may be happily sheltered, the weary may repose, and the penitent may meditate. Those retreats of prayer and contemplation have something so congenial to the mind of man that, perhaps, there is scarcely one that does not purpose to close his life in pious abstraction with a few associates serious as himself.'

'Such, said Pekuah, has often been my wish, and I have heard the princess declare, that she should not willingly die in a croud.'

'The liberty of using harmless pleasures,* proceeded Imlac, will not be disputed; but it is still to be examined what pleasures are harmless. The evil of any pleasure that Nekayah can image is not in the act itself, but in its consequences. Pleasure, in itself harmless, may become mischievous, by endearing to us a state which we know to be transient and probatory,* and withdrawing our thoughts from that, of which every hour brings us nearer to the beginning, and of which no length of time will bring us to the end. Mortification is not virtuous in itself, nor has any other use, but that it disengages us from the allurements of sense.* In the state of future perfection, to which we all aspire, there will be pleasure without danger, and security without restraint.'

The princess was silent, and Rasselas, turning to the astronomer, asked him, whether he could not delay her retreat, by shewing her something which she had not seen before.

'Your curiosity, said the sage, has been so general, and your pursuit of knowledge so vigorous, that novelties are not now very easily to be found: but what you can no longer procure from the living may be given by the dead. Among the wonders of this country are the catacombs, or the ancient repositories, in which the bodies of the earliest generations were lodged, and where, by the virtue of the gums which embalmed them, they yet remain without corruption.'*

'I know not, said Rasselas, what pleasure the sight of the catacombs can afford; but, since nothing else is offered, I am resolved to view them, and shall place this with many other things which I have done, because I would do something.'

They hired a guard of horsemen, and the next day visited the catacombs.* When they were about to descend into the sepulchral caves, 'Pekuah, said the princess, we are now again invading the habitations of the dead; I know that you will stay behind; let me find you safe when I return.' 'No, I will not be left, answered Pekuah; I will go down between you and the prince.'

They then all descended, and roved with wonder through the labyrinth of subterraneous passages, where the bodies were laid in rows on either side.*

CHAP. XLVIII

Imlac discourses on the nature of the soul

'WHAT reason, said the prince, can be given, why the Egyptians should thus expensively preserve those carcasses which some nations consume with fire, others lay to mingle with the earth, and all agree to remove from their sight, as soon as decent rites can be performed?'

'The original of ancient customs, said Imlac, is commonly unknown; for the practice often continues when the cause has ceased; and concerning superstitious ceremonies it is vain to conjecture; for what reason did not dictate reason cannot explain. I have long believed that the practice of embalming arose only from tenderness to the remains of relations or friends, and to this opinion I am more inclined, because it seems impossible that this care should have been general: had all the dead been embalmed, their repositories must in time have been more spacious than the dwellings of the living. I suppose only the rich or honourable were secured from corruption, and the rest left to the course of nature.

'But it is commonly supposed that the Egyptians believed the soul to live as long as the body continued undissolved and therefore tried this method of eluding death.'*

'Could the wise Egyptians, said Nekayah, think so grossly of the soul? If the soul could once survive its separation, what could it afterwards receive or suffer from the body?'

'The Egyptians would doubtless think erroneously, said the astronomer, in the darkness of heathenism, and the first dawn of philosophy. The nature of the soul is still disputed amidst all our opportunities of clearer knowledge: some yet say, that it may be material, who, nevertheless, believe it to be immortal.'*

'Some, answered Imlac, have indeed said that the soul is material, but I can scarcely believe that any man has thought it, who knew how to think; for all the conclusions of reason enforce the immateriality of mind, and all the notices of sense and investigations of science concur to prove the unconsciousness of matter.*

'It was never supposed that cogitation is inherent in matter,* or that every particle is a thinking being. Yet, if any part of matter be devoid of thought, what part can we suppose to think? Matter can differ from matter only in form, density, bulk, motion, and direction of motion: to which of these, however varied or combined, can consciousness be annexed? To be round or square, to be solid or fluid, to be great or little, to be moved slowly or swiftly one way or another, are modes of material existence, all equally alien from the nature of cogitation.* If matter be once without thought, it can only be made to think by some new modification, but all the modifications which it can admit are equally unconnected with cogitative powers.'

'But the materialists, said the astronomer, urge that matter may have qualities with which we are unacquainted.'*

'He who will determine, returned Imlac, against that which he knows, because there may be something which he knows not; he that can set hypothetical possibility against acknowledged certainty, is not to be admitted among reasonable beings. All that we know of matter is, that matter is inert, senseless and lifeless; and if this conviction cannot be opposed but by referring us to something that we know not, we have all the evidence that human intellect can admit. If that which is known may be over-ruled by that which is unknown, no being, not omniscient, can arrive at certainty.'

'Yet let us not, said the astronomer, too arrogantly limit the Creator's power.'

'It is no limitation of omnipotence, replied the poet, to suppose that one thing is not consistent with another, that the same proposition cannot be at once true and false, that the same number cannot be even and odd, that cogitation cannot be conferred on that which is created incapable of cogitation.'*

'I know not, said Nekayah, any great use of this question. Does that immateriality, which, in my opinion, you have sufficiently proved, necessarily include eternal duration?'

'Of immateriality, said Imlac, our ideas are negative, and therefore obscure. Immateriality seems to imply a natural power of perpetual duration as a consequence of exemption from all causes of decay:* whatever perishes, is destroyed by the solution of its contexture, and separation of its parts; nor can we conceive how that which has no parts, and therefore admits no solution, can be naturally corrupted or impaired.'

'I know not, said Rasselas, how to conceive any thing without extension: what is extended must have parts, and you allow, that whatever has parts may be destroyed.'

'Consider your own conceptions, replied Imlac, and the difficulty will be less. You will find substance without extension.* An ideal form is no less real than material bulk: yet an ideal form has no extension. It is no less certain, when you think on a pyramid, that your mind possesses the idea of a pyramid, than that the pyramid itself is standing. What space does the idea of a pyramid occupy more than the idea of a grain of corn? or how can either idea suffer laceration? As is the effect such is the cause; as thought is, such is the power that thinks; a power impassive and indiscerptible.'

'But the Being, said Nekayah, whom I fear to name, the Being which made the soul, can destroy it.'

'He, surely, can destroy it, answered Imlac, since, however unperishable, it receives from a superiour nature its power of duration. That it will not perish by any inherent cause of decay, or principle of corruption, may be shown by philosophy; but philosophy can tell no more. That it will not be annihilated by him that made it, we must humbly learn from higher authority.'

The whole assembly stood a while silent and collected. 'Let us return, said Rasselas, from this scene of mortality. How gloomy would be these mansions of the dead to him who did not know that he shall never die; that what now acts shall continue its agency, and what now thinks shall think on for ever. Those that lie here stretched before us, the wise and the powerful of antient times, warn us to remember the shortness of our present state; they were, perhaps, snatched away while they were busy, like us, in the choice of life.'

'To me, said the princess, the choice of life is become less important; I hope hereafter to think only on the choice of eternity.'*

They then hastened out of the caverns, and, under the protection of their guard, returned to Cairo.

CHAP. XLIX

The conclusion, in which nothing is concluded

IT was now the time of the inundation of the Nile: a few days after their visit to the catacombs, the river began to rise.

They were confined to their house. The whole region being under water gave them no invitation to any excursions, and, being well supplied with materials for talk, they diverted themselves with comparisons of the different forms of life which they had observed, and with various schemes of happiness which each of them had formed.

Pekuah was never so much charmed with any place as the convent of St. Anthony, where the Arab restored her to the princess, and wished only to fill it with pious maidens, and to be made prioress of the order: she was weary of expectation and disgust, and would gladly be fixed in some unvariable state.

The princess thought, that of all sublunary things, knowledge was the best: She desired first to learn all sciences, and then purposed to found a college of learned women, in which she would preside, that, by conversing with the old, and educating the young, she might divide her time between the acquisition and communication of wisdom, and raise up for the next age models of prudence, and patterns of piety.*

The prince desired a little kingdom, in which he might administer justice in his own person, and see all the parts of government with his own eyes; but he could never fix the limits of his dominion, and was always adding to the number of his subjects.

Imlac and the astronomer were contented to be driven along the stream of life without directing their course to any particular port.

Of these wishes that they had formed they well knew that none could be obtained. They deliberated a while what was to be done, and resolved, when the inundation should cease, to return to Abissinia.*

EXPLANATORY NOTES

THE elevation of Johnson to classic status by late nineteenth- and early twentieth-century scholars such as G. B. Hill, O. F. Emerson, and R. W. Chapman inaugurated traditions of commentary that have turned *Rasselas*, over the years, into the most heavily annotated work of fiction in the language. Much of this commentary, based on an implicit view of the work as a repository of wisdom comparable to, and requiring the same editorial treatment as, the literary and philosophical canon in Latin or Greek, has been invaluable in situating *Rasselas* within the overall context of Johnson's thought. But it has had the unfortunate side-effect of making the narrative seem a mere pretext for Johnsonian truth-telling, and the debates and dialogues staged in the text—especially where analogues are proposed between Imlac's dicta and Johnson's essays—as crushingly didactic reinforcements of fixed authorial dogma. Yet *Rasselas* is nothing if not an exploratory and sceptical work, and the annotations below, while enabling readers to pursue thematic connections with Johnson's writings elsewhere, are not intended to suggest that external affirmation or contradiction can be found—in the *Rambler*, say, or in Boswell's record of Johnson's conversation—for any given argument or speech. Johnson is far too subtle, mobile, and troubled a writer, and *Rasselas* too complex and unstable a work, for that to be a safe assumption.

Another consequence of Johnsonian exceptionalism and the style of annotation associated with it is that the editorial quest for analogues elsewhere in Johnson has been at the expense of broader contextualization. For the most part, points of contact with other Johnson works are recorded below only in cases of specific verbal as opposed to general philosophical resemblance, and compensating attempts have been made to relate the text to larger, sometimes unexpected, trends in the literature and culture of the day. In chapter vi of *Rasselas*, for example, the 'dissertation on the art of flying' involves not only characteristically Johnsonian reflections on the vanity of human wishes but also a wry memory of the 'rage for flying' created by tightrope-walking illusionists in the 1730s; in chapter ii, the world in which 'man preyed upon man' is not just characteristic Johnsonian pessimism but an echo of a self-taught woman poet (Mary Masters, whose work Johnson may have prepared for the press a few years beforehand) and, behind her, of Hobbes. The result of all this is that annotation remains fairly heavy, and in order to minimize textual clutter endnotes have not normally been used for simple cases of definition. Instead, a glossary of obsolete and unfamiliar words and senses is supplied at the back of the volume.

ABBREVIATIONS

Dictionary	Samuel Johnson, *A Dictionary of the English Language* (1755)
Goring	Samuel Johnson, *The History of Rasselas, Prince of Abissinia* (London: Penguin, 2007)
G. B. Hill	Samuel Johnson, *History of Rasselas, Prince of Abyssinia*, ed. G. B. Hill (Oxford: Clarendon Press, 1887)
Hardy	Samuel Johnson, *The History of Rasselas, Prince of Abissinia* (London: Oxford University Press, 1968)
Kolb	Samuel Johnson, *Rasselas and Other Tales*, ed. Gwin J. Kolb (New Haven: Yale University Press, 1990)
Letters	*The Letters of Samuel Johnson*, ed. Bruce Redford, 5 vols. (Oxford: Clarendon Press, 1992)
Life	*Boswell's Life of Johnson*, ed. G. B. Hill, rev. L. F. Powell, 6 vols. (Oxford: Clarendon Press, 1934–64)
Lives	Samuel Johnson, *The Lives of the Most Eminent English Poets*, ed. Roger Lonsdale, 4 vols. (Oxford: Clarendon Press, 2006)
OED	*Oxford English Dictionary Online*, 2008
YW	The Yale Edition of the Works of Samuel Johnson (New Haven: Yale University Press, 1958–). The following volumes are cited by number:
i	*Diaries, Prayers, and Annals*, ed. E. L. McAdam, Jr., with Donald and Mary Hyde
ii	*The Idler and The Adventurer*, ed. W. J. Bate, John M. Bullitt, and L. F. Powell
iii–v	*The Rambler*, ed. W. J. Bate and Albrecht B. Strauss
vi	*Poems*, ed. E. L. McAdam, Jr., with George Milne
vii–viii	*Johnson on Shakespeare*, ed. Arthur Sherbo, introd. Bertrand H. Bronson
ix	*A Journey to the Western Islands of Scotland*, ed. Mary Lascelles
x	*Political Writings*, ed. Donald J. Greene
xiv	*Sermons*, ed. Jean H. Hagstrum and James Gray
xv	*A Voyage to Abyssinia*, ed. Joel J. Gold
xvii	*A Commentary on Mr. Pope's Principles of Morality, or Essay on Man*, ed. O M Brack, Jr.
xviii	*Johnson on the English Language*, ed. Gwin J. Kolb and Robert DeMaria, Jr.

7 *Abissinia*: also known in SJ's day as Ethiopia, a mountainous and predominantly Christian kingdom (or federation of kingdoms) in north-
eastern Africa, bordering the Red Sea. Much of SJ's knowledge about
the region derived from his early work as translator of *A Voyage to*

Abyssinia (1735) by Jerónimo Lobo, a seventeenth-century Jesuit mission-ary involved in Roman Catholic attempts to subject the Church of Abyssinia, which had developed in isolation for many centuries, to doc-trinal and political control.

Rasselas . . . fourth son of the mighty emperour: Lobo reports that 'the kings of Abyssinia having formerly had several princes tributary to them, still retain the title of Emperor or King of the Kings of Aethiopia'. Elsewhere he notes the establishment of 'the title of *ras*, or chief', and mentions an Abyssinian general named 'Rassela Christos', who was the pro-Catholic brother of a seventeenth-century emperor (*YW* xv. 211; 213; 85). In Hiob Ludolf's *Historia Aethiopica* (1681), which SJ owned in the English trans-lation of 1682, there appears a sixteenth-century prince named variously as 'Ras-Seelaxus', 'Ras-Seelax', and 'Rasselach'; Ludolf also records the unnamed fourth son of an earlier emperor 'who Escap'd from the Rock of *Amhara*' (*A New History of Ethiopia* (1682), 328, 334, and 'A Genealogic Table of the Kings of Habessinia', between pp. 192 and 193). For further detail of names, places, and customs in this opening chapter, and SJ's likely sources of information, see Donald M. Lockhart, '"The Fourth Son of the Mighty Emperor": The Ethiopian Background of Johnson's *Rasselas*', *PMLA* 78 (1963), 516–28. See also W. L. Belcher, 'Origin of the Name Rasselas', *Notes and Queries* 56 (2009).

the Father of waters begins his course: James Bruce of Kinnaird claimed to have been the first European to have visited the headwaters of the Blue Nile (*Travels to Discover the Source of the Nile in the Years 1768 to 1773*, 5 vols. (1790), iii. 597), but he was preceded by Jesuit missionaries of the seventeenth century. Lobo writes that the Nile, 'which the natives call *Abavi*, that is, the Father of Waters, rises first in Sacala a province of the kingdom of Goiama, which is one of the most fruitful and agreeable of all the Abyssinian dominions' (*YW* xv. 81).

According to the custom . . . overhang the middle part: SJ imaginatively transforms the nature and setting of a widely noted Abyssinian practice. Describing the mountainous territory of Amhara, Lobo reports: 'In this kingdom is Guexon the famous rock on which the sons and brothers of the Emperor were confin'd till their accession to the throne. This custom establish'd about 1260, hath been abolish'd for two ages.' He later adds that 'It was on the barren summit of Ambaguexa, that the princes of the blood-royal pass'd their melancholly life, being guarded by officers who treated them often with great rigour and severity' (*YW* xv. 163, 167; see also, on the abandonment of this tradition after two centuries, pp. 212–13). Other sources probably known to SJ present the site of royal confinement in idyllic terms (see below, n. to p. 8), and the myth of an Abyssinian para-dise enters major poems of the extended period, including John Milton's *Paradise Lost* (iv. 280–4) and James Thomson's *Summer* (ll. 747–83).

8 *necessaries of life . . . superfluities were added*: this formulation may reflect the influence on SJ of the sixteenth-century theologian Richard Hooker, for whom the 'triple perfection' needed to attain happiness began with a

sensual stage 'consisting of those things which very life itself requireth either as necessary supplements, or as beauties and ornaments thereof' (Hooker, *Laws of Ecclesiastical Polity* (1594), i. xi. 4, quoted by SJ in his *Dictionary* of 1755 (s.v. Perfection)). For the argument that *Rasselas* is structured according to the sensual, intellectual, and spiritual stages set out by Hooker, see Nicholas Hudson, 'Three Steps to Perfection: *Rasselas* and the Philosophy of Richard Hooker', *Eighteenth-Century Life*, 14 (1990), 29–39.

8 *annual visit which the emperour paid his children*: SJ's source for this and other details may be Luis de Urreta's fabulous *Historia ecclesiastica, politica, natural y moral de los grandes y remotos reynos de la Etiopia* (1610), parts of which are reworked in *Purchas His Pilgrimage*, a well-known English compilation of 1613, and *The Late Travels of S. Giacomo Baratti, an Italian Gentleman, into the Remote Countries of the Abissins*, a spurious voyage narrative of 1670. Unlike other sources, Urreta and Baratti both represent the site as an earthly paradise. Baratti describes the royal offspring as confined in 'a very delicious place in the middle of a large mountain', where 'they are kept with the other precious things belonging to the Emperour' and taught 'humane Philosophy and the Principles of Christian Religion . . . The Emperour visits this place once a year with his Wives' (pp. 33–4, 36).

9 *Abissinia*: i.e. the Emperor of Abyssinia, though some sources place other ruling-class children in the royal prison: 'Hither are also sent the chief Noblemens sons of the Empire to keep company with the Royal bloud, and to receive with them the instructions which this place only affords' (*Late Travels of Baratti*, 36).

10 *man preyed upon man*: SJ may be recalling a couplet by his acquaintance Mary Masters, whose poems he subscribed to (and, according to Boswell, revised) in their second edition of 1755: 'Man preys on Man, the Tyrant gains Applause, | And few durst plead the injur'd *Widow*'s Cause' (Masters, *Poems on Several Occasions* (1733), 25). Behind this phrase lies the Latin tag *homo homini lupus*, famously translated by Thomas Hobbes as 'Man to Man is an arrant Wolfe' in his dedicatory epistle to *De Cive* (1651).

the sport of chance, and the slaves of misery: SJ may be recalling a passage from *Comus: A Mask* (1738), a much-performed adaptation of Milton's original by John Dalton and Thomas Arne, to which he contributed a new prologue for a benefit performance of 1750 in aid of Milton's granddaughter: 'That righteous *Jove* forbids, | Lest Man should call his frail Divinity | The Slave of Evil, or the Sport of Chance' (*Comus: A Mask* (1738), 51).

officiousness: 'Forwardness of civility, or respect, or endeavour. Commonly in an ill sense' (*Dictionary*, s.v. Officiousness, 1); revised in the second edition from 'endeavours' in the first, presumably to avoid repetition following 'endeavoured' in the line above.

11 *What . . . animal creation*: Rasselas's words recall the classic discussion of this topic in Cicero's *De Officiis* (*On Duties*), in which 'the greatest Distinction between a Man and a Brute' lies in the contrast between animal instinct and human reason (*M. T. Cicero His Offices*, trans. William Guthrie (1755), 8). Where Cicero stresses man's rational awareness of time and causation, Rasselas goes on to emphasize the restlessness of human desire.

I long again to be hungry . . . quicken my attention: Rasselas's plight recalls that of the retired citizen imagined by SJ in *Adventurer* 102 (27 October 1753), who spins out breakfast 'because when it is ended I have no call for my attention, till I can . . . grow impatient for my dinner'. Having longed throughout his business career for 'the happiness of rural privacy', the citizen now finds that 'the privilege of idleness is attained, but has not brought with it the blessing of tranquility' (*YW* ii. 436–40).

to morrow: often written as two words during the period. 'Before *day*, *to* notes the present day; before *morrow*, the day next coming' (*Dictionary*, s.v. To, 24).

The birds peck the berries . . . before he can be happy: Kolb cites SJ's contrast in *Rambler* 41 (7 August 1750) between insatiable human desire and the easy contentment of animals (*YW* iii. 221–2). The passage also recalls John Locke's influential discussion, first published in 1690, of the distinction between mere satisfaction and enduring happiness: 'All Men desire Happiness, that's past doubt: but . . . when they are rid of pain, they are apt to take up with any pleasure at hand, or that custom has endear'd to them; to rest satisfied in that; and so being happy, till some new desire by making them uneasy, disturbs that happiness, and shews them, that they are not so, they look no farther' (Locke, *An Essay Concerning Human Understanding*, ed. Peter H. Nidditch (Oxford: Clarendon Press, 1975), 279 (II. xxi. §68)).

not the felicity of man: Boswell reports a more robust judgement by SJ about bovine contentment, directed against an interlocutor who had 'expatiated on the happiness of a savage life' in a conversation of 1773: ' "Do not allow yourself, Sir, to be imposed upon by such gross absurdity. It is sad stuff; it is brutish. If a bull could speak, he might as well exclaim,—Here am I with this cow and this grass; what being can enjoy greater felicity?" ' (*Life*, ii. 228).

solace of the miseries of life . . . bewailed them: Hardy compares Rasselas's self-satisfaction with SJ's remark, reported by Boswell, 'that if a man *talks* of his misfortunes, there is something in them that is not disagreeable to him; for where there is nothing but pure misery, there never is any recourse to the mention of it' (*Life*, iv. 31; see also iii. 421).

12 *disease of mind*: SJ sometimes uses *disease* in its otherwise largely obsolete sense of uneasiness, disquiet, or disturbance, without necessarily implying sickness. Cf. his journal entry for 2 January 1781, in which he was 'yesterday hindred by my old disease of mind' (*YW* i. 302).

13 *my childhood . . . never had observed before*: Kolb compares SJ's account of novelty and childhood delight in *Idler* 44 (17 February 1759): 'When we first enter into the world, whithersoever we turn our eyes, they meet knowledge with pleasure at her side; every diversity of nature pours ideas in upon the soul' (*YW* ii. 137).

   miseries . . . necessary to happiness: Kolb cites SJ's observation elsewhere that 'the experience of calamity is necessary to a just sense of better fortune' (*Rambler* 150 (24 August 1751), *YW* v. 35–6); also his reversal of a motto from Seneca to propose that 'no man is happy, but as he is compared with the miserable' (*Adventurer* 111 (27 November 1753), *YW* ii. 451).

14 *run*: i.e. ran. Here and in ch. vi (p. 17) *run* is used as an alternative form, though *ran* occurs in ch. xxxix (p. 85). In the 'Grammar of the English Tongue' that SJ prefixed to his *Dictionary*, he allows *run* 'both in the preterite imperfect and participle passive' of the verb (*YW* xviii. 327).

15 *much might have been done . . . nothing real behind it*: Goring cites similar reflections from SJ's essays, notably *Adventurer* 137 (26 February 1754): 'Much of my time has sunk into nothing, and left no trace by which it can be distinguished, and of this I now only know, that it was once in my power and might once have been improved' (*YW* ii. 487–8). Cf. also the many self-reproaches in SJ's diaries, as in his entry for 18 September 1764: 'I have done nothing; the need of doing therefore is pressing, since the time of doing is short' (*YW* i. 81).

16 *what cannot be repaired is not to be regretted*: SJ reformulates, in typically resonant and abstracted style, a popular proverbial expression: ''Tis a folly to cry for spilt Milk', as Swift records the saying in *Polite Conversation* (1738), 27.

   regretted his regret: cf. SJ's similarly recursive observation in *The Patriot*, a political pamphlet of 1774: 'much time is lost in regretting the time which had been lost before' (*YW* x. 390).

   eagle in a grate: a caged eagle is traditionally an emblem of yearning. Cf. Christopher Smart's poem of 1751, 'On an Eagle confined in a College-Court', and Vicesimus Knox's account of the soul in the body, which, 'conscious of her kindred to heaven, will still be striving to escape, and will eye the golden sun, like an eagle confined in a cage' (Knox, *Winter Evenings*, 3 vols. (1788), iii. 104).

   blessing of hope: 'Hope is the chief blessing of man', SJ writes in *Rambler* 203 (25 February 1752); see also *Rambler* 67 (6 November 1750), on hope as a 'general blessing' (*YW* v. 295; iii. 354). A few weeks after publishing *Rasselas*, he writes in *Idler* 58 (26 May 1759) that 'hope itself is happiness, and its frustrations, however frequent, are yet less dreadful than its extinction' (*YW* ii. 182).

17 *art of flying*: for the background of this chapter in aspirations of human flight that reach back to the Icarus myth, see Louis A. Landa, 'Johnson's Feathered Man: "A Dissertation on the Art of Flying" Considered',

in W. H. Bond (ed.), *Eighteenth-Century Studies in Honor of Donald F. Hyde* (New York: Grolier Club, 1970), 161–78. SJ seems to have used or remembered a manual of 1648, *Mathematicall Magick; or, The Wonders That May Be Performed by Mechanicall Geometry*, written by John Wilkins, an indefatigable proponent of aviation who later became a bishop and a founding member of the Royal Society (Gwin J. Kolb, 'Johnson's Dissertation on Flying', in Frederick W. Hilles (ed.), *New Light on Dr. Johnson* (New Haven: Yale University Press, 1959), 91–106).

18 *sailing chariot*: Wilkins devotes a chapter to machines of this kind (*Mathematicall Magick*, 154–62), describing a prototype constructed and tested for the Prince of Orange by the engineer Simon Stevin in about 1600. Cf. Sterne's running joke in the first instalment of *Tristram Shandy*, published a few months after *Rasselas*, about 'the celebrated sailing chariot, which belonged to Prince *Maurice*, and was of such wonderful contrivance and velocity, as to carry half a dozen people thirty *German* miles . . . invented by *Stevinus*, that great mathematician and engineer' (Sterne, *Tristram Shandy*, ed. Ian Campbell Ross (Oxford: Oxford World's Classics, 1983), 93 (II. xiv) and n.).

19 *philosopher . . . parallel*: the mechanist's fantasy recalls the panoramic ambitions announced in the opening lines of SJ's poem of 1749, *The Vanity of Human Wishes*: 'Let observation with extensive view, | Survey mankind, from China to Peru' (*YW* vi. 91). Decades later, the inaugural balloon flights of 1783–4 held out this kind of promise in literal terms, but SJ's excitement about the potential of ballooning rapidly waned: 'We now know a method of mounting into the air, and I think, are not likely to know more', he writes on 6 October 1784: 'The vehicles can serve no use, till we can guide them, and they can gratify no curiosity till we mount with them to greater heights than we can reach without, till we rise above the tops of the highest mountains, which we have yet not done' (*Letters*, iv. 415).

tenuity: in the *Dictionary*, SJ illustrates this word ('Thinness; exility; smallness; minuteness; not grossness') with a description of the upper atmosphere from Richard Bentley's 'Confutation of Atheism from the Origin and Frame of the World' (1692). Following Isaac Newton, Bentley calculates that at 4,000 miles in altitude 'the Æther is of that wonderful tenuity, that . . . a small Sphere of common Air of one Inch Diameter . . . would more than take up the vast Orb of *Saturn*' (Bentley, *Eight Sermons Preach'd at the Honourable Robert Boyle's Lecture*, 5th edn. (Cambridge, 1724), 257).

Nothing . . . overcome: the mechanist's words recall those attributed to the Persian emperor Xerxes when advised of the difficulties and dangers of invading Greece. 'For if in each matter that comes before us you look to all possible chances, never will you achieve anything' (James A. Arieti, 'A Herodotean Source for *Rasselas*, Ch. 6', *Notes and Queries*, 28 (1981), 241, citing Herodotus, *Persian Wars*, vii. 50). In an essay on heroic failure in *Adventurer* 99 (16 October 1753), SJ moves on from Xerxes to consider cases of scientific ambition that end in defeat but also advance knowledge: 'Many that presume to laugh at projectors, would consider a flight through the air in a winged chariot, and the movement of a mighty engine by a steam of water, as equally the dreams of mechanic lunacy.' SJ concludes here that 'Those who have attempted much, have seldom failed to perform more than those who never deviate from the common roads of action . . . and, when they fail, may sometimes benefit the world even by their miscarriages' (*YW* ii. 434–5).

19 *volant*: 'Flying; passing through the air' (*Dictionary*, s.v. Volant, 1). SJ's illustrative quotation is from Wilkins's *Mathematicall Magick*: 'The *volant*, or flying automata, are such mechanical contrivances as have a self-motion, whereby they are carried aloft in the air, like birds.'

bat's wings . . . human form: Wilkins also advances the batman theory, thinking bats designed by nature 'to imply that other kinds of creatures are capable of flying as well as birds, and if any should attempt it, that would be the best pattern for imitation' (Wilkins, *Mathematicall Magick*, 223).

20 *flight of northern savages . . . rolling under them*: 'Given the setting and what is known of SJ's attitude to contemporary colonial expansion, "northern savages" could be taken to mean European imperialists' (Goring). The passage certainly resonates with SJ's critiques of European expansionism as a political journalist, and he had probably read (see note below) a magazine poem of 1740 that whimsically imagined an airborne attack on Spain. In the usage of the day, however, 'northern savages' primarily suggests the Goths and Vandals who overran imperial Rome; the term was also applied to the Jacobite Highlanders who invaded England in 1745 and to the reputedly ferocious armies of Sweden and Russia. If SJ's speaker remains in character here as a Christian Abyssinian, European imperialism was a remote prospect until Italy began colonizing the region in the late nineteenth century; the only threat from the north was the Ottoman Empire, a sprawling Muslim power that had passed its peak but still controlled much of south-eastern Europe, western Asia, and northern Africa.

dropped into the lake: the mechanist's ducking may reflect SJ's memory of the 'rage for flying' created in the English midlands in the 1730s by high-wire illusionists such as Robert Cadman, who eventually died of a fall in 1739, and an imitator of Cadman whose career ended at Kedleston Hall, Derbyshire, in 1734: 'A few young men, adepts in the art of flying . . . fastened one end of the rope to the top of the hall, the other in the park; but the unlucky performer, instead of flying *over* the river, fell *in*, [and] blasted his character' (*The Life of William Hutton*, ed. L. Jewitt (1872), 116–17, quoted by Pat Rogers, 'Johnson and the Art of Flying', *Notes and Queries*, 40 (1993), 329–30). Cadman was commemorated in the *Gentleman's Magazine* at a time when SJ was probably editing the poetry columns; his exploits prompted the versifier to joke that 'An army of such wights to

cross the main, | Sooner than *Haddock*'s fleet, shou'd humble *Spain*' ('On
the Death of the Famous Flyer on the Rope at Shrewsbury', *Gentleman's
Magazine*, 10 (1740), 89).

rainy season: Lobo describes 'the Abyssinian winter, a dreadful season', as
being at its most severe between June and September: 'The rains that are
almost continually falling in this season make it impossible to go far from
home, for the rivers overflow their banks' (*YW* xv. 55–6).

21 *Imlac*: 'Imlac in "Rasselas," I spelt with a *c* at the end, because it is less
like English, which should always have the Saxon *k* added to the *c*', SJ
later told Boswell (*Life*, iv. 31). The name may derive from 'the Emperour
Icon-Imlac', whom Ludolf identifies as inaugurating the practice of royal
confinement in the fourteenth century; Ludolf adds that this custom was
at last imprudently abolished in 1590 by the tender-hearted King Naod
(Ludolf, *New History of Ethiopia*, 195–6). In a different context, Irvin
Ehrenpreis observes that ' "Imlac" is an anagram of "Michael," the name
of Johnson's father, though I am confident that the author did not realize
the fact' (Ehrenpreis, '*Rasselas* and some Meanings of "Structure" in
Literary Criticism', *Novel* 14 (1981), 102).

rehearsed: 'To repeat; to recite' (*Dictionary*, s.v. To Rehearse, 1). The text
reads 'recited' in the first edition and was altered in the second to
'rehearsed', presumably to avoid repetition in the sentence ahead (which
has Imlac 'recite his verses').

22 *talk in publick . . . business of a scholar*: Imlac's words evoke the public
profile and presence of classical, especially Athenian, philosophical
schools. Cf. *Adventurer* 85 (28 August 1753), in which SJ declares that 'To
read, write, and converse in due proportions, is . . . the business of a man
of letters' (*YW* ii. 416); also Sermon 8 on the subject of academic pride:
'The business of the life of a scholar is to accumulate, and to diffuse,
knowledge; to learn, in order that he may teach' (*YW* xiv. 88). In practice,
SJ was already struggling with his own growing reputation as 'a kind of
publick oracle, whom every body thought they had the right to visit and
consult' (*Life*, ii. 118–19).

kingdom of Goiama . . . fountain of the Nile: on the tributary kingdom of
Goiama and the source of the Blue Nile, see above, p. 7 and n.

spoiled by the governours of the province: describing the impoverished
(despoiled) state of Abyssinia, Lobo reports that 'Theft is so established
in this country, that the head of the robbers purchases his employment,
and pays tribute to the king . . . The governors purchase their commis-
sions, or to speak properly their privilege of pillaging the provinces'
(*YW* xv. 214).

Subordination: a key term in SJ's social thought, and according to Boswell
his 'favourite subject' (*Life*, ii. 13; see also i. 408; iii. 383). Writing of his
own society, SJ thought the English 'a people . . . classed by subordination,
where one part of the community is sustained and accommodated by the

labour of the other' (*YW* xviii. 106). But he also saw hierarchy as inherently unstable: 'an equality of condition, though that condition be far from eligible, conduces more to the peace of society than an established and legal subordination; in which every man is perpetually endeavouring to exalt himself to the rank above him . . . and every man exerting his efforts, to hinder his inferiors from rising to the level with himself' (*YW* xiv. 59).

23 *This, young man . . . to waste or to improve*: Imlac's task recalls the parable of the talents in Matthew 25: 14–30, a frequent point of reference in SJ's writing: see, for example, 'On the Death of Dr. Robert Levet' (1782), lines 27–8 (*YW* vi. 35); also Paul Fussell, *Samuel Johnson and the Life of Writing* (New York: Harcourt, Brace, Jovanovich, 1971), pp. 95–7, 130.

24 *Surat*: a wealthy trading port in north-western India, but twice sacked in the 1660s by Maratha (Hindu) opponents of the Mughal Empire, and in relative decline thereafter as British mercantile interests shifted their operations to Bombay. In March 1759, at the height of the Seven Years War and weeks before the publication of *Rasselas*, British forces took military control of the city, though reports did not reach the London newspapers (e.g. the *London Chronicle* for 22 September 1759) until months later.

world of waters: echoing Milton's description of 'The rising world of waters dark and deep, | Won from the void and formless infinite' (*Paradise Lost*, iii. 11–12); SJ quotes these lines in the *Dictionary* (s.v. Mantle; see also Invest).

pleasing terrour: Imlac flirts here with the discourse of the sublime, in which 'terror is a passion which always produces delight when it does not press too close' (Edmund Burke, *A Philosophical Enquiry into the Origin of Our Ideas of the Sublime and Beautiful*, ed. Adam Phillips (Oxford: Oxford World's Classics, 1990), 42 (I. xiv); see also, on the ocean as sublime, pp. 53–4 (II. ii)). For a scholar of epic poetry in the period, 'even the frightful Raptures of *Theoclymenus*, and the *Harpye* of *Virgil*, engage the Reader with a sort of pleasing Terrour' (Joseph Spence, *An Essay on Pope's Odyssey* (1726–7), pt. II, p. 55); for a traveller crossing the Apennines, 'the very rough rocks and horrible precipices had a pleasing terror in them' (*The Travels of Thomas Broderick, Esq.* (1754), 390).

25 *injure another without benefit to himself*: motiveless malignity was a standard theme of eighteenth-century satire; cf. Fielding's ironic praise of Jonathan Wild, who 'carried Good-nature to that wonderful and uncommon Height, that he never did a single Injury to Man or Woman, by which he himself did not expect to reap some Advantage' (Henry Fielding, *Jonathan Wild*, ed. Claude Rawson and Linda Bree (Oxford: Oxford World's Classics, 2003), 32–3 (I. xi)).

Agra . . . great Mogul commonly resides: Agra, the inland terminal of the Surat trade, had been capital of the Mughal Empire until 1649, and it remained an important commercial and cultural centre. The last 'Great Mughal' to merit the name was Aurangzeb, and after his death in 1707 the Mughal Empire declined rapidly under pressure from the Hindu Maratha Empire, the Sikh Confederacy in the Punjab, and the rival Muslim power in the region, Persia. Agra lay 'about 700 miles north-east of Surat, a journey which the caravans generally perform in nine weeks' (Stephen Whatley et al., *A Complete System of Geography*, 2 vols. (1747), ii. 315).

26 *end of their studies . . . dignity of instructing*: Kolb compares SJ's *Adventurer* 126 (19 January 1754): 'He has learned to no purpose, that is not able to teach' (*YW* ii. 474).

Persians . . . eminently social: Persian sociability is a standard theme in the period, though not in the oriental tale that SJ published as *Idler* 75 (22 September 1759), which describes a talented youth frozen out of Persian society when his fortune fails (*YW* ii. 232–5). Jonas Hanway's eyewitness report of Persian manners is typical: 'In their dispositions they are chearful, but rather inclined to seriousness than loud mirth; in this they are not so much the *French of Asia*, as in their politeness and civility to strangers. Hospitality is a part of their religion; on occasions of the least intercourse, men of any distinction invite strangers, as well as their friends to their table' (Hanway, *An Historical Account of the British Trade over the Caspian Sea*, 4 vols. (1753), i. 330).

Arabia . . . war with all mankind: SJ gives a somewhat Hobbesian inflection to the standard view of nomadic tribes in the Arabian Peninsula, recalling Hobbes's state of nature as a condition of 'Warre . . . of every man, against every man' (Thomas Hobbes, *Leviathan* (1651), I. xiii). Kolb cites a seventeenth-century French witness for whom 'the *Arabs* concern themselves with nothing but their Cattle, following their Princes, going to War, and robbing Passengers' (*The Chevalier d'Arvieux's Travels in Arabia the Desart*, 2nd edn. (1723), 189). Cf. also the account given of the Barbary States in North Africa by the historian and travel writer Thomas Salmon, who describes the people of Algiers as 'being in a manner in perpetual war with all mankind' (Salmon, *Modern History; or, The Present State of All Nations*, 3rd edn., 3 vols. (1744–6), iii. 72).

27 *Poetry . . . the highest learning*: here and elsewhere, Imlac's position cannot be identified unequivocally with that of SJ, who gives a downbeat definition of poetry in the *Dictionary* ('Metrical composition; the art or practice of writing poems') and later criticizes 'Dryden's learning and genius' for failing 'to have laboured science into poetry, and have shewn . . . that verse did not refuse the ideas of philosophy' (*Lives*, ii. 134). On the overlaps, intersections, and divergences between Imlac's theories of poetry and SJ's own, see Howard D. Weinbrot, 'The Reader, the General, and the Particular: Imlac and Johnson in Chapter Ten of *Rasselas*', *Eighteenth-Century Studies*, 5 (1971), 80–96.

27 *in almost all countries . . . considered as the best*: Imlac's remark recalls the enduring 'Ancients versus Moderns' debate in neoclassical criticism. Kolb cites Swift's patron Sir William Temple, from his essay 'Upon Poetry': 'What Honor and Request the antient Poetry has Lived in, may not only be Observed from the Universal Reception and Use in all Nations from *China* to *Peru*, from *Scythia* to *Arabia*, but from the Esteem of the Best and the Greatest Men as well as the Vulgar' (Temple, *Miscellanea . . . The Second Part* (1690), 338).

Nature and Passion . . . always the same: echoing Pope's injunction in *An Essay on Criticism* (1711): 'First follow *Nature*, and your judgment frame | By her just standard, which is still the same' (ll. 68–9); cf. also SJ's assertion in *Adventurer* 99 (16 October 1753) that 'human nature is always the same' (*YW* ii. 431).

volumes . . . suspended in the mosque of Mecca: Imlac invokes the dubious tradition of the Muʹallaqat, a group of pre-Islamic poems thought to have been suspended on curtains covering the Kaʹba in the Great Mosque at Mecca. The orientalist George Sale describes 'seven celebrated poems . . . hung up on the *Caaba* . . . by public order, being written on *Egyptian* silk, and in letters of gold' (*The Koran* (1734), 28). Decades later Sir William Jones, a member of Johnson's literary 'Club' in the 1770s, published an edition and translation of *The Moallakât; or, Seven Arabian Poems, Which Were Suspended on the Temple at Mecca* (1782). For SJ's acquaintance with relevant scholarship, see Richard Eversole, 'Imlac and the Poets of Persia and Arabia', *Philological Quarterly*, 58 (1979), 155–70.

28 *Whatever is beautiful . . . inexhaustible variety*: as well as invoking the celebrated Burkean distinction between the sublime and the beautiful, Imlac emphasizes the attentive observation of life in ways that recall several of SJ's essays. Cf. *Adventurer* 95 (2 October 1753): 'Here then is the fund, from which those who study mankind may fill their compositions with an inexhaustible variety of images and allusions; and he must be confessed to look with little attention upon scenes thus perpetually changing, who cannot catch some of the figures before they are made vulgar by reiterated descriptions' (*YW* ii. 428).

idea: in the *Dictionary*, SJ defines *idea* as 'Mental imagination' or 'Mental image' (see Glossary). Boswell reports him to have been 'particularly indignant against the almost universal use of the word *idea* in the sense of *notion* or *opinion*, when it is clear that *idea* can only signify something of which an image can be formed in the mind. We may have an *idea* or *image* of a mountain, a tree, a building; but we cannot surely have an *idea* or *image* of an *argument* or *proposition*' (*Life*, iii. 196).

not the individual, but the species: cf. SJ's judgement, in his 1765 Preface to Shakespeare, that 'In the writings of other poets a character is too often an individual; in those of Shakespeare it is commonly a species' (*YW* vii. 62).

streaks of the tulip: there is no specific target behind this famous passage, but the streaks of a tulip, particularized or not, were something of a poetic cliché. SJ may have half-remembered William Hamilton of Bangour, a poet he disparaged in conversation with Boswell, in whose 'Contemplation' the hand of Nature 'Tinges with pencil slow unseen, | The grass that cloathes the valley green; | Or spreads the tulip's parted streaks, | Or sanguine dyes the rose's cheeks . . .' (Hamilton, *Poems on Several Occasions* (Glasgow, 1748), 10–11). Somewhat against the grain of Imlac's precept, Thomas Newcomb, a minor satirist, advises poets not to attempt cosmic sublimity before first learning 'To trace the wonders of a grass or flower; | The hidden beauties to unfold, that grow | On every shrub, in every field below; | Whose skill a whiteness o'er the lilly throws, | Streaks the gay tulip, and enflames the rose . . .' (Newcomb, *The Manners of the Age* (1733), 136). For background, including the consequences for poetry of seventeenth-century 'tulipomania' (a speculative market in prized bulbs that spread to the Ottoman Empire during its so-called 'tulip period' of 1718–30), see Robert Folkenflik, 'The Tulip and Its Streaks: Contexts of *Rasselas* X', *Ariel*, 9 (1978), 57–71. Folkenflik compares the descriptive overkill of two late metaphysical poems about tulips, Abraham Cowley's 'Tulipa' (1668) and Richard Leigh's 'Beauty in Chance' (1675).

29 *interpreter of nature . . . legislator of mankind*: another famous passage, anticipating Percy Bysshe Shelley's account of poets as 'the unacknowledged legislators of the world' in his 1821 *Defence of Poetry*; behind both statements lies Ben Jonson's view of the poet, in his 1607 Preface to *Volpone*, as 'the interpreter, and arbiter of nature' who 'can alone (or with a few) effect the business of mankind'. Hardy compares Imlac's expression with Joseph Warton's *An Essay on the Writings and Genius of Pope* (1756), which SJ had reviewed; at one point Warton describes an unidentified ode in which Orpheus, traditionally the father of lyric, 'is considered . . . as the first legislator and civilizer of mankind' (p. 60).

northern and western nations . . . remotest parts of the globe: *Rasselas* was published at the height of the Seven Years War (1756–63), a struggle for global supremacy that shifted in Britain's favour in 1759, the so-called 'Year of Victories'. The technological underpinnings of British and French power are SJ's subject in *Idler* 81 (3 November 1759), written in the voice of a native leader in Quebec. See also SJ's 'Observations on the Present State of Affairs' (1756), which debunks claims that European territorial acquisition in America enjoys legitimacy or genuine consent: 'We astonished them with our ships, with our arms, and with our general superiority. They yielded to us as to beings of another and higher race, sent among them from some unknown regions, with power which naked Indians could not resist, and which they were therefore, by every act of humility, to propitiate, that they who could so easily destroy might be induced to spare.' Famously, SJ concludes at this point that 'the American dispute between the French and us is therefore only the quarrel of two robbers for the spoils of a passenger' (*YW* x. 187–8).

30 *By what means . . . Supreme Being*: during a journey by carriage in June 1781, SJ 'seized . . . with avidity' on a copy of *Rasselas* that Boswell had with him, saying he had not looked at the work since publication. Pointing to the present passage, 'He said, "This, Sir, no man can explain otherwise"' (*Life*, iv. 119).

Palestine . . . continually resorting: here Rasselas typifies his people as Lobo describes them: 'The Abyssins were much addicted to pilgrimages into the Holy-Land' (*YW* xv. 207).

fields where great actions . . . holy resolutions: in a letter of *c*.19 March 1774, SJ expresses scepticism about 'local sanctity and local devotion', adding 'that the Universal Lord is every where present; and that, therefore, to come to Jona, or to Jerusalem, though it may not be useful, cannot be necessary' (*Letters*, ii. 133–4). In his *Journey to the Western Islands of Scotland* (1775), however, SJ responds more fervently to Iona, a principal site of early Christianity in Britain: 'That man is little to be envied, whose patriotism would not gain force upon the plain of Marathon, or whose piety would not grow warmer among the ruins of Iona' (*YW* ix. 148).

31 *Knowledge . . . increasing its ideas*: Hardy cites several similar judgements from SJ's conversation and letters, including his remark to Boswell that 'a desire of knowledge is the natural feeling of mankind; and every human being, whose mind is not debauched, will be willing to give all that he has to get knowledge' (*Life*, i. 458).

we grow more happy as our minds take a wider range: an Aristotelian position that SJ expanded in conversation in 1766: 'A peasant and a philosopher may be equally *satisfied*, but not equally *happy*. Happiness consists in the multiplicity of agreeable consciousness. A peasant has not capacity for having equal happiness with a philosopher' (*Life*, ii. 9).

32 *much is to be endured, and little to be enjoyed*: a familiar antithesis throughout SJ's writing and conversation; Boswell reports that in conversation 'he used frequently to observe, that there was more to be endured than enjoyed, in the general condition of human life' (*Life*, ii. 124). Cf. also SJ's earlier use of the endure/enjoy binary in *Rambler* 167 for 22 October 1751 (*YW* v. 121), *Adventurer* 111 for 27 November 1753 (*YW* ii. 451), and in his devastating review of Soame Jenyns's blandly optimistic *Free Inquiry into the Nature and Origin of Evil* (1757): 'The only end of writing is to enable the readers better to enjoy life, or better to endure it' (*YW*, xvii. 421).

the choice of life: this is the title originally projected by SJ for *Rasselas*, perhaps even before his protagonist's name had been fixed. As he told his printer William Strahan on 20 January 1759, 'The title will be The choice of Life or The History of —— Prince of Abissinia' (*Letters*, i. 178). On SJ's adaptation of the classical *vitarum electio* theme (notably as outlined by Cicero in *De Officiis*) and its role in classical allegory, see Earl R. Wasserman, 'Johnson's *Rasselas*: Implicit Contexts', *Journal of English and Germanic Philology*, 74 (1975), 1–25.

why should not life glide quietly away . . . reverence: cf. SJ's vision of ideal senescence in *The Vanity of Human Wishes*: 'An age that melts with unperceiv'd decay, | And glides in modest innocence away' (*YW* vi. 105 (ll. 293–4)).

I began to long . . . my counsels: Hardy compares *Idler* 43 (10 February 1759) on longing for the scene of lost youth: 'The man of business, wearied with unsatisfactory prosperity, retires to the town of his nativity, and expects to play away the last years with the companions of his childhood, and recover youth in the fields where he once was young' (*YW* ii. 136).

33 *remains of its ancient learning*: Egypt was widely recognized as an important source, though later overshadowed, of Greek and Roman accomplishments in the arts and sciences. In the *Dictionary* (s.v. Master, 11), SJ quotes a passage from Robert South characterizing the Egyptians as 'the first masters of learning'. In *Idler* 68 (4 August 1759), he laments the eclipse of Egyptian learning in later antiquity: 'The Greeks for a time travelled into Egypt, but they translated no books from the Egyptian language . . . and, except the sacred writings of the Old Testament, I know not that the library of Alexandria adopted any thing from a foreign tongue' (*YW* ii. 212).

mixture of all nations: Cairo was a thriving commercial centre serving three continents, and famously cosmopolitan. An English visitor whose work SJ knew gives a detailed analysis of the diverse demography of the city, adding that trade brings 'a great conflux of people to Grand Cairo . . . probably near a quarter of the souls in the city not being fix'd inhabitants' (Richard Pococke, *A Description of the East*, 3 vols. (1743–5), i. 38–9). G. B. Hill cites an earlier source in which '*Grand Cairo* is the most admirable and greatest city, seen upon the Earth, being thrice as large of bounds as *Constantinople* . . . There is great Commerce here with exceeding many Nations, for by their concurring hither, it is wonderfully peopled with infinite Numbers' (*Lithgow's Nineteen Years Travels through the Most Eminent Places in the Habitable World*, 2nd edn. (1692), 291, 293).

Suez: port at the northern end of the Red Sea. According to Pococke, 'The trade of Suez is only to Jedda on the east of the Red sea near Mecca' (*Description of the East*, i. 134), but Imlac continues south to the African coast.

I now expected . . . foreign manners: the disappointment and disillusionment of returning natives is a recurrent theme in SJ's essays of the period, notably *Idler* 43 (10 February 1759), *Idler* 58 (26 May 1759), and *Idler* 75 (22 September 1759). On 20 July 1762 he told Joseph Baretti of suffering this experience himself on returning to his birthplace, Lichfield, from which he promptly rebounded back to London: 'I found the streets much narrower and shorter than I thought I had left them, inhabited by a new race of people, to whom I was very little known. My play-fellows were grown old . . . My only remaining friend has changed his principles, and was become the tool of the predominant faction . . . I wandered about for five days, and took the first convenient opportunity of returning to a place, where, if there is not much happiness, there is at least such a diversity of good and evil, that slight vexations do not fix upon the heart' (*Letters*, i. 206).

33 *lady . . . rejected my suit, because my father was a merchant*: 'Poor Imlac! but how Dr. Johnson knew the World', wrote Hester Thrale Piozzi at this point in her 1818 edition of *Rasselas*, now at Harvard University: 'He meant Imlac as his own Representative to his own feelings; The Lady was Miss Molly Aston who sate for the Portrait of Altilia in the Rambler' (quoted by H. J. Jackson, *Marginalia: Readers Writing in Books* (New Haven: Yale University Press, 2001), pp. 107–8). On the brilliant, unattainable Molly Aston, see James Clifford, *Young Samuel Johnson* (London: Heinemann, 1955), pp. 218–20; also *Rambler* 182 (14 December 1751).

34 *images . . . combine at pleasure*: cf. SJ's oriental tale in *Idler* 101 (22 March 1760), in which the youthful Omar plans to spend his early manhood acquiring knowledge and experience. 'Twenty years thus passed will store my mind with images, which I shall be busy through the rest of my life in combining and comparing', he resolves, but then comes to understand in old age that he has 'trifled away the years of improvement' (*YW* ii. 310–11).

36 *countenance of sorrow*: the phrase suggests the aspiring but melancholy hero of *Don Quixote*, famously called 'the Knight of the Woeful Countenance' by his squire Sancho (Miguel de Cervantes, *Don Quixote*, trans. Peter Motteux et al., 2nd edn., 4 vols. (1705–6), i. 185 (I. xix)). For structural and thematic affinities between *Rasselas* and *Don Quixote*, see Eithne Henson, *The Fictions of Romantic Chivalry: Samuel Johnson and Romance* (London: Associated University Presses, 1992), 128–37.

knowledge . . . laughs at strength: cf. Ecclesiastes 9: 16: 'Then said I, wisdom is better than strength.' On the relationship between *Rasselas*, the *vanitas vanitatum* theme of Ecclesiastes, and Bishop Simon Patrick's optimistic reading of Ecclesiastes in his *Paraphrase* of 1685, see Thomas R. Preston, 'The Biblical Context of Johnson's *Rasselas*', *PMLA* 84 (1969), 274–81.

opinion of antiquity . . . instinct of animals: SJ may be recalling the following lines from Alexander Pope, which Pope's editor William Warburton annotated with references to Pliny the Elder's *Natural History* and Oppian's *Halieutica*: 'See him from Nature rising slow to Art! | To copy Instinct then was Reason's part; | Thus then to man the voice of Nature spake— | "Go, from the Creatures thy instructions take: | Learn from the birds what food the thickets yield; | Learn from the beasts the physic of the field; | Thy arts of building from the bee receive; | Learn of the mole to plow, the worm to weave; | Learn of the little Nautilus to sail, | Spread the thin oar, and catch the driving gale"' (Pope, *An Essay on Man*

(1733–4), iii. 169–78). See also the scathing commentary on this passage by Jean-Pierre Crousaz, which SJ translated for an English edition entitled *A Commentary on Mr. Pope's Principles of Morality* (1739): 'Had man, whose *prerogative* extended thro' the whole creation, hitherto been so void of reason as not to have discovered any way of supplying such pressing necessities?' (*YW* xvii. 224).

37 *Great works . . . perseverance*: Imlac echoes Cicero's treatise *De Senectute* (*On Old Age*), vi. 17: 'Great works are performed, not by strength or speed or physical dexterity, but by reflection, force of character, and determination' (George L. Barnett, '*Rasselas* and *De Senectute*', *Notes and Queries*, 201 (1956), 485–6). Cf. also *Rambler* 43 (14 August 1750): 'All the performances of human art, at which we look with praise or wonder, are instances of the resistless force of perseverance' (*YW* iii. 235).

38 *single favourite*: the favourite, Pekuah, is not obviously individualized, but it was later reported that Mary Welch, the 16-year-old daughter of SJ's friend Saunders Welch, was 'the original of Johnson's Pekuah in *Rasselas*' (Laetitia-Matilda Hawkins, *Memoirs, Anecdotes, Facts, and Opinions*, 2 vols. (1824), i. 57). Mary Welch, who went on to marry Nollekens the sculptor, was beautiful and vivacious, 'but instruction, when poured on her mind, ran off it as from polished marble, and with every advantage, she to the last remained sadly illiterate' (i. 56).

39 *shepherds in the fields . . . table spread with delicacies*: Lobo describes the Abyssinian tradition of hospitality as follows: 'when a stranger comes to a village, or to the camp, the people are obliged to entertain him and his company according to his rank . . . and there is great care taken to provide enough, because if the guest complains, the town is oblig'd to pay double the value of what they ought to have furnish'd' (*YW* xv. 50).

eat: in the *Dictionary*, SJ lists '*ate*, or *eat*' as alternative preterite forms of the verb *to eat*; cf. the same usage in ch. xxxviii below (p. 81).

40 *ruggedness of the commercial race*: in his 'Life of Dryden', SJ applies similar language—*ruggedness* here means 'Roughness; asperity' (*Dictionary*)—to the hard-nosed booksellers of Restoration London: 'To the mercantile ruggedness of that race, the delicacy of the poet was sometimes exposed' (*Lives*, ii. 117).

41 *use and nature of money*: 'There is no money in Abyssinia, except in the eastern provinces, where they have iron coin', Lobo reports: 'But in the chief provinces all commerce is managed by exchange; their chief trade consists in provisions . . . and principally in salt which is properly the money of this country' (*YW* xv. 50).

42 *I live in the crowds . . . to shun myself*: cf. Sermon 16: 'Men are often driven, by reflection and remorse, into the hurries of business, or of pleasure, and fly from the terrifying suggestions of their own thoughts to banquets and courts' (*YW* xiv. 178). SJ often makes this admission in his own case, telling Joseph Baretti that he frequents the theatre 'only to escape from

myself' (*Letters*, i. 199; 10 June 1761) and envying Hester Thrale her family life when 'here sit poor I, with nothing but my own solitary individuality' (*Letters*, ii. 256; 21 July 1775). 'It is again Midnight, and I am again alone', he tells Hill Boothby on 30 December 1755: 'If I turn my thoughts upon myself what do [I] perceive but a poor helpless being reduced by a blast of wind to weakness and misery' (*Letters*, i. 117).

42 *Every man . . . tyranny of reflection*: cf. *Adventurer* 120 (29 December 1753): 'He that enters a gay assembly [and] beholds the chearfulness displayed in every countenance . . . would naturally imagine, that he had reached the metropolis of felicity, the place sacred to gladness of heart, from whence all fear and anxiety were irreversibly excluded . . . but who is there of those who frequent these luxurious assemblies, that will not confess his own uneasiness, or cannot recount the vexations and distresses that prey upon the lives of his gay companions? The world, in its best state, is nothing more than a larger assembly of beings, combining to counterfeit happiness which they do not feel . . . and to hide their real condition from the eyes of one another' (*YW* ii. 467–8).

causes of good and evil . . . inquiring and deliberating: cf. *Rambler* 63 (23 October 1750): 'The good and ill of different modes of life are sometimes so equally opposed, that perhaps no man ever yet made his choice between them upon a full conviction, and adequate knowledge' (*YW* iii. 337–8).

Very few . . . willingly co-operate: cf. *Rambler* 184 (21 December 1751): 'It is not commonly observed, how much, even of actions considered as particularly subject to choice, is to be attributed to accident, or some cause out of our own power' (*YW* v. 202).

43 *I have here the world before me*: SJ plays on Milton's famous conclusion to *Paradise Lost*, following the expulsion from Eden of Adam and Eve: 'The world was all before them . . .' (xii. 646). Also perhaps in play is the equivalent moment in *Tom Jones*, when Fielding's hero is expelled from Paradise Hall: '*The world*, as Milton phrases it, *lay all before him*' (Henry Fielding, *Tom Jones*, ed. John Bender and Simon Stern (Oxford: Oxford World's Classics, 1996), p. 288 (VII. ii)).

Happiness . . . without uncertainty: cf. *Rambler* 53 (18 September 1750): 'To make any happiness sincere, it is necessary that we believe it to be lasting; since whatever we suppose ourselves in danger of losing, must be enjoyed with solicitude and uneasiness' (*YW* iii. 287–8).

44 *government of the passions*: this expression signals the Stoic position that the wise and virtuous pursue happiness 'by the free Guidance of their Reason, and the due Government of their Passions' (George Stanhope, *Epictetus His Morals*, 3rd edn. (1704), 56). For the remainder of this chapter, the sage's speeches paraphrase and exaggerate English Stoic and neo-Stoic writing of the seventeenth and eighteenth centuries: see Gwin J. Kolb, 'The Use of Stoical Doctrines in *Rasselas*, Chapter XVIII', *Modern Language Notes*, 68 (1953), 439–47.

45 *My daughter . . . died last night of a fever*: the philosopher's bereavement reworks a comic scene from Fielding's *Joseph Andrews* (1742), in which Parson Adams, a Christian Stoic who 'was a great Enemy to the Passions, and preached nothing more than the Conquest of them by Reason and Grace', is overwhelmed by grief when told of the drowning of his favourite son—a son he then meets, 'in a wet Condition indeed, but alive, and running towards him'. See Henry Fielding, *Joseph Andrews*, ed. Thomas Keymer (Oxford: Oxford World's Classics, 1999), 270–1 (iv. 8); also, for a further variation on this episode by Oliver Goldsmith, George L. Barnett, '*Rasselas* and *The Vicar of Wakefield*', *Notes and Queries*, 202 (1957), 303–5.

46 *Has wisdom no strength . . . against calamity*: Rasselas's disappointment echoes SJ's critique elsewhere of 'the Stoics, or scholars of Zeno . . . who proclaimed themselves exalted, by the doctrines of their sect, above the reach of those miseries, which embitter life to the rest of the world. They therefore removed pain, poverty, loss of friends, exile, and violent death, from the catalogue of evils; and passed, in their haughty stile, a kind of irreversible decree, by which they forbad them . . . to give any disturbance to the tranquillity of a wise man' (*Rambler* 32 (7 July 1750), *YW* iii. 174); see also *Rambler* 6 (7 April 1750), *YW* iii. 30; *Idler* 41 (21 January 1759), *YW* ii. 130–1.

lowest cataract of the Nile: the Nile has six cataracts (shallows or rapids rather than waterfalls) between Aswan and Khartoum. The lowest, at Aswan, is more than 400 miles south of Cairo; Rasselas and his companions work wonders to reach it below (p. 52) 'on the third day'.

Their way lay through fields . . . pastoral simplicity: cf. *Idler* 71 (25 August 1759), which recounts the disillusionment of Dick Shifter, a pastoral-loving Londoner who, retiring the country, finds the inhabitants 'coarse of manners, and . . . mischievous of disposition'. Within days he 'began to be tired with rustick simplicity . . . and bad farewell to the regions of calm content and placid meditation' (*YW* ii. 223–4). The same trajectory is described in SJ's *Life of Savage* (1744), when Savage, on retiring to Wales, 'imagined that he should be transported to scenes of flowery felicity, like those which one poet has reflected to another' (*Lives*, iii. 173).

48 *The shrubs . . . harmless luxury*: the passage recalls an earlier and shorter exercise in oriental fiction by SJ, the tale of 'Seged, lord of Ethiopia' in *Rambler* 204–5 (29 February–3 March 1752), in which Seged enjoys the 'harmless luxury' of roaming his pleasure gardens (*YW* v. 301); cf. also the gardens of Almamoulin in *Rambler* 120 (11 May 1751). In the present passage, however, little attempt is made to represent a distinctively eastern landscape, and SJ instead evokes the naturalistic fashions of gardening in England at the time. G. B. Hill compares the passage with SJ's later account of William Shenstone's *ferme ornée* at The Leasowes, Shropshire, laid out from the mid-1740s onwards, where Shenstone contrived 'to point his prospects, to diversify his surface, to entangle his walks, and to wind his waters' (*Lives*, iv. 127).

48 *laws of eastern hospitality . . . liberal and wealthy*: see above, n. to p. 39. These traditions of hospitality, Lobo adds, are 'so well establish'd, that a stranger goes into a house of one he never saw, with the same familiarity, and assurance of welcome, as into that of an intimate friend' (*YW* xv. 50).

Bassa: a variant form of *pasha*, a Turkish-appointed viceroy and 'the highest official title of honour in the Ottoman Empire' (*OED*); the term was a byword in the eighteenth century for despotic rule. Kolb cites Pococke on the corrupt and exploitative nature of colonial rule in Egypt, which had been annexed to the Ottoman Empire in 1517: 'the little officers oppress the people; the great officers squeeze them; and out of Egypt, the Pasha all the people under him; the Pasha himself becomes a prey to the great people of the Porte [i.e. Constantinople, the imperial capital]; and the Grand Signor at last seizes the riches of the great officers about him' (Pococke, *Description of the East*, i. 171).

50 *For some time . . . relaxation or diversion*: Hardy cites SJ's account in *Rambler* 6 (7 April 1750) of the Restoration poet Abraham Cowley, who retired to the country in his last years to seek 'the happiness of leisure and retreat . . . He forgot, in the vehemence of desire, that solitude and quiet owe their pleasures to those miseries, which he was so studious to obviate; for such are the vicissitudes of the world, through all its parts, that day and night, labour and rest, hurry and retirement, endear each other; such are the changes that keep the mind in action' (*YW*. iii. 34–5). See also *Rambler* 207 (10 March 1752) on human dissatisfaction with extreme states: 'if by the necessity of solitary application he is secluded from the world, he listens with a beating heart to distant noises, longs to mingle with living beings, and resolves to take hereafter his fill of diversions' (*YW* v. 312).

51 *life led according to nature*: the chapter title suggests the primitivism of Jean-Jacques Rousseau, but parallels identified in the body of the chapter by Hardy and other editors are inconclusive, and firm evidence of SJ's hostility to Rousseau postdates *Rasselas* by several years. The chapter is now usually read as satirizing the comfortable platitudes of English deism, or freethinking in general, in earlier decades: see Gwin J. Kolb, 'Rousseau and the Background of the "Life Led According to Nature" in Chapter 22 of *Rasselas*', *Modern Philology*, 73 (1976), S66–S73.

Some talked . . . purify his heart: SJ articulates both these views in essays written shortly before *Rasselas*. In *Idler* 19 (19 August 1758), 'mankind is one vast republick, where every individual receives many benefits from the labour of others, which, by labouring in his turn for others, he is obliged to repay' (*YW* ii. 59). In *Idler* 38 (6 January 1759), retirement is permissible 'to those who have paid their due proportion to society, and who, having lived for others, may be honourably dismissed to live for themselves' (*YW* ii. 119–20).

52 *But the time . . . his own fault*: the speaker repeats the religious consolation held out by SJ in *Adventurer* 120 (29 December 1753): 'there will surely

come a time, when every capacity of happiness shall be filled, and none shall be wretched but by his own fault' (*YW* ii. 470).

a philosopher: According to Hester Thrale Piozzi, the philosopher was modelled on John Gilbert Cooper (1722–69), a minor poet whose philosophical verse was influenced by Shaftesbury's *Characteristics*. Annotating this chapter in her 1818 edition of *Rasselas*, Piozzi called him 'a Man now I think wholly forgotten, tho' a very showy Talker in his Time' (Jackson, *Marginalia*, p. 108).

The time is already come . . . within our reach: Kolb finds echoes here of Antoine Le Grand, a French philosopher active in London in the later seventeenth century, whose early work attempts to reconcile stoic and epicurean doctrines. In *Man without Passion; or, The Wise Stoick* (1675), Le Grand sees man as 'a Conspirator against his own Felicity' who 'emploies all [Nature's] benefits to make himself unhappy' (p. 115); happiness is available to all who seek it, for 'Nature is too liberal to deny us our Desires: She is too Noble to refuse us a gift which she preserves for us in the Cabinet of our Soul' (p. 16).

The way to be happy . . . infused at our nativity: this passage was identified by an early reviewer (Owen Ruffhead in the *Monthly Review* for May 1759) as a paraphrase of Cicero's oration for Milo, sect. iv, in which Cicero makes an appeal to natural law. As the passage reads in a free eighteenth-century translation, 'This . . . is a Law not adopted by Custom, but inherent to our Being; a Law not received, learned, or read, but an essential, cogenial, inseparable Character of Nature; a Law which we have not by *Institution* but by *Constitution*, not derived from Authority, but existing with Consciousness' (*The Orations of Marcus Tullius Cicero*, trans. William Guthrie, 2nd edn., 3 vols. (1745–52), i. 38–40). More immediately, the sage typifies the glib adoption of this terminology in eighteenth-century arguments for natural religion. An influential example is the deist Matthew Tindal, for whom 'there's a Religion of Nature & Reason written in the hearts of every one of us from the first Creation'. This religion is 'universal, unchangeable, & indelibly implanted in human-nature', Tindal goes on; 'the end for which God implanted this Religion in human-nature, was to make Men happy here as well as hereafter; (God's will in relation to Man & human happiness being equivalent terms)' (Tindal, *Christianity as Old as the Creation* (1731), 52, 257).

He that lives . . . reason of things shall alternately prescribe: here the sage employs a notorious Tindal catchphrase, adopted in the first place from the Anglican theologian Samuel Clarke, whose arguments for the conformity of Christianity with 'the reason of things' gave inadvertent support to the deist project of dispensing altogether with revealed religion. Citing Clarke's *Discourse Concerning the Unchangeable Obligations of Natural Religion* (1706), Tindal insists '"that the *Will of God* always determines itself to act according to the eternal *Reason of Things*, & that all *rational Creatures* are oblig'd to govern themselves in all their actions

by the same eternal *Rule* of Reason"'. Tindal then reinforces his point
from Clarke's *Demonstration of the Being and Attributes of God* (1705):
'"They, who are not govern'd by this Law, are for setting up their own
unreasonable self-will, in opposition to the Nature, and Reason of
things"' (Tindal, *Christianity*, 324).

52 *Let them learn to be wise . . . deviation from happiness*: on human reason and
animal instinct, see above, p. 36 and n. Tindal employs the same argument: 'When we see with what skill & contrivance, Birds, without being
taught by any, but the God of Nature, build their nests . . . must we not
own, that what we call *instinct*, is a certain & infallible Guide for inferior
Animals? And can we doubt, whether Man, the Lord of the Creation, has
not from his superior Reason, sufficient notices of whatever makes
for his greatest, his eternal happiness?' Earlier Tindal maintains that 'The
Happiness of all beings whatever consists in the perfection of their
nature', and that in the case of rational human nature 'every deviation
from the rules of right reason being an imperfection, must carry with it a
proportionable unhappiness' (Tindal, *Christianity*, 252, 19).

53 *To live according to nature . . . present system of things*: at this point the
sage's opaque platitudes recall the freethinking tutor Square in Fielding's
Tom Jones (1749), who 'measured all actions by the *unalterable rule of
right*, and the *eternal fitness of things*' (Henry Fielding, *Tom Jones*, ed.
Bender and Stern, 109 (III. iii)). Underlying both characterizations is
the heavy use of ill-defined notions of 'fitness' by eighteenth-century
deists, perhaps in particular the notoriously obfuscating Thomas Chubb,
who explains his terminology thus: 'By the *moral* Fitness of things,
I mean that Fitness, which arises from, and is founded in the *Nature*
and the *Relations of Things*; taking it for granted, that there is an essential
Difference betwixt Good and Evil, or Fitness and Unfitness, arising from
the Nature and the Relations of Things, antecedent to, and independent
of any divine or human Determination concerning them' (Chubb, *The
Previous Question, with Regard to Religion* (1725), 7).

understand less as he heard him longer: 'In the character of this sage, [SJ]
intends to expose the absurdity of the Epicurean doctrine . . . by making
the philosopher found a system of happiness upon a maxim which he is
incapable of explaining intelligibly' (*Monthly Review*, May 1759). Kolb
cites several challenges to deism along these lines, some of which identified Samuel Clarke as the source of the problem. In one explicit critique
of 'Dr. *Clarke* and his Followers', Thomas Johnson protests that 'the
Maintainers of this *natural, necessary, or independent Fitness* of Things
and Actions, have constantly declined letting us know what they mean
by *Moral Obligation* . . . and when they are called upon for a Reason, why
these Fitnesses or Relations *must be obeyed*, or our Actions regulated by
them, their Answer is that "'tis self-evident . . . 'tis contain'd in our own
Ideas, and the like"' (Johnson, *An Essay on Moral Obligation* (1731), 25).

as he was yet young: Rasselas is 'in the twenty-sixth year of his age' in ch.ii (p. 10); if the time scheme is to be taken seriously, he is now about 32.

54 *middle fortune*: the period saw the emergence in England of a wealth-based class system, replacing older structures and designations based on inherited rank. For SJ's role in 'defin[ing] the values and social role of what later became known as the "middle class," the stratum of professionals, writers, and men of commerce distinct from both the nobility and upper gentry above and the lower orders below', see Nicholas Hudson, *Samuel Johnson and the Making of Modern England* (Cambridge: Cambridge University Press, 2003), 11 and *passim*.

law of subordination . . . the lot of one: on subordination, see above, p. 22 and n. SJ later told Boswell that 'subordination is very necessary for society, and contensions for superiority very dangerous' (*Life*, i. 442), but this view did not imply endorsement of autocratic power: 'I agree . . . that there must be a high satisfaction in being a feudal Lord', he teased Boswell on another occasion, 'but we are to consider that we ought not to wish to have a number of men unhappy for the sake of one' (*Life*, ii. 178).

55 *letters of revocation . . . chains to Constantinople*: in the *Dictionary*, SJ's primary definition of *revocation* is 'Act of recalling'; the term was used especially in the eighteenth century for 'the recall of a representative or ambassador from abroad; also in *letters of revocation*' (*OED*). Here the Bassa is summoned back to Constantinople (also known as the Porte, now Istanbul), the capital of the Ottoman Empire. His precarious position is indicated by Aaron Hill, an early eighteenth-century visitor, who notes that the viceroy of Egypt is 'full Possessor of an arbitrary Power' and 'the first *Bashaw* of all the Turkish Empire', but 'continues seldom in his Government above three Years' (Hill, *A Full and Just Account of the Present State of the Ottoman Empire* (1709), 228).

Janisaries: originally formed in the fourteenth century as a corps of royal guards, the Janissaries steadily evolved into a standing army. By the time of Sultan Osman II, whom the Janissaries assassinated in 1622, they had become a large, powerful, and unreliable force, and they remained so until disbanded in 1826. 'They are often mutinous, and sometimes their fury has arose to such a height, as to depose the sultan', notes a mid-eighteenth-century visitor (*Familiar Letters from a Gentleman at Damascus, to His Sister in London* (1750), 153); SJ sums up their reputation in the 'hungry Janizary' of his tragedy *Irene* (1749), 'Tainted by sloth, the parent of sedition' (*YW* vi. 184 (IV. v)).

56 *Answer . . . great father of waters*: Nekayah's address to the Nile recalls an apostrophe to the Thames from Thomas Gray's 'Ode on a Distant Prospect of Eton College' (1747), which SJ was later to ridicule. 'His supplication to father *Thames*, to tell him who drives the hoop or tosses the ball, is useless and puerile', SJ writes of lines 21–30 of the ode ('Say, Father Thames, for thou hast seen . . .'): 'Father *Thames* has no better

means of knowing than himself' (*Lives*, iv. 181). See also, on a similar moment in Pope's *Windsor Forest*, *Lives*, iv. 67.

56 *fury*: 'One of the deities of vengeance, and thence a stormy, turbulent, violent, raging woman' (*Dictionary*, s.v. Fury, 4); the first edition reads 'fiend' at this point.

among the poor . . . could not be found: SJ had little time for Horatian clichés about the happy poor. As he wrote when reviewing Soame Jenyns, 'The poor indeed are insensible of many little vexations which sometimes imbitter the possessions and pollute the enjoyments, of the rich . . . but this happiness is like that of a malefactor who ceases to feel the cords that bind him when the pincers are tearing his flesh' (*YW* xvii. 407); cf. also *Rambler* 53 (18 September 1750) and 57 (2 October 1750), *YW* iii. 284–5 and 306.

It is the care . . . conceal their indigence from the rest: cf. *Adventurer* 120 (29 December 1753): 'There is in the world more poverty than is generally imagined . . . great numbers are pressed by real necessities which it is their chief ambition to conceal' (*YW* ii. 468).

some have refused . . . forgive their benefactress: on the pains and resentments of obligation, see *Rambler* 87 (15 January 1751), *YW* iv. 96; also *Rambler* 166 (19 October 1751), *YW* v. 118.

57 *if a kingdom . . . exposed to revolutions*: Imlac's principle is traceable to Aristotle, and was central to British political debate in the decades following Robert Filmer's *Patriarcha* (1680). Nekayah develops the domestic implications in ways that recall *Rambler* 148 (17 August 1751): 'since, as Aristotle observes . . . "the government of a family is naturally monarchical," it is like other monarchies too often arbitrarily administered. The regal and parental tyrant differ only in the extent of their dominions, and in the number of their slaves' (*YW* v. 25).

each child endeavours . . . fondness of the parents: in childhood, according to Hester Thrale Piozzi, SJ and his brother Nathaniel were 'always rivals for the mother's fondness; and many of the severe reflections on domestic life in Rasselas, took their source from its author's keen recollections of the time passed in his early years' (Piozzi, *Anecdotes of the Late Samuel Johnson, LL.D.* (1786), 7).

colours of life . . . spring and winter: cf. *Rambler* 69 (13 November 1750): 'So different are the colours of life, as we look forward to the future, or backward to the past; and so different the opinions and sentiments which this contrariety of appearance naturally produces, that the conversation of the old and young ends generally with contempt or pity on either side' (*YW* iii. 365); see also *Rambler* 50 (8 September 1750), *YW* iii. 272.

58 *scrupulosity*: G. B. Hill identifies this as 'a favourite word with Johnson', and it recurs below, p. 100; see also Glossary. Observing its use in Samuel Richardson's novel *Sir Charles Grandison* (1753–4), an anonymous critic had fired a shot across SJ's bows by deploring the likelihood that such

'new-coin'd words . . . may possibly become current in common Conservation, be imitated by other writers, or by the laborious industry of some future compiler, transferred into a Dictionary' (*Critical Remarks on Sir Charles Grandison* (1754), 4). When his *Dictionary* appeared the following year, however, SJ was able to illustrate the term from earlier and more venerable authorities (Thomas Hooker, Robert South).

59 *Marriage . . . pleasures*: cf. SJ's conversational remark that 'even ill assorted marriages were preferable to cheerless celibacy' (*Life*, ii. 128). He also compares the two states in several essays, including *Rambler* 18 (19 May 1750), *Rambler* 115 (23 April 1751), and, most characteristically, *Rambler* 45 (21 August 1750): 'I am afraid that whether married or unmarried, we shall find the vesture of terrestrial existence more heavy and cumbrous, the longer it is worn' (*YW* iii. 244).

If he gratifies one . . . always discontented: SJ amplifies this point in his 'Life of Swift': 'every man of known influence has so many petitions which he cannot grant, that he must necessarily offend more than he gratifies, because the preference given to one affords all the rest a reason for complaint. *When I give away a place*, said Lewis XIV, *I make an hundred discontented, and one ungrateful*' (*Lives*, iii. 197, quoting Voltaire's *Le Siècle de Louis XIV* (1751), ch. xxv; cf. also *Life*, ii. 167).

60 *the more destructive bribery of flattery and servility*: resuming a standard theme from SJ's anti-Walpole satires of the 1730s, which describe a corrupted environment 'Where looks are merchandise, and smiles are sold, | Where won by bribes, by flatteries implor'd, | The groom retails the favours of his lord' (*London* (1738), ll. 179–81; *YW* vi. 56). Elsewhere SJ writes of flatterers as 'perverters of reason, and corrupters of the world', while those who hire them 'confirm error, and harden stupidity' (*Rambler* 66 (3 November 1750), *YW* iii. 353; *Rambler* 58 (6 October 1750), *YW* iii. 313). Cf. also SJ's rebuke when Boswell boasts that he cannot be bribed: 'Yes, you may be bribed by flattery' (*Life*, v. 306).

61 *visible happiness . . . the bad and good*: SJ frequently considers Aristotelian notions of 'the happiness of virtue' (*Rambler* 157 (17 September 1751), *YW* v. 71), but at issue here is the more banal eighteenth-century trope of 'virtue rewarded', which SJ frequently debunks. Cf. *Adventurer* 120 (29 December 1753): 'But surely, the quiver of Omnipotence is stored with arrows, against which the shield of human virtue, however adamantine it has been boasted, is held up in vain . . . A good man is subject, like other mortals, to all the influences of natural evil' (*YW* ii. 468–9).

All that virtue can afford . . . patience must suppose pain: the wording recalls, alongside the biblical Job, SJ's earlier interrogation of the status of Stoics as 'teachers of patience; for if pain be not an evil, there seems no instruction requisite how it may be borne' (*Rambler* 32 (7 July 1750), iii. 175). Cf. also his letter to Boswell of 3 July 1778: 'Without asserting Stoicism, it may be said, that it is our business to exempt ourselves as much as we can from the power of external things. There is but one solid basis of happiness; and that is, the reasonable hope of a happy futurity' (*Letters*, iii. 119).

61 *siege like that of Jerusalem*: the siege and destruction of Jerusalem by the Roman army in AD 70, best known in the harrowing account of the historian Josephus, was a byword for catastrophe in SJ's day. The following evocation is typical: 'Famines, Plagues, Earthquakes, ominous Voices, Armies and flaming Swords in the Air, were the fatal Presages of the Ruin of that glorious City and Temple; and there never was the like signal Instance of Heaven's Visitation of a People' (*The Travels of the Late Charles Thompson, Esq.*, 3 vols. (1744), iii. 239–40).

62 *bursts of universal distress . . . wonted revolutions*: on the indifference of daily existence to public calamity, see SJ's letter to Joseph Baretti of 21 December 1762: 'The good or ill success of battles and embassies extends itself to a very small part of domestic life: we all have good and evil, which we feel more sensibly than our petty part of public miscarriage or prosperity' (*Letters*, i. 213); also Sermon 1 (*YW* xiv. 5).

various forms of connubial infelicity: see above, n. to p. 59. Some of these forms are exemplified in *Rambler* 18 (19 May 1750); see also Sermon 1: 'That marriage . . . sometimes condenses the gloom, which it was intended to dispel, and encreases the weight, which was expected to be made lighter by it, must, however unwillingly, be yet acknowledged' (*YW* xiv. 6).

63 *To the mind . . . memory or fancy*: a characteristic expression of Johnsonian scepticism. Cf. *Adventurer* 107 (13 November 1753): 'As a question becomes more complicated and involved, and extends to a greater number of relations, disagreement of opinion will always be multiplied, not because we are irrational, but because we are finite beings, furnished with different kinds of knowledge, exerting different degrees of attention, one discovering consequences which escape another, none taking in the whole concatenation of causes and effects, and most comprehending but a very small part' (*YW* ii. 441); see also *Rambler* 125 (28 May 1751), *YW* iv. 300.

65 *Long customs . . . labours in vain*: cf. SJ's description of the chains of habit in his allegorical fiction 'The Vision of Theodore, the Hermit of Teneriffe' (1748): 'Each link grew tighter as it had been longer worn, and when by continual additions they became so heavy as to be felt, they were frequently too strong to be broken' (*YW* xvi. 202).

66 *No man . . . Nile*: a pithier articulation of a moral that SJ had previously outlined in *Rambler* 178 (30 November 1751): 'Of two objects tempting at a distance on contrary sides it is impossible to approach one but by receding from the other; by long deliberation and dilatory projects, they may be both lost, but can never be both gained' (*YW* v. 173).

67 *a country . . . domestick life*: on Egypt as a cradle of civilization, see above, p. 33 and n. Kolb cites the following passage from *The Preceptor*, an educational manual by Robert Dodsley to which SJ contributed: 'we find in

the records of antiquity, no nation celebrated more early for carrying all arts to perfection than the inhabitants of Egypt' (*The Preceptor*, 3rd edn., 2 vols. (1758), ii. 393).

my business is with man: the same priority is articulated in *Idler* 97 (23 February 1760): 'He that would travel for the entertainment of others, should remember that the great object of remark is human life' (*YW* ii. 300).

things that are now before us . . . deserve it: cf. Milton, *Paradise Lost*, viii. 191–4: 'not to know at large of things remote | From use, obscure and subtle, but to know | That which before us lies in daily life, | Is the prime wisdom' (cited in *Dictionary*, s.v. Life, 11). Hardy notes Piozzi's judgement that all SJ's conversational precepts 'were chiefly intended to promote the cultivation of "That which before thee lies in daily life" ' (Piozzi, *Anecdotes*, 198).

no mind . . . almost all our moments: cf. *Rambler* 203 (25 February 1752): 'The time present is seldom able to fill desire or imagination with immediate enjoyment, and we are forced to supply its deficiencies by recollection or anticipation' (*YW* v. 291; see also *Rambler* 41 (7 August 1750), *YW* iii. 221).

68 *revolutions of the intellectual world*: Kolb compares SJ's 'Account of the Harleian Library' (1742), which recommends descriptive catalogues of books to those 'who think the intellectual revolutions of the world more worthy of their attention than the ravages of tyrants, the desolation of kingdoms, the rout of armies, and the fall of empires . . . those that amuse themselves with remarking the different periods of human knowledge, and observe how darkness and light succeed each other, by what accident the most gloomy nights of ignorance have given way to the dawn of science'.

Example is always more efficacious than precept: a commonplace of the period. The *locus classicus* is Seneca's maxim, from his *Epistles*, vi. 5 that 'the way by precept is long and tedious; whereas that of example is short and powerful' (*The Epistles of Lucius Annaeus Seneca*, ed. Thomas Morell, 2 vols. (1786), i. 17). Cf. also Matthew Prior's *The Turtle and the Sparrow* (1723), 7: 'Examples draw where Precept fails, | And *Sermons* are less read than Tales.'

When the eye . . . means by which it was performed: as SJ later asked of Samuel Butler's satire *Hudibras*: 'When any work has been viewed and admired, the first question of intelligent curiosity is, how was it performed?' (*Lives*, ii. 7).

earliest narratives . . . uncertain traditions: hieroglyphics were not understood until the deciphering of the Rosetta Stone in the 1820s; the narratives in question are those of Herodotus and later classical geographers and historians such as Strabo and Pliny the Elder. On these and the modern sources about Egypt seemingly used by SJ, see Arthur J. Weitzman, 'More Light on *Rasselas*: The Background of the Egyptian Episodes', *Philological Quarterly*, 48 (1969), 42–58.

69 *pyramidal form . . . dissolution of the continent*: cf. Sir William Temple's
'Essay upon the Original and Nature of Government', according to which
'the rules of *Architecture* . . . teach us that the *Pyramid* is of all figures
the firmest, and least subject to be shaken or overthrown by any concus-
sions, or accidents from the Earth or Air: and it grows still so much the
firmer, by how much broader the bottom and sharper the top' (Temple,
Miscellanea (1680), 83–4).

Next day . . . dreadful gloom: this and later passages may draw on an
eyewitness account of the Great Pyramid of Giza by Aaron Hill, whom SJ
probably knew in the 1730s or 1740s, and who believed himself (though
he was anticipated in *Pyramidographia*, a treatise of 1646 by John Greaves)
to be the first European to describe the interior. 'We enter'd after certain
Guides, who undertook our Conduct thro' this dismal Passage, and
descended, as upon the steepness of some narrow Hill, almost one hundred Foot before we reach'd the bottom, and were all that while oblig'd
to *stoop*, or rather *crawl* along with *Torches* in our Hands', Hill writes. He
and his companions then pass along 'the *bottom* of this *close* and *gloomy*
way' to reach 'the Brink of a most dreadful *Well*, a strange Descent of
such *forbidding horror* in its black appearance, that the very apprehensions
of its *Depth* and *Danger*, has for many Ages frightned the desire of
Curious Men' (Hill, *Ottoman Empire*, 250).

70 *apparitions of the dead . . . related and believed*: Kolb compares Imlac's
opinion with that of Joseph Addison, for whom a person afraid of ghosts
was 'much more reasonable, than one who contrary to the Reports of all
Historians sacred and prophane, ancient and modern, and to the
Traditions of all Nations, thinks the Appearance of Spirits fabulous and
groundless' (*Spectator* 110; Friday, 6 July 1711). SJ himself more pithily
remarked of the reality of apparitions that 'All argument is against it; but
all belief is for it' (*Life*, iii. 230).

71 *passed through the galleries . . . supposed to have been reposited*: here SJ may
have been recalling Greaves, who describes passing through a 'Gallery or
Coridore . . . built of white, and polished marble' to reach a 'very sumptu-
ous, and well-proportioned room' at the centre of the pyramid. 'This
rich, and spacious chamber, in which art may seem to have contended
with nature', contains 'the monument of Cheops, or Chemmis, of one
peece of marble, hollow within, and uncovered at the top' (John Greaves,
Pyramidographia (1646), 91, 93, 95). Greaves also mentions the tradition
that the sarcophagus had never housed a body, and that Cheops and the
founder of a nearby pyramid had been privately buried elsewhere: 'For
the people being exasperated against them, by reason of the toilsomnesse
of these works, and for their cruelty, and oppression, threatned to teare in
pieces their dead bodies, and with ignominy to throw them out of their
Sepulchers' (p. 95).

wall of China: 'To this Wall there is no Work equal in the known World',
according to a summary of Jean-Baptiste Du Halde's *General History of*

China probably compiled by SJ for the *Gentleman's Magazine*, 12 (1742), 322. According to Boswell, 'he expressed a particular enthusiasm with respect to visiting the wall of China', and rebutted Boswell's remark that he would make the journey himself were it not for duty to his children: ' "Sir, (said he,), by doing so, you would do what would be of importance in raising your children to eminence . . . They would at all times be regarded as the children of a man who had gone to view the wall of China" ' (*Life*, iii. 269).

this mighty structure . . . insufficiency of human enjoyments: cf. SJ's rejoinder when Boswell observed, in a conversation of September 1777 about SJ's poem *The Vanity of Human Wishes*, 'that things were done upon the supposition of happiness; grand houses were built, fine gardens were made . . . JOHNSON. Alas, Sir, these are all only struggles for happiness' (*Life*, iii. 198–9).

survey the pyramids, and confess thy folly: as in the chapter on poetry, Imlac's words look forward to a well-known moment in Shelley, this time from 'Ozymandias' (1818): 'Look on my Works ye Mighty, and despair!' But reflections of this kind were a standard response to the pyramids in both ancient and modern sources. As Greaves reports, '*Pliny* . . . judges them *to be an idle, and vaine ostentation of the wealth of Kings*' (*Pyramidographia*, A4); Aaron Hill notes that the pyramids have 'long amus'd the World, with strange Reflections on the strong *Ambition*, and vain-glorious *Aim* of their aspiring *Founders*' (Hill, *Ottoman Empire*, 245). On leaving the burial chamber, Hill adds that 'the strange disorder'd heaps of *Dust* and *broken Stones*, o'er which we walk'd, and the uncertainty we had, of knowing, when those massy Piles were built, and to what *Founder* they have owed their *Origin*, then struck me deeply with a melancholy Thought . . . on the arbitrary Power, which *Time*'s Prerogative entitles him to exercise o'er *frail Mortality*' (p. 252).

73 *Next day . . . petition for redress*: SJ may be remembering the Bassa's role as described by Lobo in response to a murder ordered by a Sudanese king: 'A memorial was likewise given to the Bassa . . . entreating him to lend his assistance in the punishment of the King of Sanaar for a crime committed against the law of nations' (*YW* xv. 148).

74 *sunk*: i.e. sank. As with *run* in ch. iv (see p. 14 and n.), SJ lists *sink* in his 'Grammar' as an anomalous verb producing *sunk* 'both in the preterite imperfect and participle passive' (*YW* xviii. 327); see also ch. xxxv (p. 75), where he makes participial use of the same form ('She was . . . sunk').

76 *irrevocable determinations*: Kolb cites several examples of SJ's hostility to vows; see also his criticism of monastic seclusion in *Rambler* 202 (22 February 1752), in which a monk 'preclud[es] himself by an irrevocable vow from the pursuit and acquisition of all that his fellow beings consider as worthy of wishes and endeavours' (*YW*, v. 290).

77 *fabulous inhabitants . . . day would never return*: various sources for this myth have been noted by E. E. Duncan-Jones (*TLS*, 3 April 1959, 193), including a passage from Manilius, *Astronomicon*, i. 66–70, which read as follows in Thomas Creech's translation of 1697: 'The *Sun*, when Night came on, withdrawn, they griev'd, | As *dead*, and joy'd next Morn when He reviv'd' (p. 5). Duncan-Jones also cites Statius, *Thebaid*, iv. 282–4; Lucretius, *De Rerum Natura*, v. 973–6; see also Marvell, *The First Anniversary* (1655), ll. 325–42, and the editor's note in *The Poems of Andrew Marvell*, ed. Nigel Smith (Harlow: Longman, 2007), 296.

life to stagnate . . . current of the world: the same images appear in SJ's *Rambler*, where sorrow is 'the putrefaction of stagnant life' and 'the stream of life, if it is not ruffled by obstructions, will grow putrid by stagnation' (No. 47 (28 August 1750), *YW* iii. 258; No. 165 (15 October 1751), *YW* v. 111).

78 *common cares . . . suspension of her sorrows*: cf. SJ's remarks on the healing effects of time in *Rambler* 47 (28 August 1750), where 'sorrow is to a certain point laudable, as the offspring of love . . . but must give way, after a stated time, to social duties, and the common avocations of life' (*YW* iii. 255).

79 *happiness itself is the cause of misery . . . lose again what I have lost in Pekuah*: cf. SJ's warning against any such attempt 'to preserve life in a state of neutrality and indifference' in *Rambler* 47 (28 August 1750): 'however we may debar ourselves from happiness, misery will find its way at many inlets . . . it cannot be reasonable not to gain happiness for fear of losing it.' (*YW* iii. 256–7).

79 *Nubia*: a fragmented, predominantly Islamic group of kingdoms occupying the northern half of modern Sudan and part of southern Egypt. 'Nubia is bounded on the north by Upper Egypt . . . on the east by the Red Sea, on the south by Aethiopia' (Whatley et al., *Geography*, ii. 396).

the lower country: 'Egypt is commonly divided into Upper, Lower, and Middle, with respect to the course of the river Nile' (Whatley et al., *Geography*, ii. 381). Hence the 'lower country' is northern Egypt, where Ottoman power was most secure and pervasive.

St. Anthony: traditionally the founder, in the third and fourth centuries, of Christian monasticism, which originated in the Egyptian desert. The remote monastery of St Anthony was established in the Red Sea Mountains following the saint's death, and is now the oldest active monastery in the world, housing Coptic Christians. A first-hand description is given by Richard Pococke, who visited the embattled community in 1738: 'The convent is encompass'd by a wall to defend them against robbers . . . the country is very little inhabited above the convent of St. Antony; and those that are on the east side are mostly Arabs, who submit to no government' (Pococke, *Description of the East*, i. 70–1).

80 *laws of hospitality . . . into his power*: cf. the account given of Arab hospitality by a French visitor to Egypt in the 1720s: 'Their Light-Horse scour
the Country, most humanely stripping and plundering such Travellers as
fall in their Way: But, notwithstanding their whole Subsistence is by
Theft and Rapine, there are no People in the Universe who exercise
Hospitality with so much Generosity, or more Fidelity, than do the *Arabs*
in general. All Travellers, be they of what Nation or Belief soever, who
put themselves under their Protection, or go to visit them, are in the
utmost Security' (Charles de Sainte-Maure, *A New Journey through
Greece, Ægypt, Palestine . . .* (1725), 67).

81 *splendour of my cloaths . . . embroidery*: the costly dress of the Abyssinian
elite is noted by Lobo: 'the people of quality especially those that frequent
the court . . . wear all sorts of silks, and particularly the fine velvets of
Turkey . . . Their robes are always full of gold and silver embroidery'
(*YW* xv. 49).

82 *sons of Ishmael . . . denied to justice*: traditionally, the Bedouin Arabs were
descended from Ishmael, the outcast son of Abraham in Genesis 16:
11–15 and 21: 9–21: 'Ishmael . . . was the father of the Arabian Ishmaelites,
of whom some few tribes apply'd themselves to trade and husbandry; the
others . . . possess'd the desarts, and led a sort of life, which they thought
the most agreeable to their condition and original' (*Familiar Letters from
Damascus*, 204 n.). Arab customs of plunder were thought to derive from
this source: 'as to their living altogether upon plunder, they, especially
the Ishmaelites, are so far from disowning it, or being asham'd of it, that
they think themselves the only nation that is entitled to that way of living;
because Abraham, the father of their progenitor, is recorded to have sent
him away without any portion, from which they infer that he left him the
whole world to range in at pleasure' (Whatley et al., *Geography*, ii. 126).
The classic statement of this view is by Edward Gibbon, for whom 'the
poverty of the land has introduced a maxim of jurisprudence, which they
believe and practise to the present hour. They pretend, that in the division of the earth the rich and fertile climates were assigned to the other
branches of the human family; and that the posterity of the outlaw Ismael
might recover, by fraud or force, the portion of inheritance of which he
had been unjustly deprived' (Gibbon, *The Decline and Fall of the Roman
Empire*, ed. David Womersley, 3 vols. (London: Penguin, 1996), iii. 162
(ch. 1)).

83 *Walls supply stones . . . cottages of porphyry*: SJ revisits this point in *A Journey
to the Western Islands of Scotland*, where the ruined cathedral of Elgin was
not destroyed by Reformation zealots 'but more shamefully suffered to
dilapidate by deliberate robbery and frigid indifference'. Following the
Reformation, SJ writes, cathedrals in general 'were first neglected, and
perhaps, as the stone was wanted, afterwards demolished' (*YW* ix. 24).

84 *crocodiles and river-horses*: detailed descriptions of crocodiles and hippo-
potami are given by Lobo, who notes that 'the Nile has at least as great

numbers of each as any river in the world'. Of the hippopotamus (literally 'river horse' in Greek) Lobo adds 'that he hath no resemblance of an horse, and indeed nothing could give occasion to the name, but some likeness in his ears, and his neighing and snorting like an horse when he is provoked, or raises his head out of water' (*YW* xv. 86).

85 *mermaids and tritons . . . my credulity*: sirens and tritons had been recorded in Lake Tana, source of the Blue Nile, by the seventeenth-century Dutch cartographer Jan Jansson, prompting a scathing contradiction from the Portuguese historian Balthazar Telles: 'It is most certain there are no *Tritons* nor *Sirens* in this Lake, as *Johnson* [i.e. Jansson] was inform'd, and he tells us in his map of *Ethiopia*, in his *Atlas*' (Telles, *The Travels of the Jesuits in Ethiopia* (1710), 15; quoted by Lockhart, 'Egyptian Background', 524).

   At night the Arab . . . courses of the stars: on eastern astronomy, see below, p. 88 and n.

86 *intercepting the tale*: in the *Dictionary*, SJ defines *intercept* as 'To obstruct; to cut off; to stop from being communicated', and illustrates this sense from *Titus Andronicus*; here Titus addresses stones rather than men 'For that they will not intercept my tale' (*Dictionary*, s.v. Intercept, 2, citing Shakespeare, *Titus Andronicus*, III. i. 39).

   tediousness of life: a stock phrase, as in SJ's flippant remark that 'the notion of liberty amuses the people of England, and helps to keep off the *taedium vitae*' (*Life*, i. 394). His observation in *Idler* 24 (30 September 1758) that 'the passage of life will be tedious and irksome to him who does not beguile it by diversified ideas' (*YW* ii. 77) is one of several recommendations of intellectual activity as a remedy.

88 *one of the most learned astronomers . . . endless calculations*: the science of astronomy was thought to have originated in Babylonia or Egypt, and it continued to be associated with the East. SJ knew, and paraphrased in the *Dictionary*, an account of European astronomy that stressed Egyptian and Arab transmission: '*Pythagoras . . .* living in a close Community with the *Egyptian* Priests for seven Years, and being initiated into their Religion, was here let into the true System of the Universe; which he afterwards taught in *Greece* and *Italy*'. Astronomy then fell into neglect in Europe, but survived at Alexandria under 'those Patrons of Learning, the *Ptolemys*, Kings of *Egypt* . . . The *Sarazens*, on their Conquest of *Egypt*, got a Tincture of *Astronomy*, which they carried with them out of *Africa* into *Spain*; and by this means *Astronomy*, after a long Exile, was at length introduced afresh into *Europe*' (Ephraim Chambers, *Cyclopaedia*, 2 vols. (1728), i. 164; cf. *Dictionary*, s.v. Astronomy).

89 *To man is permitted . . . virtue is commanded*: cf. SJ's 'Life of Milton': 'The knowledge of external nature, and the sciences which that knowledge requires or includes, are not the great or the frequent business of the human mind . . . the first requisite is the religious and moral knowledge of right and wrong' (*Lives*, i. 248). A comparable earlier formulation

comes in *Rambler* 180 (7 December 1751), where SJ comments approvingly on *Paradise Lost*, viii. 159–78: 'Raphael, in return to Adam's enquiries into the courses of the stars and the revolutions of heaven, counsels him to withdraw his mind from idle speculations, and employ his faculties upon nearer and more interesting objects'; these objects include 'the knowledge of duties which must daily be performed' (*YW* v. 183).

90 *rage of the dog-star . . . fervours of the crab*: the Dog Star (Sirius) was proverbially associated with heat-induced madness, as in the opening lines of Pope's *Epistle to Arbuthnot* (1735), which SJ quotes in the *Dictionary*: 'The dog-star rages! . . . | They rave, recite, and madden round the land' (s.v. To Madden). The Crab means the constellation of Cancer, entered by the sun in high summer and thus also associated with tropical heat. See, for example, Boethius, *The Consolation of Philosophy*, 1. vi, which in H. R. James's translation of 1897 contains a memory of SJ's wording: 'When the Crab with baleful fervours | Scorches all the plain . . . ' (p. 26).

91 *southern mountains . . . inundation*: Lobo canvasses various theories about the Nile inundation, which occurs 'regularly about the month of July'. He credits his Portuguese predecessors with the correct explanation, based on rainfall patterns in the Abyssinian mountains to the south: 'all the winter, from June to September, no day is without rain . . . the Nile receives in its course all the rivers, brooks and torrents which fall from those mountains; these necessarily swell it above the banks, and fill the plains of Egypt with the inundation' (*YW* xv. 89). SJ also knew Sir Thomas Browne's report in *Pseudodoxia Epidemica* (1646) that the ancient Egyptians attributed the inundation to the appearance of the Dog Star, 'the overflow of Nylus happening about the ascent hereof' (Browne, *Works*, ed. Geoffrey Keynes, 4 vols. (London: Faber, 1964), ii. 325; a related passage is quoted in the *Dictionary* to illustrate the adverb *bountifully*).

92 *position of the earth and sun . . . world may be advantaged*: Hardy compares *Adventurer* 45 (10 April 1753), in which SJ ridicules unnamed philosophers who 'have been foolish enough to imagine, that improvements might be made in the system of the universe, by a different arrangement of the orbs of heaven' (*YW* ii. 360). Cf. also *Idler* 43 (10 February 1759), in which, discussing 'the natural advantages which arise from the position of the earth which we inhabit with respect to the other planets', SJ concludes 'that no other conformation of the system could give such commodious distributions of light and heat, or imparted fertility and pleasure to so great a part of the revolving sphere' (*YW* ii. 134–5).

For us the Nile is sufficient: Lobo is less sanguine about the reliability of the Nile inundation: 'The different degrees of this flood are such certain indications of the fruitfulness or sterility of the ensuing year, that it is publickly proclaim'd in Cairo, how much the water hath gain'd each night' (*YW* xv. 89).

93 *Of the uncertainties . . . uncertain continuance of reason*: a similar formulation occurs in the opening chapter of Adam Smith's *The Theory of Moral*

Sentiments (1759), published within days of *Rasselas*: 'Of all the calamities to which the condition of mortality exposes mankind, the loss of reason appears . . . by far the most dreadful' (p. 12). Cf. also SJ's observation about the poet William Collins in a letter of 15 April 1756: 'The moralists all talk of the uncertainty of fortune, and the transitoriness of beauty; but it is yet more dreadful to consider that the powers of the mind are equally liable to change, that understanding may make its appearance and depart, that it may blaze and expire' (*Letters*, i. 134). SJ's early biographers associated this passage in *Rasselas* with his fears concerning his own mental state. Citing the astronomer, Sir John Hawkins comments that 'the peril he describes he believed impending over him' (Hawkins, *The Life of Samuel Johnson, LL.D.* (1787), 370); Boswell adds that 'to Johnson, whose supreme enjoyment was the exercise of his reason, the disturbance or obscuration of that faculty was the evil most to be dreaded' (*Life*, i. 66).

93 *was recollected*: i.e. had recovered her composure. *OED* cites the present sentence to illustrate this obsolete sense of the verb (s.v. *recollect*, v., 6b), which SJ probably used to mirror the passive construction 'was abashed'. Elsewhere in *Rasselas* he uses the verb in the more conventional active mode: 'Here he recollected himself' (ch. iv, p. 14); 'he recollected his powers' (ch. xlvi, p. 99).

There is no man . . . at his command: here and in the following sentences SJ develops Locke's notorious observation that involuntary connections between unrelated ideas disrupt rational thinking in all human minds, and thus constitute a form of madness shared by us all. As Locke writes in his chapter on the association of ideas (exploited for its comic potential by Sterne at about the same time), this kind of 'opposition to Reason . . . is really Madness; and there is scarce a Man so free from it, but that if he should always on all occasions argue or do as in some cases he constantly does, would not be thought fitter for *Bedlam*, than Civil Conversation' (Locke, *Essay*, 395 (II. xxxiii. §4)). On the relationship between this episode in *Rasselas* and ideas of madness between Locke and William Battie's pioneering *Treatise on Madness* (1758), see John Wiltshire, *Samuel Johnson in the Medical World* (Cambridge: Cambridge University Press, 1991), 165–94.

All power of fancy over reason . . . influences speech or action: cf. SJ's comment, recorded by Boswell, that 'many a man is mad in certain instances, and goes through life without having it perceived:—for example, a madness has seized a person of supposing himself obliged literally to pray continually—had the madness turned the opposite way and the person thought it a crime ever to pray, it might not improbably have continued unobserved' (*Life*, iv. 31). The allusion here is to the poet Smart, whose religious mania led to incarceration between 1756 and 1763 in St Luke's Hospital and later a private madhouse, where he was almost certainly visited by SJ. Further conversations recorded by Boswell, Piozzi, and others indicate that Smart's predicament crystallized SJ's understanding of madness as a relative and unstable term, or even as an artificial category. Piozzi later invoked Smart and SJ himself to illustrate the distinction between visible and concealed insanity (Piozzi, *British Synonymy*, 2 vols. (1794), ii. 4–5).

When we are alone . . . idleness or satiety: SJ describes the same processes in *Rambler* 89 (22 January 1751), citing Locke: 'It is certain that, with or without our consent, many of the few moments allotted us will slide imperceptibly away, and that the mind will break, from confinement to its stated task, into sudden excursions. Severe and connected attention is preserved but for a short time, and when a man shuts himself up in his closet, and bends his thoughts to the discussion of any abstruse question, he will find his faculties continually stealing away to more pleasing entertainments' (*YW* iv. 105).

94 *who is pleased . . . cannot bestow*: SJ describes the same resort to compensating fantasy in *Rambler* 5 (3 April 1750): 'Every man is sufficiently discontented with some circumstances of his present state, to suffer his imagination to range more or less in quest of future happiness, and to fix upon some point of time, in which, by the removal of the inconvenience which now perplexes him, or acquisition of the advantage which he at present wants, he shall find the condition of his life very much improved' (*YW* iii. 25). Cf. also SJ's account of the 'invisible riot of the mind' in *Rambler* 89 (22 January 1751): 'The dreamer retires to his apartments, shuts out the cares and interruptions of mankind, and abandons himself to his own fancy; new worlds rise up before him, one image is followed by another, and a long succession of delights dances around him' (*YW* iv. 106).

feasts on the luscious falsehood . . . bitterness of truth: SJ resumes this formulation in his Preface to Shakespeare: 'The mind, which has feasted on the luxurious wonders of fiction, has no taste of the insipidity of truth' (*YW* vii. 82). Cf. also *Idler* 34 (9 December 1758), on 'the bitterness of unwelcome truth' (*YW* ii. 108).

fictions begin to operate . . . rapture or anguish: cf. SJ's warning in *Rambler* 4 (31 March 1750) that in novels the power of imagination can be 'so great, as to take possession of the memory by a kind of violence, and produce effects almost without the intervention of the will' (*YW* iii. 22).

95 *possibility of a perfect government*: Rasselas's confession recalls SJ's scepticism about utopian politics in a conversation of October 1769: 'Why, Sir, most schemes of political improvement are very laughable things' (*Life*, ii. 102).

visionary schemes . . . lose sight of their folly: Kolb compares Imlac's judgement about the quixotism of his companions with *Rambler* 2 (24 March 1750), in which, while laughing at the grandiose fantasies of Don Quixote, 'very few readers, amidst their mirth or pity, can deny that they have admitted visions of the same kind' (*YW* iii. 11). Cf. also *Rambler* 207 (10 March 1752): 'Such is the pleasure of projecting, that many content themselves with a succession of visionary schemes, and wear out their allotted time in the calm amusement of contriving what they never attempt or hope to execute' (*YW* v. 310).

96 *ease*: the pitch of this term is clarified by *Rambler* 85 (8 January 1751), in which SJ defines ease as 'the utmost that can be hoped from a sedentary and unactive habit; ease, a neutral state between pain and pleasure' (*YW* iv. 83).

what I remember . . . vicissitudes of life: cf. SJ's account of the pains of memory in *Idler* 44 (17 February 1759): 'Every revived idea reminds us of a time when something was enjoyed that is now lost, when some hope was yet not blasted, when some purpose had yet not languished into sluggishness or indifference' (*YW* ii. 139).

Praise . . . rivals: the sage echoes the melancholy conclusion to SJ's Preface to the *Dictionary*: 'I may surely be contented without the praise of perfection, which, if I could obtain, in this gloom of solitude, what would it avail me? I have protracted my work till most of those whom I wished to please, have sunk into the grave, and success and miscarriage are empty sounds' (*YW* xviii. 112–13). Cf. also SJ's *Idler* paper on bereavement (No. 41, 27 January 1759), written a few days after the death of his mother: 'what is success to him that has none to enjoy it. Happiness is not found in self-contemplation; it is perceived only when it is reflected from another' (*YW* ii. 130).

retrospect of life . . . attempts unfinished: the passage recalls several similar retrospects in SJ's own voice, including a letter of 21 September 1773: 'I can now look back upon threescore and four years, in which little has been done, and little has been enjoyed, a life diversified by misery, spent part in the sluggishness of penury, and part under the violence of pain' (*Letters*, ii. 75). Cf. also his Preface to the *Dictionary*, in which 'much of my life has been lost under the pressures of disease; much has been trifled away; and much has always been spent in provision for the day that was passing over me' (*YW* xviii. 110).

97 *that happiness which here I could not find*: cf. the religious consolation held out at the close of *The Vanity of Human Wishes*, where SJ lists the benefits of life: 'With these celestial wisdom calms the mind, | And makes the happiness she does not find' (*YW* vi. 109).

querulous and malignant: discussing old age in *Rambler* 50 (8 September 1750), SJ notes 'the querulousness and indignation which is observed so often to disfigure the last scene of life' (*YW* iii. 270).

98 *visits from women . . . European liberty*: the condition of women in the Ottoman Empire was generally seen as a state of confinement that functioned, in Aaron Hill's words, to 'rob them barbarously of those indifferent Liberties, without whose tast 'tis morally impossible for Man or Woman to be truly happy' (Hill, *Ottoman Empire*, 97). This view was famously overturned by Lady Mary Wortley Montagu, whose letters

from Constantinople SJ read and admired after their posthumous publication in 1763. As a European woman, Montagu enjoyed personal freedom of movement during her visit of 1717–18, but she represents the veil, with the opportunities it offered for disguise and intrigue, as even more liberating for Turkish women: 'Now I am a little acquainted with their ways, I cannot forbear admiring either the exemplary discretion or extreme Stupidity of all the writers that have given accounts of 'em. Tis very easy to see they have more Liberty than we have' (Montagu, *Complete Letters*, ed. Robert Halsband, 3 vols. (Oxford: Clarendon Press, 1965–7), i. 327–8).

imposture . . . chills benevolence: cf. SJ's essay on imposture in *Adventurer* 50 (28 April 1753), in which perpetrators of falsehood 'destroy the confidence of society, weaken the credit of intelligence, and interrupt the security of life' (*YW* ii. 366); similar observations survive in SJ's recorded conversation (*Life*, iii. 293; iv. 305–6).

100 *passed my time . . . useful to mankind*: Kolb glosses this passage with reference to the preference expressed for ethics over natural science in *Rambler* 24 (9 June 1750). Here SJ praises Socrates for redirecting Greek intellectual endeavours 'from the vain persuit of natural philosophy to moral inquiries, and turn[ing] their thoughts from stars and tides, and matter and motion, upon the various modes of virtue, and relations of life' (*YW* iii. 132).

102 *when scruples importune you . . . fly to business or to Pekuah*: cf. SJ's warnings in conversations recorded by both Piozzi and Boswell against 'load[ing] life with unnecessary scruples', and his recommendations of work or society as a remedy (Piozzi, *Anecdotes*, 228; see also 112; also *Life*, ii. 421 and n.; 423).

dissipate the gloom . . . surrounded me: SJ applies the same language to himself when acknowledging to Boswell in 1763 that melancholy had obliged him 'to fly from study and meditation, to the dissipating variety of life' (*Life*, i. 446).

none are happy . . . change again: cf. *Rambler* 207 (10 March 1752) on the restlessness of human desire: 'So certainly is weariness the concomitant of our undertakings, that every man, in whatever he is engaged, consoles himself with the hope of change' (*YW* v. 312).

Variety . . . necessary to content: on the relationship between variety and happiness, see *Rambler* 80 (22 December 1750): 'The poets have numbered among the felicities of the golden age . . . a perpetual spring; but I am not certain that in this state of imaginary happiness they have made sufficient provision for that insatiable demand of new gratifications, which seems particularly to characterize the nature of man' (*YW* iv. 56).

103 *monks of St. Anthony . . . uniform hardship*: in practice this hardship had as much to do with poverty as with monastic discipline. On his visit of 1738, Richard Pococke found several of the monks 'employ'd in bringing stones

to repair their convent, and thinking we were officers come to demand the poll tax, when we ask'd how many there were in the convent, they acknowledged no more than those we saw . . . they are very poor' (Pococke, *Description of the East*, i. 70).

103 *Their devotion . . . endless felicity*: elsewhere, SJ urges the performance of religious duties because 'That mind will never be vacant, which is frequently recalled by stated duties to meditations on eternal interests; nor can any hour be long, which is spent in obtaining some new qualification for celestial happiness' (*Rambler* 124 (25 May 1751), *YW* iv. 299). But he was also sceptical of the assumption (in a letter of 10 June 1761) that submission to monastic discipline was a selfless choice: 'Men will submit to any rule, by which they may be exempted from the tyranny of caprice and of chance. They are glad to supply by external authority their own want of constancy and resolution, and court the government of others, when long experience has convinced them of their own inability to govern themselves' (*Letters*, i. 200).

He that lives well . . . may properly retreat: Imlac anticipates SJ's remark to Boswell (made while visiting the ruins of St Andrews Cathedral) allowing withdrawal from the world as a remedy for insecure virtue: 'those who cannot resist temptations, and find they make themselves worse by being in the world, without making it better, may retire' (*Life*, v. 62).

many are dismissed . . . duties of society: cf. *Idler* 38 (6 January 1759), in which the choice of monastic withdrawal over social engagement 'ought rarely to be permitted, except to those whose employment is consistent with abstraction, and who, tho' solitary, will not be idle; to those whom infirmity makes useless to the commonwealth, or to those who have paid their due proportion to society, and who, having lived for others, may be honourably dismissed to live for themselves' (*YW* ii. 119–20).

104 *harmless pleasures*: 'Harmless pleasure is the highest praise', SJ told Boswell in 1779: 'Pleasure is a word of dubious import; pleasure is in general dangerous, and pernicious to virtue: to be able therefore to furnish pleasure that is harmless, pleasure pure and unalloyed, is as great a power as man can possess' (*Life*, iii. 388).

state . . . transient and probatory: in Sermon 22 (which may be collaborative), SJ articulates the standard Christian view that 'the whole life of man is a state of probation; he is always in danger, and may be always in hope' (*YW* xiv. 233).

Mortification . . . allurements of sense: cf. *Rambler* 110 (6 April 1751): 'Austerities and mortifications are means by which the mind is invigorated and roused, by which the attractions of pleasure are interrupted, and the chains of sensuality are broken' (*YW* iv. 224–5).

catacombs . . . without corruption: among several descriptions of the Egyptian catacombs available to SJ was Aaron Hill's 'strange, but true Account of those vast *Catacombs*, wherein the Old *Egyptians* were

Embalm'd and Buried, and whose black, horrid Wombs do yet contain a formidable Proof, how long our Humane Bodies may preserve their Substance, when defended by the help of *Art*, from the destructive Power of a *Natural* Corruption' (Hill, *Ottoman Empire*, 264).

hired a guard . . . visited the catacombs: the most frequently visited catacombs were at Saqqara, originally the necropolis of the ancient city of Memphis, about 15 miles south-west of Cairo. The need for guards is explained by an anecdote of Aaron Hill, who in 1701 stumbled on the corpses of two recently dead Italians in an underground passage. The remoteness of the catacombs, he explains, 'exposes frequently the *unwary* Traveller, to the barbarous Violence of the Inhumane *Arabs*, who, watching secretly for a favourable Opportunity, will often close the Mouth of the *Sepulchre*, and by that means Starving the *unhappy* Strangers, return some few Days after, to divide the Plunder of those *Miscarried* Gentlemen' (Hill, *Ottoman Empire*, 265).

105 *labyrinth . . . rows on either side*: cf. Aaron Hill's somewhat more florid description of the catacombs as 'a Gloomy *Labyrinth* of Death and Horrour: For on either side, lie rang'd in *measur'd* Order, at near Three Foot distance from each other, promiscuous Bodies of *Men*, *Women*, and *Children*' (Hill, *Ottoman Empire*, 264).

commonly supposed . . . method of eluding death: as Imlac's wording indicates, it was widely assumed that ancient embalming 'sprung from the theology of the Ægyptians, who . . . believed that *as long as the body endured so long the soule continued with it . . . Hence the Ægyptians skilfull in wisedome do keepe their dead imbalmed so much the longer, to the end that the soule may for a long while continue, and be obnoxious* [i.e. subject] *to the body, least it should quickly passe to another*' (Greaves, *Pyramidographia*, 45). Likewise, Sir Thomas Browne records the theory that mummification originated 'in the desire to prevent the separation of the soul', and adds the Christian objection that 'all this was but fond insideration. The soul . . . is not stayed by bands and cerecoths, nor to be recalled by Sabæan odours, but fleeth to the place of invisibles' (Browne, *Works*, iii. 469).

nature of the soul . . . immortal: Imlac's words point to a series of debates in the period, with high philosophical and theological stakes, concerning the immateriality or materiality, and hence the immortality or mortality, of the human soul. These were generated especially by Locke's contro-versial suggestion in 1690 that matter might be endowed by God with the power to think, and intensified by the radical materialism of La Mettrie's *L'Homme Machine*, translated in 1749 as *Man a Machine*. For the impact on *Rasselas* of specific contributions to the 'thinking matter' debate, see Gwin J. Kolb, 'The Intellectual Background of the Discourse on the Soul in *Rasselas*', *Philological Quarterly*, 54 (1975), 357–69; also Robert G. Walker, *Eighteenth-Century Arguments for Immortality and Johnson's Rasselas* (Victoria, BC: University of Victoria, 1977). For the larger con-text, see John W. Yolton, *Thinking Matter: Materialism in Eighteenth-Century Britain* (Minneapolis: University of Minnesota Press, 1983).

106 *soul is material . . . unconsciousness of matter*: SJ's own position in this controversy is evident from his *Dictionary*, where the primary definition of
soul is 'The immaterial and immortal spirit of man'. On the immateriality
of mind and the unconsciousness of matter, Kolb cites Isaac Watt's
Logick, a source of many illustrative quotations in the *Dictionary*: 'When
we have judged that matter cannot think, and that the mind of man doth
think, we then infer and conclude, that therefore the mind of man is not
matter' (10th edn., 1755, p. 5). Cf. also Samuel Clarke's various demon-
strations, in opposition to the materialist arguments of Anthony Collins
and others, that it is 'ridiculous to imagine that any *Motion*, or any other
Quality of Matter void of Consciousness, should have any *Tendency*
towards being *Consciousness*' (Clarke, *A Third and Fourth Defense of an
Argument . . . To Prove the Immateriality and Natural Immortality of the
Soul*, 2nd edn. (1712), 69).

cogitation is inherent in matter: in the *Dictionary*, SJ defines *cogitation* as
'Thought; the act of thinking' (sense 1) and turns for an illustration to
Richard Bentley's celebrated Boyle lecture of 4 April 1692, entitled
'Matter and Motion Cannot Think': 'So that if these powers of Cogitation,
and Volition, and Sensation, are neither inherent in Matter as such, nor
producible in Matter by any motion and modification of it; it necessarily
follows, that they proceed from some cogitative Substance, some incor-
poreal Inhabitant within us, which we call Spirit and Soul' (Bentley, *Eight
Sermons*, 58).

round or square . . . nature of cogitation: again, SJ may be remembering
particular philosophical manoeuvres by Samuel Clarke, though the
analogy with squareness and circularity (see note below) goes back to
Locke. Cf. especially Clarke's *Third and Fourth Defense*, in which he
attempts a *reductio ad absurdum* of materialist arguments about thinking
matter to the proposition '*that Circular Motion is one Species of Motion,
and Motion in a Square a second, and Motion in an Ellipsis a third, and
Thinking or Consciousness a fourth*; (which Consequence, I think, is abun-
dantly absurd)' (p. 94).

But the materialists . . . qualities with which we are unacquainted: in the
Dictionary, SJ defines *materialist* as 'One who denies spiritual substances';
to be a materialist in the period was to hold that nothing exists except
matter and its movements or modifications, and to view mental phenomena
such as thought and feeling as simply matter in motion. Proponents of
the material soul drew regularly on Locke's guarded statement about the
limitations of human knowledge on this question: 'We have the *Ideas* of a
Square, a *Circle*, and *Equality*; and yet, perhaps, shall never be able to find
a Circle equal to a Square, and certainly know that it is so. We have the
Ideas of *Matter* and *Thinking*, but possibly shall never be able to know,
whether any mere material Being thinks, or no; it being impossible for us . . .
to discover, whether Omnipotency has not given to some Systems of Matter
fitly disposed, a power to perceive and think, or else joined and fixed to

Matter so disposed, a thinking immaterial Substance' (Locke, *Essay*, 540–1 (IV. iii. §6)).

Yet let us not . . . incapable of cogitation: Imlac's reply to the astronomer is also a direct challenge to Locke's original hypothesis that 'GOD can, if he pleases, superadd to Matter a Faculty of Thinking . . . I see no contradiction in it, that the first eternal thinking Being should, if he pleased, give to certain Systems of created sensless matter . . . some degrees of sense, perception, and thought' (Locke, *Essay*, 541 (IV. iii. §6). Comparable earlier responses to this provocative suggestion include William Wollaston's insistence that 'the *accidents* of matter are so far from being made *by any power* to produce cogitation, that some *even of them* shew it incapable of having a faculty of thinking superadded' (*The Religion of Nature Delineated*, 6th edn. (1738), 236). Cf. also, for wording closer to Imlac's, Lawrence Smith, *The Evidence of Things Not Seen; or, The Immorality of the Human Soul*, 2nd edn. (1703): 'Neither, secondly, are the Powers of Cogitation, Volition, Sensation, put into Human Matter or Body by God, as Powers of no essentially distinct Substance from that Matter; for this would be for God to put Powers into Matter . . . of which Matter is naturally incapable' (p. 84).

107 *Immateriality . . . exemption from all causes of decay*: Christian materialists had attempted to reconcile arguments for the soul as a material substance with belief in its immortality, but most saw immateriality as the primary guarantor of the immortal soul, and indeed as the basis for morality. As Addison summed up the orthodox view, faith in spiritual immortality derived 'from the Nature of the Soul it self, and particularly its Immateriality; which tho' not absolutely necessary to the Eternity of its Duration, has, I think, been evinced to almost a Demonstration' (*Spectator* 111, 7 July 1711).

substance without extension: in philosophical (specifically Lockean) usage, *substance* is a slippery term denoting 'that which underlies phenomena; the permanent substratum of things'; *extension* is 'the property of being extended or of occupying space; spatial magnitude' (*OED*). Substance can thus be immaterial, and 'is supposed always *something* besides the Extension, Figure, Solidity, Motion, Thinking, or other observable *Ideas*, though we know not what it is' (Locke, *Essay*, 297 (II. xxiii. §3).

108 *choice of eternity*: cf. Elizabeth Carter's poem of 1744, 'To Miss D'Aeth', in which Nature 'directs our choice | To long eternity and purer joys' (*Memoirs of the Life of Mrs. Elizabeth Carter, With a New Edition of Her Poems*, ed. Montagu Pennington, 3rd edn., 2 vols. (1816), ii. 52).

college of learned women . . . patterns of piety: echoing the widely discussed proposals for female education set out in Mary Astell's *A Serious Proposal to the Ladies* (1694). Young women would be educated 'under the tuition of persons of irreproachable Lives, of a consummate Prudence, sincere Piety, and unaffected Gravity', Astell writes, and the proposed institution would work 'to revive the antient Spirit of Piety in the World, and to transmit it to succeeding Generations' (pp. 100, 59). For SJ's views on female learning in general, see Claudia Thomas, 'Samuel Johnson and Elizabeth Carter: Pudding, Epictetus, and the Accomplished Woman', *South Central Review*, 9/4 (1992), 18–30.

109 *resolved . . . to return to Abissinia*: but not necessarily to the Happy Valley. For the implications of this ambiguity, see George Sherburn, 'Rasselas Returns—To What?', *Philological Quarterly*, 38 (1959), 383–4.

GLOSSARY

JOHNSON completed his monumental *Dictionary of the English Language* in 1755, and the rigorous lexical habits that he cultivated in the process are evident throughout *Rasselas*, written four years later. Sometimes his usages involve meanings that were standard in the eighteenth century and have now shifted or disappeared (*riot*; *speculation*), but elsewhere he employs common words in strict senses that already seemed archaic or idiosyncratic (*idea*; *image*), and occasionally he indulges in the kind of arcane latinism for which the *Dictionary* drew fire at the time (*excogitation*; *indiscerptible*). Unless otherwise stated, all the definitions given below are from the first edition of the *Dictionary*, which Johnson later revised for a fourth edition of 1773. The purpose is to gloss words and senses that are now obsolete or unfamiliar, and no attempt has been made to record the more easily recognizable senses in which some of the listed words are also used. Thus the adjective *wild* is defined as 'Meerly imaginary' (the preceding number indicates that this is the *Dictionary*'s eleventh sense) to clarify Rasselas's engagement 'in wild adventures' while still confined within the Happy Valley (p. 14). Elsewhere the meaning coincides with modern usage ('wild beasts', 'wild and cultivated nature') and no definition is supplied. Square brackets indicate editorial insertions, and page numbers have been added to specify the relevant occurrences in cases where confusion might arise.

accommodations (1) provision of conveniencies; (2) in the plural, conveniencies, things requisite to ease or refreshment

acquaintance (4) the person with whom we are acquainted; him of whom we have some knowledge, without the intimacy of friendship. In this sense, the plural is, in some authors, *acquaintance*, in others *acquaintances* (pp. 41, 58, 95)

admiration (1) wonder; the act of admiring or wondering

airy (6) wanting reality; having no steady foundation in truth or nature; vain; trifling (p. 93); (8) gay; sprightly; full of mirth; vivacious; lively; spirited; light of heart (p. 55)

allay (2) to join any thing to another, so as to abate its predominant qualities

anon (2) sometimes; now and then; at other times

artist (1) the professor of an art, generally of an art manual

auditory (1) an audience; a collection of persons assembled to hear

avocation (2) the business that calls; or the call that summons away

awful (1) that which strikes with awe, or fills with reverence

bason (2) a small pond [SJ notes that the word 'is often written *bason*, but not according to etymology']

Bassa a title of honour and command among the Turks; the viceroy of a province; the general of an army [s.v. *bashaw*, 'sometimes written *bassa*']

blast (1) a gust or puff of wind

candour sweetness of temper; purity of mind; openness; ingenuity [i.e. ingenuousness]; kindness

casuist one that studies and settles cases of conscience

chimera a vain and wild fancy, as remote from reality as the existence of the poetical chimera, a monster feigned to have the head of a lion, the belly of a goat, and the tail of a dragon

collect (4) to infer as a consequence; to gather from premises (p. 64); (5) to recover from surprise; to gain command over his thoughts; to assemble his sentiments [usually but not always with a reflexive pronoun in this sense] (p. 107)

compact a contract; an accord; an agreement; a mutual and settled appointment between two or more, to do or to forbear something

compose (7) to adjust the mind to any business, by freeing it from disturbance

condition (6) rank (pp. 60, 75)

controvertist disputant; a man versed or engaged in literary wars or disputations

convenience (4) fitness of time or place (p. 75)

converse (1) to cohabit with; to hold intercourse with; to be a companion to: followed by *with* (pp. 29, 103)

cony a rabbit; an animal that burroughs in the ground

countenance (6) patronage; appearance of favour; appearance on any side; support (p. 56)

desert (1) qualities or conduct considered with respect to rewards or punishments; degree of merit or demerit (p. 60)

dignity (1) rank of elevation (p. 39)

discover (1) to shew; to disclose; to bring to light (pp. 11, 72, 74, 89); (2) to make known (pp. 23, 100)

discovery (2) the act of revealing or disclosing any secret (p. 41)

disgust (2) ill-humour; malevolence; offence conceived

dissipation (3) scattered attention

emersion the time when a star, having been obscured by its too near approach to the sun, appears again

engine (1) any mechanical complication, in which various movements and parts concur to one effect

enthusiasm (1) a vain belief of private revelation; a vain confidence of divine favour or communication

enthusiastic (2) vehemently hot in any cause

envy (3) to grudge; to impart unwillingly; to withhold maliciously (p. 19)

erratick (1) wandering; uncertain; keeping no certain order; holding no established course

excogitate to invent; to strike out by thinking [*excogitation* does not appear]

excursion (4) digression; ramble from a subject (p. 76)

fabrick (1) a building; an edifice

familiar (3) unceremonious; free, as among persons long acquainted (pp. 47, 61)

fatal (3) appointed by destiny (p. 10)

fatally (2) by the decree of fate; by inevitable and invincible determination (p. 58)

fountain (4) the head or first spring of a river (p. 22)

grate (1) a partition made with bars placed near to one another, or crossing each other: such as are in cloysters or prisons

gross (5) thick; not refined; not pure (p. 18)

horrid (1) hideous; dreadful; shocking (p. 61); (3) rough; rugged (p. 70)

humour (4) present disposition (p. 10)

idea mental imagination [revised in the fourth edition to 'Mental image']

illiterate unlettered; untaught; unlearned; unenlightened by science

image [n.] (5) an idea; a representation of any thing to the mind; a picture drawn in the fancy

image [v.] to copy by the fancy; to imagine

imbecility weakness; feebleness of mind or body

impassive exempt from the agency of external causes

indiscerptible not to be separated; incapable of being broken or destroyed by dissolution of parts

Janisary one of the guards of the Turkish king

lawn (1) an open space between woods

literature learning; skill in letters

luxury (4) delicious fare (pp. 10, 15)

materialist one who denies spiritual substances

meat (2) food in general

mechanist a man professing or studying the construction of machines [s.v. *mechanician*; *mechanist* does not appear]

modification the act of modifying any thing, or giving it new accidental differences of form or mode

negociate, negotiate to have intercourse of business; to traffick; to treat

obsequiousness obedience; compliance [not normally a pejorative term in the period]

offend (2) to assail, to attack (p. 40)

officious (1) kind; doing good offices

officiously (2) kindly; with unasked kindness

pace (5) a measure of five feet

parallel (2) lines on the globe marking the latitude

passenger (1) a traveller; one who is upon the road; a wayfarer

periodical (3) regular; performing some action at stated times

physical (1) relating to nature or to natural philosophy; not moral

policy (2) art; prudence; management of affairs; stratagem

pompous splendid; magnificent; grand

portion (3) part of an inheritance given to a child; a fortune

prevalence superiority; influence; predominance

probatory serving for trial

province (2) the proper office or business of any one (pp. 27, 56)

punctuality nicety; scrupulous exactness

radical (2) implanted by nature

recollect (2) to recover reason or resolution (pp. 14, 93, 99)

recreate (3) to relieve; to revive

repose (2) to place as in confidence or trust (p. 37)

riot [n.] (1) wild and loose festivity

riot [v.] (1) to revel; to be dissipated in luxurious enjoyment

salute (1) to greet; to hail

science (1) knowledge (pp. 68, 88, 106); (4) any art of species of knowledge (pp. 18, 24, 29, 67, 100, 108)

scruple doubt; difficulty of determination; perplexity; generally about minute things

scrupulosity (2) fear of acting in any manner; tenderness of conscience

sensitive having sense or perception, but not reason

speculation (1) examination by the eye; view (p. 19)

spoil (2) to plunder; to strip of goods

stay (3) to wait; to attend; to forbear to act (p. 99)

straggler a wanderer; a rover; one who forsakes his company; one who rambles without any settled direction

sublime (5) lofty of mien; elevated in manner (p. 89)

subtile (1) thin; not dense; not gross (p. 18); (4) cunning; artful; sly; subdulous. In this sense it is now commonly written *subtle* (p. 8)

suffrage vote; voice given in a controverted point

support (2) to endure any thing painful without being overcome (pp. 20, 44, 91, 103)

suppose (3) to imagine; to believe without examination (p. 95)

suspense (1) uncertainty; delay of certainty or determination; indetermination

terrour (1) fear communicated (p. 22)

traffick (1) commerce; merchandising; large trade; exchange of commodities

vacation (2) leisure; freedom from trouble or perplexity

vicissitudes (1) regular change; return of the same things in the same succession (p. 9)

voluptuous given to excess of pleasure; luxurious

wild (11) meerly imaginary (p. 14)

The Oxford World's Classics Website

www.worldsclassics.co.uk

- Browse the full range of Oxford World's Classics online

- Sign up for our monthly e-alert to receive information on new titles

- Read extracts from the Introductions

- Listen to our editors and translators talk about the world's greatest literature with our Oxford World's Classics audio guides

- Join the conversation, follow us on Twitter at OWC_Oxford

- Teachers and lecturers can order inspection copies quickly and simply via our website

www.worldsclassics.co.uk

American Literature

British and Irish Literature

Children's Literature

Classics and Ancient Literature

Colonial Literature

Eastern Literature

European Literature

Gothic Literature

History

Medieval Literature

Oxford English Drama

Poetry

Philosophy

Politics

Religion

The Oxford Shakespeare

A complete list of Oxford World's Classics, including Authors in Context, Oxford English Drama, and the Oxford Shakespeare, is available in the UK from the Marketing Services Department, Oxford University Press, Great Clarendon Street, Oxford OX2 6DP, or visit the website at www.oup.com/uk/worldsclassics.

In the USA, visit www.oup.com/us/owc for a complete title list.

Oxford World's Classics are available from all good bookshops. In case of difficulty, customers in the UK should contact Oxford University Press Bookshop, 116 High Street, Oxford OX1 4BR.

Travel Writing 1700–1830

Women's Writing 1778–1838

WILLIAM BECKFORD	**Vathek**
JAMES BOSWELL	**Life of Johnson**
FRANCES BURNEY	**Camilla** **Cecilia** **Evelina** **The Wanderer**
LORD CHESTERFIELD	**Lord Chesterfield's Letters**
JOHN CLELAND	**Memoirs of a Woman of Pleasure**
DANIEL DEFOE	**A Journal of the Plague Year** **Moll Flanders** **Robinson Crusoe** **Roxana**
HENRY FIELDING	**Jonathan Wild** **Joseph Andrews** and **Shamela** **Tom Jones**
WILLIAM GODWIN	**Caleb Williams**
OLIVER GOLDSMITH	**The Vicar of Wakefield**
MARY HAYS	**Memoirs of Emma Courtney**
ELIZABETH INCHBALD	**A Simple Story**
SAMUEL JOHNSON	**The History of Rasselas** **The Major Works**
CHARLOTTE LENNOX	**The Female Quixote**
MATTHEW LEWIS	**Journal of a West India Proprietor** **The Monk**
HENRY MACKENZIE	**The Man of Feeling**

A SELECTION OF   OXFORD WORLD'S CLASSICS

ALEXANDER POPE	Selected Poetry
ANN RADCLIFFE	The Italian The Mysteries of Udolpho The Romance of the Forest A Sicilian Romance
CLARA REEVE	The Old English Baron
SAMUEL RICHARDSON	Pamela
RICHARD BRINSLEY SHERIDAN	The School for Scandal and Other Plays
TOBIAS SMOLLETT	The Adventures of Roderick Random The Expedition of Humphry Clinker
LAURENCE STERNE	The Life and Opinions of Tristram Shandy, Gentleman A Sentimental Journey
JONATHAN SWIFT	Gulliver's Travels Major Works A Tale of a Tub and Other Works
JOHN VANBRUGH	The Relapse and Other Plays
HORACE WALPOLE	The Castle of Otranto
MARY WOLLSTONECRAFT	Mary and The Wrongs of Woman A Vindication of the Rights of Woman

A SELECTION OF   **OXFORD WORLD'S CLASSICS**

	Late Victorian Gothic Tales
JANE AUSTEN	**Emma**
	Mansfield Park
	Persuasion
	Pride and Prejudice
	Selected Letters
	Sense and Sensibility
MRS BEETON	**Book of Household Management**
MARY ELIZABETH BRADDON	**Lady Audley's Secret**
ANNE BRONTË	**The Tenant of Wildfell Hall**
CHARLOTTE BRONTË	**Jane Eyre**
	Shirley
	Villette
EMILY BRONTË	**Wuthering Heights**
ROBERT BROWNING	**The Major Works**
JOHN CLARE	**The Major Works**
SAMUEL TAYLOR COLERIDGE	**The Major Works**
WILKIE COLLINS	**The Moonstone**
	No Name
	The Woman in White
CHARLES DARWIN	**The Origin of Species**
THOMAS DE QUINCEY	**The Confessions of an English Opium-Eater**
	On Murder
CHARLES DICKENS	**The Adventures of Oliver Twist**
	Barnaby Rudge
	Bleak House
	David Copperfield
	Great Expectations
	Nicholas Nickleby
	The Old Curiosity Shop
	Our Mutual Friend
	The Pickwick Papers